Sandra Balzo

A Cup of Jo

WORLDWIDE®

TORONTO • NEW YORK • LONDON
AMSTERDAM • PARIS • SYDNEY • HAMBURG
STOCKHOLM • ATHENS • TOKYO • MILAN
MADRID • WARSAW • BUDAPEST • AUCKLAND

Recycling programs
for this product may
not exist in your area.

A Cup of Jo

A Worldwide Mystery/February 2015

First published by Severn House Publishers Limited

ISBN-13: 978-0-373-26930-3

Printed in U.S.A.

ONE

'A MIME IS a terrible thing to waste,' Sarah Kingston snarled. 'But damned if we shouldn't take a machine gun to this one, Maggy.'

She gestured toward the white-gloved performer not three feet in front of us.

'Be nice,' I said, shushing my friend and business partner.

'Mimes probably have a very tough time of it.' Ignoring us, a lanky guy who looked as improbable a mime as Will Ferrell did an elf, outlined an invisible door in the air, then rapped on it.

I cleared my throat. 'Socially, I mean.' And no small wonder.

'Then why hire…it?'

'Him,' I corrected. After all, mimes must have feelings, too. Even this string bean, wearing a green beret, white face paint, red-and-white striped gondolier shirt, black short pants and puce suspenders.

No taste, apparently, but feelings. 'And I didn't hire the man, Sarah. JoLynne Penn-Williams must have, because she's responsible for our Brookhills end of the Milwaukee commuter-train dedication.'

'Oh, yeah?' My partner looked around. 'Then where is she? You can't unleash a mime on an unsuspecting populace and just walk away. There should be conse-quences.' Sarah had a point. If not about the 'entertain-

ment', at least about the event manager not being present
to manage her own event.

After all, this was a big deal for Brookhills. As of
today, September 1st, a regular train would connect
downtown Milwaukee on the shores of Lake Michigan
to our Brookhills Junction depot fifteen miles west. I
say 'our' because—also, as of today—the depot was
the new location of Uncommon Grounds, the gourmet
coffeehouse Sarah and I co-owned.

The first train had departed quietly around dawn
on a special run to carry our Brookhills County dignitaries—JoLynne presumably included—to the Milwaukee dedication. Following that, the 'big city' hotshots
would climb aboard for the trip back to our celebration.

Since Milwaukee was far larger than our little sub-
urb, I grudgingly had to admit their event should have
priority. Besides, despite Jo Penn-Williams's temporary
absence, everything for the combination commuter-
train dedication and grand reopening of Uncommon
Grounds had been in place when Sarah and I arrived.

The *piece de resistance* of the celebration, at least in
my mind, was the giant, inflatable Uncommon Grounds
cup and saucer situated atop the wooden framework—
or 'gallows'—above us.

I had commissioned the 'advertising balloon' from
JoLynne's husband, staging and props professional
Kevin Williams. Balloon, inflatable, blow-up—whatever you chose to call it, the thing was magnificent,
with just the right dash of kitchen kitsch.

Fifteen feet in diameter by five feet high and capable of holding nearly 5,000 gallons of coffee, should
someone, not mentioning names, have considered filling it. A continual, varying flow of air made the cup

and streamers of 'steam' shimmy and beckon like an animated snowman on a Christmas-tree lot.

In fact, the cup was odds-on favorite to be the most animated part of the ceremony, which would feature the requisite dry as dust speeches by our own Brookhills' County Executive Brewster Hampton and his counterpart from Milwaukee County, Wynona Counsel. Brewster was a long-time acquaintance and I knew Wynona through WoPro, a group of high-profile women in the metropolitan area.

Nice people, you understand, but not exactly lightning rods. Nonetheless, the metro newspapers and television stations had sent teams to cover our event and they were spread out interviewing anyone they could find. In the distance I could see Mary, our town's head librarian, talking to a dark-haired female reporter and her camera operator, while a passing dogwalker held court for a print reporter.

I was itching to get down there and revel in my own fifteen seconds of fame now that I was satisfied our cup—elevated ten feet above the boarding platform on the aforementioned gallows—was high enough to be seen by the crowd, but not so high it would be outside a camera's frame.

'So,' said Sarah, head tilted toward the mime, tone laced with impatience and uneasiness, 'can't we just make it leave?'

'For the last time, it's a *he*.' The mime had abandoned his knocking on the make-believe door and instead opened it and stepped through. Once his second foot landed, he nearly collided with Kevin Williams as the props and staging guru came out a real door from the depot and on to the porch.

'Sorry,' Kevin said, seemingly instinctively, then looked the other guy up and down.

Obligingly, the mime began a clockwise pirouette.

'You sure that's a guy?' Sarah asked. 'It's got a braid of hair sticking out the back of its beret.'

'And a lump pushing out the front of *his* pants.' Emphasis on 'his'.

'There is that,' Sarah said admiringly as we watched the spinning mime reverse direction.

Kevin, though, had apparently had his fill of the whirling dervish. Keeping the door partially open with his foot, he gestured toward the narrow makeshift stairs leading up to the cup. 'For safety reasons, this part of the porch and boarding platform are closed.' The mime stopped and stared deadpan, a jolly red, white and green giant.

Kevin folded his arms, biceps the girth of tree trunks.

'If a mime falls in the forest...' Sarah speculated.

I'd already been cheated—by a homicide—out of *one* grand opening. Damned if I was going to let it happen again. 'Knock it off,' I told the mime.

Sarah cocked her head. 'I think that's exactly what Kevin plans to do.' Evidently coming to the same conclusion, the mime held up both hands in what could be interpreted as either surrender or surprise, depending on whether you were French or not.

Kevin and his massive arms stayed where they were.

One white-gloved hand dropped, the other slid down to shake.

The props man turned a gimlet eye to the offer, then reluctantly took it. 'Apology accepted. Now beat it.' A salute by index finger to the rim of his beret, and the mime was gone.

Kevin turned to us. 'Just to let you know, the saucer part is fully inflated and sealed, so it'll provide a stable base. The air compressor for your cup—to keep it a-movin' and a-shakin'—is behind this depot wall, so the engine noise shouldn't override the dedication speeches.' Pity.

'I ran the air supply hose—' he pointed toward a thick, blue snake '—up the gallows steps.' My eyes followed the hose to the plywood decking the cup and saucer rested on. The more you heard the word, the more like a man-made 'hanging tree' our framework looked.

'Gallows?' Sarah had a foot on the first step of its staircase. 'Do we have a trapdoor thingy, too? You know, like in the movies?'

'Nah.' Kevin shrugged. 'We don't want uneven spots supporting the cup and saucer. Sorry.'

'I'm not.' This from me. Trapdoors undoubtedly cost extra. And think of the liability. 'However, we do need to keep people away somehow so they don't trip over the hose or try to climb up to the balloon.'

'Not to mention walk off with my equipment,' said Kevin.

'Equipment?' Sarah was looking at the sun-faded, ratty hose, then tracked it through our depot door to a grubby, oil-blotched air compressor. 'You're telling me there are lamebrains who actually *steal* this stuff?'

'Equipment and decorations, lights and even batteries. That's why we don't set up anything but the scaffolding and stage itself until the day of the event. My crew and I have been here since four a.m. erecting everything else. It's either schedule that way or post, and pay, a security guard.' I looked up at our oversized tea service. 'I'd dare them to get that out of here.'

'You'd be surprised. I was telling someone last night about an event I did in a corporate boardroom. Picture this: two guys get off the elevator, broad daylight. They roll up a twelve-foot by fifteen-foot Oriental rug and just walk off with it.'

'Count your blessings,' Sarah said. 'If Maggy was running that show, there would've been a corpse wrapped up in—' I dug an elbow into my 'friend's' side.

'Just ignore her,' I said to Kevin who seemed a little taken aback. 'She has a macabre sense of humor.' Sarah tipped her head toward the high framework. 'You might even say "gallows humor".' Before our conversation could degenerate any further, I pulled out my cell phone and checked the time. 7:40 a.m.

'Kevin, do you have somebody to put here? Sarah and I need to be onstage for the ceremony, and Amy and Tien are busy.' Barista Amy Caprese and Chef Tien Romano were providing complimentary food and coffee for the attendees at a table under our big 'Now Open!' banner facing the street.

'Yeah,' Sarah said. 'We'd better get over there. Hate to keep any…body…hanging.'

Oh, boy. 'You don't intend to let this "gallows" thing go, do you?'

'Not on your…life.' A giggle.

'Why don't you two head out?' Kevin wisely suggested.

'I'll get some yellow caution tape from my truck to rope off this whole side of the porch.' He ducked back inside the depot.

'It's too late.' Startled, I turned toward the direction of the new voice. Kate McNamara, editor and publisher of the *Brookhills Observer*, and now—God help us—

occasional on-air reporter for a regional cable news operation, dug her three-inch heels into the gravel slope to the track side of our stage. Apparently it was Kate I'd seen interviewing Mary the Librarian.

'What's too late?' I asked.

'The train,' supplied Kate's camera operator, trudging up the loose rocks to join her. 'I know they're not on a regular schedule until tomorrow, but if the locomotive and cars don't get here soon, our live coverage'll be bumped into the eight o'clock hour.' Nobody wanted that, especially me. Commuters heading downtown—our coffee and cream, if not our bread and butter—would already have left home by eight.

Then I did a double-take. 'Jerome, is that you?' The camera operator had the same freckled face and glasses I remembered from his college internship, but now the short blonde hair had matured into a longish man-shag, and the head it was attached to stood a good deal higher than the last time he and I were together.

'Great to see you again, Maggy.' Jerome set down his camera and extended his hand. 'It's been awhile.' We shook.

'About a year. And six inches of height, by my guess-timation. I barely recognized you.'

'A real job *and* a growth spurt at twenty-two,' Jerome said, flashing a grin. 'Crazy, huh?'

'Hey, you're not such a shrimp anymore,' Sarah said, leaning over the porch railing. 'In fact, you've jumped enough rungs on the studly ladder to be entering its "hot" zone.' I wanted to smack her for embarrassing Jerome, but...despite a peculiar way of expressing herself, Sarah was right. The nerdish Brookhills Community College kid who operated a camera at last year's coffee convention (don't ask: the gathering didn't end well) was now a handsome young man.

Jerome pushed a hank of hair out of his eyes, looking more pleased than embarrassed. His boss, on the other hand, seemed downright annoyed.

'Leave him alone,' Kate snapped.

'Whoa.' Sarah held up her hands theatrically like the mime had earlier. 'No offense meant.' The news team moved away, Kate throwing us a dirty look that Jerome tried to dilute with an apologetic smile. Sarah leaned into me. 'So, Maggy, what do you think? Mama Bear or Katie Cougar?'

'Katie what?' I was scanning the eastern horizon for a sign of smoke. On the other hand, did locomotives still produce skyward plumes? I really should Google that, given our business was now located in a train station.

'Cougar,' repeated Sarah.

Still not tumbling to it, I swiveled back to my partner. 'Her name is not...ohhh.'

'"Ohhh" indeed. Tell me you didn't have the same dirty thought.' We both turned to watch Kate and Jerome, heads close together as the on-air talent gave the off-air technician an earful. Of something.

'Honestly?' I felt a convulsive shiver. 'I did not.' No need to see the eye-roll. 'They're both adults. You are *so* naive, Maggy.'

Naive?

I'd been married for twenty years to the same man and, on the day our son Eric went off to college, my dentist husband said he was leaving me for a twenty-I-forget-how-old.

Ted had been screwing his hygienist, and, eventually, she screwed him right back in an entirely different and—at least from my standpoint—infinitely more satisfying way.

Meanwhile, I'd quit my well-paying public relations job at First National Bank in a fit of pique and started a coffeehouse with two friends, one of whom was found dead in a pool of skim milk the morning we opened. The other abandoned me after we'd been forcibly closed by, euphemistically put, an 'act of God'.

Currently, I was reopening Uncommon Grounds in a century-and-a-half-old train station with Sarah Kingston, my insufficiently medicated, bipolar friend, with whom I had stumbled on not one, not two, but at least *four* (give or take) dead bodies in the prior eleven months. Oh, and I was dating our county sheriff, who, understandably perhaps, was beginning to fear he, as a law-enforcement officer, was wooing the female equivalent of a Jonah.

So, naive? I think not. Certifiable? Perhaps.

'C'mon,' Sarah continued. 'You just don't want to accept the "cougar concept" because when you look at Jerome, you really see Eric.' My son was only— what, three years younger than the camera operator? The thought of someone Kate's age hitting on him… ugh. No, *beyond* ugh.

A change of subjects seemed best. 'Look, there's Rebecca.' I pointed out into the crowd. 'Maybe she knows where JoLynne is.' Rebecca Penn, JoLynne Penn-William's younger sister, was one of our business neighbors in Brookhills Junction. Rebecca and her significant other, Michael Inkel, owned Penn and Ink, a graphics and marketing firm across the street from the depot.

As siblings, JoLynne and Rebecca were eerily identical, except for their respective sizes. If they

were pure-bred dogs, JoLynne would be the miniature poodle, Rebecca the standard. Both impeccably
groomed, but in different classes.

And with vastly different…temperaments.

'You really think Rebecca is keeping tabs on Jo?'
Sarah asked. 'I mean, except to keep her away from
Michael?' Rebecca (tall, gorgeous and brunette) was
walking next to Michael (taller, more gorgeous and
blonde). She was wearing an electric-blue wrap-dress,
he a black suit. As usual, Rebecca appeared to be giving Michael hell for something as the two made their
way to the stage.

I said, 'Our Rebecca sees red any time Michael so
much as talks to another woman. Including her own
sister.'

'And you.' Sarah slewed her eyes toward mine.
'Grrrrrrowl.'

'Now, *I'm* a cougar?' I shook my head. 'Sorry, but no.
Nor a puma or mountain lion, either. And I'm certainly
not interested in Michael. He just likes to occasionally
talk to a woman who doesn't give him shit.'

'So where *is* the man you're interested in?' Sarah
asked, looking around. 'No Brookhills County Sheriff Jake Pavlik at his own jurisdiction's celebration?'

I checked my cell again for the nth time. 7:51. 'He
should be here soon. Pavlik's driving back from a two-
day conference in Chicago. He's been gone since Sun-
day afternoon.'

'Chicago? But that's just a ninety-minute cruise on
the Interstate. I'm surprised your Romeo didn't come
back last night. You two could have had a sleepover.'

I shrugged. 'Pavlik planned to, but called early evening to say he was beat. He'd checked in with his office

and found nothing pressing, so decided to stay for one more night and start back early this morning. You know, to avoid the Tuesday afternoon rush hour?'

'Right. And good luck avoiding rush hour—morning or afternoon. It's round-the-clock for that city.' Couldn't argue with Sarah's traffic logic, but I wasn't liking the greater implication 'What do you mean by "right"?'

'I just figured you might be skeptical, what with your ex having used his fake "dental conferences" to shack-up with Rachel.' Rachel. Once Ted's illicit lover and now, for better or worse—mostly worse—his wife. Leave it to Sarah to pinch where she thought it might hurt.

'Pavlik is *not* Ted,' I said.

'Right,' she repeated. Damn right, I was right.

Glancing around restlessly, I caught sight of the mime scuttling after Rebecca and Michael. The poor guy didn't know what he was getting himself into.

'Why are you so antsy?' Sarah asked. 'There's nothing for us to do before the train arrives. And, speaking of which, your old friend Anita Hampton will be on it with her husband and the rest of the "dignitaries".'

'I'll notify Reuters.' Anita Hampton, married to Brookhills County Executive Brewster Hampton, was coordinating the Milwaukee celebration at the east end of the fifteen-mile route. Both counties employed event managers—JoLynne for Brookhills, Anita for Milwaukee.

I'd introduced Anita to her husband Brewster when she took over First National's public relations department. Very quickly I'd learned to ignore most of my new boss's hyperactive kibitzing and extract the ten per cent of criticism that made a positive difference.

I could picture Anita now, fashionably slim, tapping one manicured finger on a pursed lip as she contemplated our depot. 'Are you truly satisfied with this, Maggy? Wouldn't moving the entire building just a foot to the south-west make a world of difference?'

'Maggy, shouldn't our lettering have been bigger?' I jumped thanks to reflexive memory, but the words had come from Sarah. Taking a deep breath, I looked up at the navy-blue stenciling against our signature white cup.

'I'd have preferred bigger,' I admitted. 'Problem is, "Uncommon" and "Grounds" are both fairly long words. Any larger and, even stacked one above the other, they'd wrap around the entire circumference of the cup. All the cameras would see in one frame is "omm ound".'

'Gotcha.' Now, however, Sarah was looking around uneasily.

'Do you see Kevin with his tape? That mime is heading toward us again.'

'Is this a phobia of some kind?' I asked. 'Do clowns scare you, too?' I traced an exaggerated smile on my lips and leered.

'Or maybe the evil doll from those *Chucky* movies?'

'Stop that,' my friend said, swatting my hand away. 'Go take care of your mime.'

'For the last time, he's not *my* mime. Besides, the guy's harmless. He collects a paycheck for pretending he's doing something. Just like a politician.'

'You call that harmless?' Sarah muttered as we watched the red-and-white striped torso approach.

Apparently he'd been sent packing by Rebecca and Michael, who now stood on the stage with Art Jenada. Art ran the catering business next to their Penn and Ink shop. JoLynne must have asked them to participate in the dedication. Or maybe they'd just invited themselves, like Sarah and I had.

'You're not supposed to be back here,' I reminded the pesky performer when he reached us. 'Remember the guy with the muscles?' The mime nodded solemnly.

'You don't want him to come back, do you?' Yes, I was talking as though he were a two-year-old, but it's hard to take seriously someone in a braid, white face-paint and puce suspenders. Even if he is six-feet tall with a schlong in his short pants.

An 'uh-unh' motion of the head on the issue of Kevin's return.

'Good.' Sarah was standing behind me, like I was a human shield against the big, bad mime. 'Now, depart, foul spirit!' Ignoring her, the performer put the tips of his right index finger and thumb together, raised them to his mouth and let out an air-splitting, nerve-curdling whistle.

'Isn't that against mime union rules?' Sarah demanded from the far end of the porch's corner, to which she'd bolted at the sound. 'You know: No noise is good noise?' The mime shrugged, hands palm up, as the media whose attention he had just commanded, converged on us. Apparently satisfied, the mime waved to them and then oh-so theatrically tipped his head waaay back, toward the cup on the gallows above us.

'Don't even think about it.' I started toward him. 'You keep your mitts off my cup.' Sarah restrained me.

'Relax, Maggy. He's "harmless", remember?' Do not mock me. *Never* mock me.

The camera operators—including Jerome—had their lenses focused on our wannabe Marcel Marceau,

I guessed for want of anything else to film before the train arrived. Maybe I was being short-sighted: Uncommon Grounds could use the publicity.

Arms stretched wide and knees bent, the mime made like he was hefting our coffee cup balloon. Then, crooking his right little finger, he turned toward the media and pretended to take a sip for the cameras.

'Yes!' I called to Sarah, pumping my fist. 'We'll be on every TV newscast in southeastern Wisconsin.' My last word was still echoing off the depot wall when the wretched mime spit out our make-believe coffee.

'Damn that rat-bastard.' I started for him again.

A train whistle sounded. Everyone turned toward the noise. Everyone, that is, except Mr Mime and me.

I shook my finger at him. He shook his.

I dropped my hand. Ditto.

'Stop that.' I stamped my foot. Guess what?

Sarah sing-songed from the corner, 'He's rubber, you're glue, whatever you say bounces off him and sticks to...*you*.'

'Yeah? Well, let's see how he likes being pasted.' The mime edged away as the train slid to a halt. Since Sarah was on one end of the porch and I the other, he was trapped like a rat at the foot of the gallows framework that held the cup and saucer.

I advanced on him as he made for the depot door Kevin had used.

'Not that way,' I said, catching up with him.

The mime turned back, or at least his head did. One hand held the beret steady so both it and his body were facing away from me.

'Cool trick,' Sarah said, apparently feeling braver now that we had him boxed. 'How'd you pull that off?'

The mime winked one very blue eye at Sarah, looked down at his bulging short pants, and then held his hand to his heart, mirroring the beating with his hand. Thud-thud. Thud-thud.

Sarah giggled, albeit uneasily.

The mime batted his eyes and did a coy finger-flutter, even as the doors of the first train car slid back and dignitaries began pouring out on to the platform.

Mime romance. Sweet. But Sarah and I needed to be on stage to bask in the commuter-rail's reflected glory.

Anita Hampton stepped off the train. She was even thinner and more fashionable than the last time I'd seen her. Her eyes darted around imperiously and then she seemed to catch sight of someone. She gave a little, beckoning head gesture.

Following her gaze, I saw Kevin Williams at ground level, but sans our caution tape. The props guy abruptly detoured to Anita's edge of the stage, where she crouched down to speak to him.

The Grand Inquisitor. Oh, Kevin, wouldn't *this* be better, wouldn't *that* be better? And, true to form, she didn't seem happy with any of his answers, sweeping her hand disdainfully toward the spare set-up of our Brookhills' celebration.

Surveying it myself, I didn't see what she was complaining about. The stage-decorations might consist only of a couple clusters of Mylar balloons, tethering ribbons anchored in pots filled with stones, but the true centerpiece of the event was meant to be the commuter-line. The train itself would provide the backdrop for the television cameras.

With our giant, strikingly photogenic coffee cup and saucer at stage right.

Whatever Anita's problem might be, it better not have anything to do with my cup. The conversation between the two ended with a prolonged handshake, Anita holding Kevin's hand hostage as she spouted further instructions or criticisms. Finally released, the props man loped off in the direction of his truck.

'He'd better be getting that tape for us,' I grumbled to Sarah.

'And *before* he does Her Majesty's bidding. That woman *always* has to be first. And where is JoLynne? *She's* the one who's supposed to be in charge here.'

'Chillax. She'll show,' Sarah said, uncharacteristically mellow all of a sudden.

Unfortunately for Sarah, Anita never failed to put me in a bad mood. '"Chillax"? What the hell is "chillax"?'

'The kids use it. It means chill and relax. Chillax, you know?' No, I didn't know. Eric was my one lifeline to things current and he now lived three hundred long and, in my case, suffering miles away. So when Sarah exchanged a 'what a dinosaur' look with the mime, it set a match to my already shortened fuse.

'You!' I said, wheeling on him, 'I don't want to see you here again, is that understood?' At my tone, the mime convulsively stepped back, then back again. Because his face was still toward me, he couldn't see where his body was going.

Whoosh went Kevin's air hose. Down went JoLynne's mime.

And my giant cup? It shuddered more than shimmied, the jet stream of escaping air itching to topple the balloon off its perch and onto the boarding platform and adjacent stage beneath it.

I began scrambling up the stairs to the gallows. Halfway there, I made a grab for the edge of the saucer. It seemed to be weighted at the bottom and maybe adding my poundage (no wisecracks) could keep the thing in place.

'Are you crazy?' Sarah yelled from two steps behind me.

'That Paul Bunyan-size mug will take you with it.' She grabbed the back of my Uncommon Grounds T-shirt to hold me stable, but even as she did, the overall load of the inflatable shifted, sending the top of the imploding cup tipping over the edge like the leading coil of a Slinky.

Sarah was right. I let go of the saucer.

The two county execs—Brewster Hampton of Brookhills in a neat dark suit, Wynona Counsel of Milwaukee, a conservative slate-gray dress—came off the train and on to the platform as Anita Hampton moved to meet them.

'Look out below,' Sarah bellowed.

Both execs obeyed her immediately and saw the huge, white balloon sliding over the edge of the gallows like an avalanche down the wintry slope of a mountain.

Not so, Anita. 'No, no,' she was saying to them. 'Better you pose facing each—' Brewster dove to the right, Wynona the left.

Anita glanced one way, then the other, before finally looking up herself.

The deflating inflatable missed her nose by maybe eight inches, landing saucer-first with a thud at her feet.

Anita stared down at the now collapsed coffee cup, seeming dazed. 'Joe?' Talk about dinosaurs.

I might not know what 'chillax' meant, but I was

damned if I was going to let my old boss brand my new endeavor a Depression era 'joe-joint'.

'LaMinita,' I corrected as I climbed to the top of the newly vacated gallows. 'A delicious brew of hand-roasted beans from Costa Rica.' A hundred faces were tilted up as Sarah joined me on the plywood platform and peered over the edge.

'Wow. Shriveled like that, it looks less like Paul Bunyan's coffee cup and more like his used condom.' God, what a public relations nightmare. Lynched on our own gallows.

'Sorry,' I said weakly to the crowd below. 'But—' gesturing toward the fallen cup—'it's not just "joe".'

'Oh, but it *is*.' Anita Hampton ignored the solicitous hand Brewster laid on her shoulder. Delicately, she nudged aside a wall of our collapsed cup with the toes of one impeccably-shod foot.

A tangle of dark hair was exposed. Not joe.

Jo.

TWO

Missing Brookhills event manager JoLynne Penn-Williams was sprawled in the bottom of our cup. The lip of the still-inflated saucer made her look like a rag doll left behind in an empty kiddy pool.

I felt a full-body shudder, fearing history was repeating itself. Again.

'JoLynne, damn it!' Rebecca Penn said, marching over to look at her fallen sister. 'Must you always be the center of attention?' JoLynne wasn't rising to the bait. In fact, she didn't look like she was rising, period. Not that it stopped Rebecca.

'Really. Popping out of this cup like it was a giant cake at a bachelor's party?' She leaned down to give her older sister's shoulder a shake. 'Jo, do you have no sense of decorum? No professional pride?'

'Probably depends on the profession,' Sarah observed.

'Slut.' Rebecca pivoted to Sarah and me on our perch above the stage. 'I wouldn't blame Uncommon Grounds for suing your butt, besmirching their business like this.'

'Besmirch?' Sarah blinked. 'I don't feel "besmirched". You?'

I shrugged. 'Besieged, maybe. And beleaguered, with a little bemused thrown in. But besmirched? Not so much.' Unless, of course, Uncommon Grounds could be sued for personal injury or something. I looked down next to the gallows, but there was no sign of the mime. Apparently he hadn't been injured in his tumble. At least, not sufficiently that he couldn't flee the scene he'd destroyed.

Our Brookhills event manager, on the other hand, wasn't going anywhere for the time being. Could JoLynne be playing possum for some reason? And what in hell had she been doing in my coffee cup, anyway?

'Is Jo OK?' I called down.

No answer, at least from Anita Hampton and company.

Anita had nudged Brewster and Milwaukee County Executive Wynona Counsel back, probably to keep them out of the way. Or, more likely, beyond the range of probing television cameras.

Rebecca, though, was still in soliloquy mode. 'Oh, please. Don't give Drama Queen here the satisfaction. Get up, Jo, so we can drag your mess out of the way and get on with the dedication.'

'She's right,' Sarah agreed from on high. 'JoLynne made her cup, now let her lie in it.' Actually, 'Drama Queen's' husband had made the cup. Which reminded me: Kevin had disappeared. I didn't see a sign of him or his Williams Props and Staging truck.

'Calm down, Becc.' Michael Inkel had crossed the stage to his partner.

'Don't call me "Becc",' Rebecca snapped. 'You know I hate it. And you, of all people, have no right to tell me to calm down about my sister.'

'I told you…' Michael spread his hands. 'She and I never—'

'Not relevant,' Art Jenada interrupted, damn him.

Not only did he cut Michael off before Rebecca did, but he was standing over JoLynne, effectively blocking our view.

'Hey, Mr Toad,' Sarah yelled down. 'You make a better door than a window.'

Art twisted his undeniably toadish body to glare at her, but it was me he addressed. 'Can't you keep her muzzled?'

'Muzzled?' Sarah sputtered. 'Why, you…' I held up one hand. Miraculously, it silenced both of them.

'Art, what's wrong? Does JoLynne have the wind knocked out of her?' I'd found in the past that the caterer, though he tended to be a bit of a busybody, could also come through in a pinch.

As to this particular pinch, I was hoping for confirmation that JoLynne was just momentarily stunned. Given the way my life had been going lately, though, I feared betting on it.

Art turned back to the woman lying motionless. 'Can't tell. Should I…?' He reached toward her.

'Don't touch her!' Brewster Hampton had stepped forward, despite his wife's efforts to stop him. 'Jo might have a neck injury.'

'Yeah, like it's broken,' Sarah murmured.

God, I hoped not. 'Don't even think that.'

'Paramedics are on their way.' Anita stepped up to join her husband, flipping closed the cell phone in her hand.

'Shouldn't take 'em long.' I gestured toward the red and white Brookhills Fire and Rescue unit I could see parked in front of the depot. Presumably it was out of Anita's line of vision, otherwise she could have just whistled and waved the EMTs over.

One way or the other, though, her message got through and the lights of the unit started to revolve. A med-tech piled out of each side of the truck and, pausing to grab their cases, trotted around the building to the train platform.

As they mounted the stairs, Art moved away. Rebecca still stood to the side giving Michael 'what-for'—for what, I wasn't sure. An imagined affair with her sister? Most likely.

But blood apparently was thicker than water—or other bodily fluids—because the reproachful looks Rebecca had been tossing JoLynne throughout the tirade were increasingly mingled with concern as the EMTs continued to kneel, hunkered over the inert body.

'Dang it,' Sarah said irritably, 'I can't see with all the Yellow Jackets swarming.' Despite the fact that yellow jackets are a kind of wasp, I knew Sarah was talking about the slickers of the firefighters who had joined the group around the cup. EMTs, firefighters and town police officers were always sent out as a team on a Brookhills' call. Two uniformed officers were at the bottom of the steps up to the stage, keeping the crowd and media back.

Including a pretty ticked-off Kate McNamara. 'What do you mean I can't go up there?' she said, nearly foaming at the mouth. 'I'm a news reporter.'

'And I'm the king of the world.' Sarah puffed out her chest and threw her arms wide like we were in that scene from *Titanic*.

'Hey, watch it,' I said, ducking her flying right hand. To get a better view of our cup on the crowded platform below, we had dropped to the prone position, our heads and shoulders cantilevered over the edge of the gallows.

Kate continued her harangue. 'My camera operator has every right—'

'Oh, yeah? What camera operator?' The cop's facial expression implied he dealt with a dozen Kates per day.

Poor cop.

She looked around. 'Where the…?'

'Ouch!' The cry came from Sarah, so I turned my head to look at her.

There was a foot on her right hand. Not attached, merely pinning it down.

'Oops, sorry. Just getting a shot.'

'Jerome?' I said, as he tried to find a place to stand close enough to the edge to videotape down, but not atop one of our collective body parts.

'Jerome?' Sarah parroted as she sat up and rubbed her hand.

'What was the giveaway? The camera on his shoulder?'

'The feet.' As I recalled, Jerome had huge feet for someone his size. I should have known he was going to grow into them like a golden retriever does its paws. 'They're huge.'

'Tell me about it.' My friend struggled to hold up her injured wing.

Jerome activated the light atop his camera, flooding artificial sunshine over the scene below, shaded until then by the depot. Kate shielded her eyes and waved delightedly.

'Geez, if he's young enough to be your son, he's not old enough to be anything *else* to you.'

'You talking to Kate or to yourself?' Sarah needled.

'Neither,' I retorted, trying to keep my temper. 'I was—'

'Who's that?' Jerome interrupted.

Sarah and I followed the direction of his camera lens. With a view blocked by humanity—both in the form of the firefighters and EMTs as well as an innate moral code—Jerome had swung toward the other players on the stage. The one I guessed to be currently in his sights was female and midtwenties, with a fresh-scrubbed face in direct contrast to the spiky rainbow hair, tattoos and multiple ear-piercings.

The woman was our barista, Amy Caprese, and her heart was as big as the oversized hoops that swung from each ear. She was standing with Art Jenada, wringing her hands as she watched the paramedics working on JoLynne.

'Beauty and the beast,' Jerome said as he gazed through the viewfinder.

'Art's a nice guy.' I stood up and wiped my hands on my jeans. 'He's just an endomorph.'

'He looks like a russet potato,' Sarah contributed, 'only with just the two eyes.' Since I'd always thought Art resembled an amphibian, I didn't have much standing to criticize her tuber-take. I noticed Kate looking back and forth between Amy and Jerome's camera lens, trying to figure out what her videographer was shooting.

And then succeeding.

'Jerome,' she yelled, tapping her index finger to her temple.

'Camera eyes on the prize, you got it?'

'Guess that depends on your definition of "prize",' Jerome muttered, but he did as his boss ordered.

'Can you see anything?' I asked him.

'I'm trained on the emergency personnel right now. I don't think it's ethical to shoot a patient while they're receiving medical treatment unless you have their permission.' The way Jerome said it, Kate and he didn't necessarily agree on that point.

'Sure is taking them long enough,' Sarah said. 'What can they be doing?' To be honest, they didn't seem to be *doing* much of anything. Which I didn't think was a good sign.

Jerome took a step forward. 'Best I can tell, one of them is talking on a cell phone.'

I grabbed the back of his shirt. 'Careful. You don't want to join them down there.' As I said it, one of the EMTs got up from his knees. Everyone on the stage froze, all conversation halted. Anita Hampton started forward and then, changing her mind, turned and whispered something to Brewster. Probably suggesting he take the lead since we were in Brookhills, but also because both Penn-Williams and the emergency personnel were working for him and/or the county. Brewster shook his head, but then, as always, Anita seemed to get her way.

The Brookhills county executive buttoned his suit jacket and approached the upright EMT. The two of them spoke, the EMT gesturing to JoLynne and then up to where we were. Brewster turned his gaze on us, and then flicked it back down. He nodded and went to the podium.

Adjusting the microphone to lip level, he tapped it twice, producing that electronic thump-thump that indicates an operational sound system.

'Ladies and gentlemen—' he was unbuttoning his coat again—'I am afraid there's been a—' he cleared his throat—'a tragic accident.'

'No shit,' Sarah hissed in my ear.

I didn't pay attention. The EMTs hadn't attempted to transport JoLynne. Even assuming a neck injury, by now they'd have brought out a backboard, stabilized her spine, and carefully loaded her on to a gurney and truck for the trip to the hospital. They hadn't done any of those things.

'Mrs JoLynne Penn-Williams,' Brewster's voice boomed into the mic, 'our county's coordinator for this event, has been badly injured. We are going to ride with her to—' He interrupted himself as the coroner's wagon pulled to the bottom of the boarding platform stairs.

A collective intake of breath. Rebecca started to wail, burying her face in her partner's suit jacket, all suspected infidelity immediately forgotten. If not forgiven.

I looked around for JoLynne's husband, Kevin, trying not to think of insurance and liability and all those nasty possibilities you can't avoid considering when someone dies on your property. Or in your property, should that be a giant coffee cup.

'Where's Kevin?' I asked Sarah. 'He went running toward his truck and I haven't seen him since.'

'Good question,' Sarah said. 'But I have a better one.' Pausing—just, I suspected, to irk me—she gestured first to the coroner's wagon and then to where JoLynne Penn-Williams lay, clearly visible to us now that everyone had moved back as an amorphous herd.

'How'd she die, Maggy?'

THREE

'BLUNT-FORCE TRAUMA?' I offered.

Sarah and I had abandoned the gallows' bird's-eye view and I now stood behind the county coroner. Although I'd seen the short, gray-haired man at a number of crime scenes, I doubted my name had ever come to his— 'Maggy Thorsen.' The coroner didn't bother to turn around. So, my 'Jonah' reputation had preceded me. This did not seem a good omen.

'Yes, sir.' I took a step back. For the life of me, I couldn't remember the guy's name.

Sarah and I had managed to talk our way past a municipal police officer by explaining that our giant coffee cup was involved. He didn't seem to think this was as interesting as we did, but waved us on anyway.

The coroner was squatting and now he pivoted on his Allen Edmonds brogues to face me. 'The sheriff is not going to be happy.' Like I didn't know that Pavlik would be less than pleased to find me at yet another death scene. Then again, this 'death' had happened on my 'scene', so I figured to merit an indulgence for that. And, on the third hand, Brookhills County—aside from the coroner—shouldn't need to be involved anyway. We were in the town of Brookhills and the local police had already arrived.

Sarah sidled up to me. 'Hey, Lucy. Ricky's home.' She chin-gestured to a dark-gray unmarked that had just

braked to a stop, off-center detachable roof-light flashing red. Sheriff Jake Pavlik climbed out of the driver's
seat and scanned the area before approaching the stage.
He paused to say a few words to the cop who'd let us
pass and then mounted the stairs.

Traditionally, his deputies and, apparently, the coroner himself got a kick out of keeping Pavlik informed
as to my whereabouts. At first I think it ticked him off.
Now, it probably served as a warning of where *not* to
go. At least until after work hours.

Still, here he was. 'Traffic bad, sheriff?' I asked him
as Sarah made herself scarce.

'Terrible.' Pavlik—voice and visage—was all business.

'Did someone call you?' The fact that he'd arrived
with lights flashing indicated they had.

'Yup.' He slanted his blue-gray eyes toward the tri-
umvirate of Anita, Brewster and Wynona Counsel. The
two women were talking on cell phones, hopefully *not*
to each other. Brewster, like a man in a fog, was staring at the coroner's back. 'My *boss*.' Of course. While
both the sheriff and the county executive posts were
separate, elected positions, Brewster Hampton liked to
believe he was master of all things 'county'.

Pavlik turned to the coroner. 'What do we have,
Doc?' No wonder I didn't remember the official's name.

'The victim, JoLynne Penn-Williams, was in the inflatable. Up there.' Doc pointed at the gallows Sarah
and I had just vacated. I didn't think I'd be telling either
the coroner or the sheriff the nickname for that framework any time soon.

Pavlik lifted a portion of the decidedly deflated
inflatable.

'What was this thing?'

'A nine-hundred-fifty dollar, five-thousand-gallon coffee cup,' I said glumly. I pointed to what was showing of the Uncommon Grounds logo near JoLynne's right leg.

'Why did you...?' Pavlik seemed to rethink his question.

'Why was Ms Penn-Williams in there?'

'Beats me,' I said. 'She wasn't supposed to be.' Pavlik looked relieved that though I might be idiot enough to spend nearly a thousand dollars on a gimmick, I wasn't stupid enough to place a woman—dead or alive—in it.

Which begged the question. How had JoLynne gotten into the cup? The thing had sides five feet high—way too challenging to scramble over, especially if you were wearing a pencil skirt, silk blouse and heels as she was. Besides, someone at the dedication should have seen her trying.

I opened my mouth to ask the question, but Pavlik had one of his own. 'So, she died in the fall?' He was looking at the roughly ten-foot height differential between the gallows and the train platform below.

'Don't know,' Doc said. 'There's no apparent cause of death. We'll have to see what we find once she's on the slab.'

I was accustomed to cop-talk, even found myself using it occasionally, so I didn't cringe. 'Blunt-force trauma, I bet,' I said, for the second time that morning.

Both men looked at me.

I shrugged. 'No blood in the white cup.'

'How was that thing secured up there?' Doc asked in a grumpy tone.

'It wasn't secured so much as weighted,' I admitted. 'From what I could tell when I was up there—'

'Wait,' Pavlik interrupted. 'You were up there?'

'Yes.'

'When?'

'As the cup and saucer fell. I tried to catch it—them. Sarah, too.'

Pavlik looked terribly confused. 'You caught Sarah?'

'Who's Sarah?' Doc asked.

'My partner,' I explained. 'And no, I didn't catch Sarah. She hung on to me so I wouldn't go over with the inflatable.'

Doc was eyeing both Pavlik and moi curiously. 'I thought you two were...' He cleared his throat. 'An item.'

'We...' I finally got it. 'Sarah's not that kind of partner. We just own the coffee shop together.'

'Ahh.' Our coroner seemed relieved that his county's chief law enforcement officer wasn't into three-ways.

Two uniformed men with a gurney had made their way to the stage and now Doc waved them over. 'So the cup was just sitting there, unsecured? Seems like a hazard to me.' I told you Doc was grumpy. The other five dwarfs had yet to put in an appearance.

I held up my hands. 'Williams Props and Staging did the work, both here and at the Milwaukee celebration. They're the experts. Bonded and everything. The thing was connected to an air hose and weighted at its bottom.'

'Evidently.' Pavlik was nodding toward JoLynne's body. Then he looked across the stage and waved to someone. 'Gotta go see the county exec. I'll talk with both of you later.' Doc motioned for me to move back.

As I did so, Sarah joined us. I didn't bother to introduce them.

'Is Pavlik in charge?' she asked.

'Yup. Guess I should have known: ruined Brookhills County event, dead Brookhills County event planner.' I was watching JoLynne's remains being lifted on to the gurney. 'So the Brookhills County Sheriff is talking to the Brookhills County Exec.' All Brookhills, all the time.

'No, he's not. He's with Wynona Counsel.' I turned to see Pavlik, not with Brewster, as I'd assumed, but with the Milwaukee county executive. This wouldn't have bothered me if Wynona was old and squat, but she was pretty. Not to mention younger than yours truly, noticeably taller and, probably, smarter.

I mean, who was the one running the county and who was the one running the coffee shop?

Bet I slept better, though.

Pavlik laid his hand on Wynona's arm.

Except maybe tonight. Damn Sarah for bringing up Ted's cheating.

'Pretty friendly,' my business partner observed.

The woman could read my mind. Not that I would ever admit to any of the unsavory things she might find there.

'Hey, men and women *can* be friends.'

'Thank you, Meg Ryan.' The actress who played opposite Billy Crystal in *When Harry Met Sally*. The whole gist of the film was that Sally believed men and women could be friends without involving sex. Harry, of course, disagreed. And he…well, go rent the movie.

But Sarah was right. I was being stupid and I was reminded of it when I looked at Rebecca, now in Michael's arms as they watched her sister being wheeled away.

When the gurney reached Pavlik, he waved the tenders to a halt and lifted a corner of the opaque plastic sheet that covered JoLynne's body. He squinted down at her face for a count of five before dropping the cover so the coroner's people could proceed.

Wynona Counsel said something in his ear. The sheriff nodded and they moved to join Anita and Brewster Hampton. The four spoke and seemed to reach consensus on something. Anita jotted some notes, handed them to her husband and all but Wynona stepped to the podium.

Brewster looked down at his wife's notes, Pavlik and Anita standing slightly behind him and to the right.

'As you may know, I'm Brewster Hampton, Brookhills County Executive. We came here this morning, along with Milwaukee County's Wynona Counsel, to dedicate the new commuter-train serving our two counties.

'As many of you sadly witnessed, one of our ranks, event coordinator JoLynne Penn-Williams, has died in an accident. If Kevin Williams is within the sound of my voice, please see the officer at the bottom of the stairs.

'I should stress that we don't know how JoLynne, uh…came to be…where she was, but, uh, I expect, that is…'

Sarah said, 'Aw, and Brew-boy was doing so well 'til now.' I could see Anita Hampton's lips forming, 'Oh, for God's sake,' before she laid her hand on Pavlik's arm and whispered earnestly into his ear.

'Can you tell us the cause of death?' someone called out from the audience.

'No, uh…' Brewster continued to stammer. 'I…umm, thought I just said that?'

'Not exactly light—nor enlightening—on his feet, is he?' said Sarah.

'Don't worry—' me still watching his wife—'Anita'll have him whipped into shape in no time.'

'Brewster already looks pretty whipped to me.' I laughed, probably too loudly, given the circumstances. Pavlik's head jerked toward me. Then he nodded to Anita, slipped his arm from under her hand and moved toward the podium himself.

Our sheriff edged his mouth near the mic. 'I'd be happy to handle that question.' The relief on the county exec's face was palpable. Sarah had pegged him perfectly. Though he was handsome enough—tall and a good physique for suits, square jaw and a cleft chin—Brewster Hampton seemed incapable of stringing words together without a teleprompter. Or maybe he was just nervous. Take it from me, having Anita breathing down your neck could have that effect.

Pavlik was now centered at the microphone and looking mighty handsome himself. I'd never trade my sheriff's dark hair and dangerous blue-gray eyes for Brewster's faded, Ivy-League quarterback vibe. It would be like dating Dudley Do-Right, when I aspired to do oh-so-wrong.

'As our county executive told you, we'll have no way of knowing the cause of death until after a full autopsy and possibly some resulting lab tests.'

'Sheriff?'

'Yes?' Pavlik shaded his eyes. 'Where are you?'

'Up here.' It was Jerome, on the gallows. Kate was nowhere in sight, but the videographer didn't seem to need her.

He pushed hair out of his eyes. 'My question is actually for Mr Hampton, if I could.'

'Certainly, but can you speak up? We have quite a bit of background noise.' Pavlik stepped away from the microphone, Brewster moved—reluctantly—back to it.

Somebody must have left the depot door open because I could hear the compressor—Pavlik's 'background noise'—chugging away.

'Mr Hampton.' Jerome ratcheted up his volume. 'You said you're looking for Kevin Williams.'

'That's not a question,' I heard Anita Hampton snap. Brewster threw a sideways glance at Pavlik, like he was hoping for a lifeline. I didn't quite understand why, and I wasn't sure Brewster did either. He just sensed that his mate was displeased enough to bite *her* mate's head off like he was a copulating praying mantis. And poor Brewster probably hadn't even gotten any.

The sheriff's expression didn't change, meaning no help from that quarter. I knew from experience that Pavlik was of the 'you-got yourself-into-this' persuasion.

'Yesss,' Brewster said slowly.

'Why? Is he a person of interest?' Jerome spoke the last phrase as though the words were bracketed by quotation marks.

Brewster was in a bind. Calling on Pavlik to answer the question would mean that the sheriff's department was the entity wanting to talk with Kevin. Pavlik, looking straight ahead, continued to stay out of it.

You could almost see a bulb come on over Brewster's head as an idea struck him. Or maybe it was just

the glare from Jerome's strong camera light on high.
'That air-pump's making so much noise,' Brewster said,
raising his voice to make the point. 'I was hoping Mr
Williams could turn it off, spare all your microphones.'
OK. You had to hand it to Brewster: He did have his
moments, though rivulets of perspiration were running
down his face during this one.

And, as he lifted a hand to swipe at a drop, the offending compressor went silent.

FOUR

SILENCE, SQUARED.

Finally, an over-hearty, 'Thanks, Kevin.' A weak grin pasted on Brewster Hampton's face, he gave a wave toward the off-stage props man. Then, maybe remembering that, as county exec, he was supposed to be presiding over an event that had gone from dedication to debacle, he said, 'Sheriff, if you would like the micro...' Brewster looked around as a cloud seemed to pass over, but his potential savior had disappeared. I turned to check the gallows.

Sure enough, Jerome was clattering down its steps, light and camera no longer fixed on the stage.

In the meantime, Pavlik had signaled the officer at the steps with a head-jerk that presumably meant 'cover the front of the building', and was making for the depot's open door.

I followed, arriving there the same time as Jerome.

'Oops,' I said, holding my hands up to stave off getting smacked by the gear bag swinging from Jerome's left shoulder.

He caught it just in time. 'Sorry, Maggy.' Jerome started into the depot.

'Whatever happened to ladies first?' And what had happened to the polite young intern I'd met a year ago?

Answer: Kate McNamara had turned him into a newsman, confirmed by Jerome's 'Gotta get the shot.'

The door had started to close behind him, so I shoved it open. Damn it, this was *my* depot. Or at least Sarah's.

The scene before me was less than climactic.

Pavlik and Jerome stood staring at the compressor. With a yell, county sheriff brought city cop running from the front.

'No one got past me, sir,' the formerly bored officer said, a little short of breath. You could tell he was happy to being doing something, *any*thing other than keeping officious suburbanites and politicians in order.

'Figures. There was no one here in the first place.'

'But how…?' Then I forced myself to concentrate. 'It's a machine powered by gasoline, not electricity. The thing just ran out of fuel.' To prove my point, Pavlik yanked at the black-handled pull cord. The compressor gave a weak cough and died.

'I thought you weren't supposed to use gasoline engines indoors,' Jerome said.

I had a sinking feeling he was right. Kevin Williams had put the compressor, probably meant for outdoor festivals where electrical power wasn't readily available, indoors because of sensitivity to the noise issue. Or maybe he'd brought the wrong compressor and was trying to compromise. Whatever, he'd likely broken some kind of code by having the gasoline-powered beast inside.

That certainly wouldn't be appreciated by OSHA, the Occupational Safety and Health Administration. A thought struck me.

'Wait. Could the compressor have been pumping carbon monoxide into the cup?' I asked.

'And killed Ms Penn-Williams?' Pavlik said, closing the circle on my theory. 'Well, if she died of carbon monoxide poisoning, the autopsy results will show signs of it.'

'A complexion approaching cherry-red,' Jerome supplied eagerly.

'Only JoLynne wasn't inside the balloon.' I bursted a bubble of my own making. 'She was just cradled in the cup.' Pavlik and Jerome looked at me.

'I mean, JoLynne was lying at the bottom of the cup, like riding an inflatable boat. She wasn't in the path of any air inflating it.'

Pavlik seemed tired of talking cop—or 'cup'—with noncops. 'Listen, I have a lot on my plate. We're not going to know what killed Ms Penn-Williams until her autopsy. It could even be a natural death.'

I couldn't hold my tongue. 'A healthy thirty-something just keels over inside a giant coffee cup?'

'And you think the far-fetched part is the natural death?'

'Maybe it was auto-erotic asphyxiation,' Jerome interjected. Now it was his turn to get the look from the two of us.

'What?' he protested, turning a tad cherry himself. 'I hear things.'

'But there aren't any ligature marks around her neck,' I said. 'Or plastic bags or—'

'Not to mention she was fully clothed.' Pavlik's patience had hit the wall. 'Now I suggest you both get back outside and we let—' he nodded at the momentarily forgotten city officer, who was looking bored again—'the Brookhills Police do their job.'

The uniform perked right up. 'Yes, sir.' Pavlik ushered out Jerome and me. 'Why does that officer call you "sir"?' I asked. 'He doesn't work for you.'

'It's a sign of what's known as respect,' Pavlik said dryly as Jerome rejoined Kate. 'You should try it sometime.'

'Yes, sir. I was thinking handcuffs, and—'

'You're completely transparent, Maggy. Get your mind out of the gutter.' But the grin on the sheriff's face belied his words.

'Sooo…' he resumed after a count of five, 'what are you doing tonight?' I glanced around to see if anyone was looking, and then gave him a quick kiss on the lips. 'You, I hope. Just be sure to bring the cuffs.' Before he could protest, I whisked myself away.

The wind had been taken out of my expensive inflatable. And our entire Brookhills celebration.

'From 'ell and back,' Sarah said as she joined me in front of the stage.

'I'm not sure of the "back", but it sure is a hell of a mess.'

'Not hell, Maggy. "L"—like the first letter in lake.'

'Oh.'

'Oh, my foot,' Sarah said. 'You don't get it, do you?' Well, honestly? No. I was watching Anita Hampton wave Pavlik over to where she and Brewster stood. Wynona Counsel joined them as well.

As I said, I first met Wynona during my brief, not-so-recent stint as a member of WoPro, an organization for high-powered female professionals.

Why, you might ask, was I included to start with? Damned if I know. As second-in-command to Anita at the bank, I was a mere vice president in a land saturated with *first* vice presidents, *senior* vice presidents and *executive* vice presidents. And don't even get me started on presidents of various types and chairmen and vice chairmen.

My point is that VPs—in banking, at least—were a dime a dozen. Certainly not typical WoPro material. Still, Anita insisted that I apply. Even sponsored me. This sounds better than it was. I'd hoped for lifelong job security and all I got was this stupid organization.

After attending a few 'last Tuesday of the month' meetings, I quit, resigned to the fact that I was never going to achieve lofty corporate status. It helped not to give a shit.

But a lot of people did and, for them, WoPro was able to unlock doors, even drill holes in glass ceilings. Someone knew somebody, who needed something, which had to be provided by a living, breathing person and, hey! Why *shouldn't* it be a WoPro?

If the overall effort involved families, it might be considered 'nepotism'. If in government, 'partisanship' or 'cronyism'. For men in general...well, let's just say 'golf'.

For some women, it was a lifeline.

JoLynne Penn-Williams, for one. She came after my time in WoPro, but I understood that Anita had met Kevin Williams through his staging business and invited Kevin's wife to join the organization. From there, JoLynne had snagged the Brookhills marketing and events position.

Not that it was all support and sweetness and light. Kate McNamara was a member, too, after all.

'Hey, Maggy?' I held up a wait-a-second index finger to Sarah, as the knot of officials broke up. Evidently, Wynona and Brewster had acquiesced to whatever bill of goods Anita, with Pavlik's help, had been trying to sell them. Brewster turned toward the train door and, as he did, Anita gave Pavlik's arm a grateful squeeze. Anyone not watching carefully might have missed how long her hand lingered.

Pavlik glanced away and caught me looking. Again. Embarrassed, I turned to Sarah. 'I'm sorry. Where were we?'

Sarah gave me a jaundiced look. 'I don't know where *you* were, but I was telling you about my entry.'

Time to admit I'd been lost in space. 'Entry?' Anita and Brewster Hampton were boarding the train. Wynona Counsel hung back for a quick chat with Pavlik before she followed.

'"From…L…and…back."' Sarah emphasized each word. Or, to be accurate, three words and one letter.

'And what does "L" stand for again?' I asked, still puzzled.

'*Lake*, you idiot. "To L and Back". To Lake and Back. It's a play on words.' More like a dirty trick on them. The words deserved better.

'Are you talking about a slogan, Sarah?' Every couple of years, one of the commerce groups in town launched a new campaign aimed at getting people to visit Wisconsin.

Me? I believe in the old adage that a picture is worth a thousand words. Show potential tourists the lakes and hills, formed by glaciers long-receded. The art and culture of a big city. The charm and friendliness of countless smaller ones. The convenient transportation—especially now. And then there was Lake Michigan…

'Oh,' I said, as the train departed the station. 'The contest for naming the commuter line. You entered?'

'Yes, and they were supposed to announce the winner here today,' Sarah said. 'This better not screw things up for me.' Don't you just hate it when a corpse comes between your contest money and you?

'"To L and Back",' she continued. 'Nobody's going to top that. Says exactly what the train does. Takes folks to the lake and back.' Did I want to explain to Sarah that the subliminal identification she was counting on—'L', working only when derived from the word 'hell'—was rather negative, and therefore the very *last* motto Milwaukee County would want? Did I want to point out that a good number of riders would be reverse-commuters from Milwaukee, who might resent the insinuation that everyone would be commuting from west (Brookhills and environs) to east (Milwaukee)?

Or that TLAB was a crappy acronym?

Put slightly differently, did I want to suggest Sarah had a snowball's chance in 'L' of winning?

Nah.

'Brilliant,' I said.

When Sarah and I stepped through the main entrance of Uncommon Grounds—the *new* Uncommon Grounds—the place, thanks be to the Norse gods, was a madhouse.

We entered facing the service windows, though that characterization had to be taken on faith because of the crowd. I could see only the three original depot clocks set high on the wall behind them. Seattle to the left, New York City to the right and, in the middle, a restored Brookhills clock, indicating it was just past nine a.m.

Offending just about everyone—getting between somebody and their first coffee of the day is taking your life in your hands—I waded to the counter with an 'excuse me', a couple of 'sorry's, and the occasional 'just passing through'.

'Tien. Are you doing OK?' Tien Romano was the only one staffing the order window. An exotic mix of her late Vietnamese mother and Italian father, she held up a scruffy steno pad. 'I didn't know how to run the cash register, so I borrowed this from one of the reporters. I'm trying to keep track, but…' She shrugged.

We hadn't trained Tien on the cash register, because she was our caterer/chef. Part our employee and part her own, she provided us with baked goods and prepackaged food that our commuter customers could take to work in the morning or pick up upon their return to have for dinner after a long day.

Samples of her fresh coffee cake and muffins were served for our Grand Opening this morning, and she had volunteered to work behind the Uncommon Grounds stand outside.

Sarah and I didn't expect Tien to be pressed into service in the store itself later, but bless her for stepping up and helping Amy.

I'd thought we'd have a brisk outdoor business and then a fairly light 'lull' introductory morning. Little did I know that we would turn out to be the 'it' spot.

And a nice surprise, 'it' was. Locals everywhere, interspersed with men and women holding steno pads, smart phones or cameras. Meaning the media, of course.

The depot building itself is a big rectangle. The service area, with the kitchen, storeroom and office behind it, constitutes a square within the perimeter, aligned in the back right-hand corner. That meant our seating area formed an 'L', the larger leg fronting on Junction Road and the other running at a right angle. That second side led to the door of the train's boarding platform, where the air-compressor was stashed, so as not to interfere with the dedication ceremony.

The best-laid plans... Still, I couldn't complain about the caffeine frenzy.

'Thank you so much, Tien,' I said, rounding the counter.

'You have gone above and beyond *any* call of duty. I can take over now.' Too late, I realized who was next in line. Kate McNamara.

'I need a medium iced latte and a fat-free bran muffin.' Her tone implied 'and I need it now'.

I looked down at the keys on the new cash register. The codes seemed to be in a foreign language.

Tien handed me the notebook. I took it gratefully.

'I'll be back later to start tomorrow's food,' she assured me.

Tien had suggested she use our kitchen after closing. That way, we wouldn't be tripping over each other and, like magic, fresh pastries, sandwiches and soups would await us when we arrived to open at six a.m.

And, smart woman that she was, Tien wouldn't be interrupted by frantic calls for help out front. While I filed this under 'good problems', in that it meant business was booming, counter service certainly wasn't Tien's responsibility. If needed, we'd add more staff.

Or, bright idea, train Sarah to open.

'Uh-hum.' A clearing of the throat from Kate.

Tien gave me a pat on the shoulder and got going while the going was good.

I turned back to Ms McNamara. She raised her eyebrows at me.

'Yes?'

'My order?' Apparently Kate had mistaken me for someone with a steel-trap memory that extended beyond the prior five seconds. I poised my pen over the pad.

'That was…' A put-upon sigh. 'Medium…iced… latte…fat-free…bran…muffin.'

I scribbled the latte details and looked up. 'We don't have bran muffins. How about chocolate chip?'

'Fat-free?'

'If you don't count the chocolate.' Or the vegetable oil.

I wrote it down. 'Did you want that for here or to go, Kate?' Guess which I was hoping for.

'Here.' Damn.

Amy, our young, but uber-experienced barista, was spinning her magic on the espresso machine. I handed her a mug and relayed the drink order.

'Milk?' she asked.

'Of course.' A latte is one-third espresso and two thirds milk. Amy knew that.

My barista gave me a patient smile. 'I meant what kind of milk? Whole? Skim? Two-per cent? Soy?' Oh. It had been a while—four months, to be exact—since I'd been behind the counter, resulting, apparently, in losing a yard off my fast-ball.

I turned to Kate.

'Skim,' she said. 'And no ice.'

'No ice in the iced latte?' I asked.

'It costs the same as a hot latte and ice takes up room.' Kate had been trying to peer out the side window and now turned back. 'Why would I pay for ice?'

'To make the drink cold?' I hazarded. Espresso was brewed and, therefore, hot. Add cold milk and you have something just this side of tepid.

'Just swirl a few ice cubes around and then fish them out,' Kate said. 'Amy knows.' She does, huh?

'Got it,' my barista said brightly and started the drink. I was seriously considering a no-ice surcharge.

'With a Splenda,' Kate added.

As Amy pulled the shots for the drink, I tongued the biggest muffin in the bakery case and centered the calorie-bomb on a plate.

'I need a bag, too,' Kate said. 'In case I'm called away on assignment.'

'Shouldn't you be somewhere working the story right now?' I asked, hope trumping experience.

'The station wants me to monitor things back here.' Kate has the light-skinned complexion of her Irish mother and father. Her emotions showed plainly on her face, like a freckled mood ring.

And right now the tip of Kate's nose was red. Equals: not happy.

Wonder why.

'Really,' I said, probing delicately. 'I have to say I was surprised to see you weren't at the morgue or wherever they took JoLynne.'

Cheeks went bright pink, in patches, like an invisible Lilliputian was serially slapping her. 'We have a police reporter on that,' she said stiffly. 'Someone needs to be here to follow the "body-found" continuing story, and I'm the one who's most familiar with it.'

A twist of the metaphorical knife now, even as I laid a real knife and three pats of butter on her plate. 'Local stuff, huh? I understand completely. Station management probably doesn't think you're quite ready yet.'

Houston, we have lift-off. Kate's entire face erupted into flames. 'I—I...'

'Excuse me.' Amy elbowed her way in and passed Kate the quasi-iced iced latte. I slid the well-equipped muffin plate toward her as well, plus the bag she'd asked for.

Kate started away and then stopped. 'Oh, and a to-go cup with some ice in it?' I opened my mouth, but Amy reached across me and handed her the cup.

As Kate took her leave, our barista confronted me. 'Maggy, we've talked about this. You know you're not supposed to torture the customers.'

I shrugged. 'She's just such easy pickings.' And cheap.

'That's no excuse.' With a stern look, Amy returned to her espresso machine.

I hadn't seen Sarah since we'd walked in together, but she was my next customer.

'What are you doing in line?' I asked.

'Getting a coffee.'

'You own the place.'

'I know, but if I go behind the counter, you'll make me work.' Damn right, I would. Trained or not.

'What did you do, jump the line?' The queue had been practically out the door when we came in. There was no way Sarah should be this close to ordering already.

'Christy let me in.' She slid sideways to let me see Christy Wrigley. Christy taught piano in a small house-cum-studio directly across the road. A germ-a-phobic, she wore yellow rubberized gloves and cleaned compulsively, her keyboard and anything else within reach of her sturdy, laminated hands. Eccentric as a loony bird, but Christy seemed like a good person.

OK, a good crazy person.

'Were you away?' I asked her. 'You look like you have a tan.'

Christy smiled self-consciously. 'Does it look all right?'

'Great,' I said. The tan took her from bony, pale, carrot-topped territory to bony, tanned and carrot-topped. I'd defy anybody to say it wasn't an improvement.

'Sarah was telling me about JoLynne. What a tragedy.' Christy's wrinkled-up nose indicated that it was probably a messy, smelly event she was glad to have missed.

And our germ-a-phobic was right as rain on that point. Death—violent or peaceful, homicidal or natural—is always a real stinker.

'You weren't here?' I asked. Admittedly, I hadn't seen Christy in the crowd, but she was a person easily overlooked.

'No, I wasn't.' Christy's voice dropped to a whisper. 'I was in jail.' Pouring Sarah's cup of coffee, I paused in midstream.

'Christy went to see my Cousin Ronny,' Sarah explained.

'I didn't know Ronny and you were…close,' I told Christy. At least close enough for Ms Clean to brave a place as predictably filthy as a jail.

Ronny Eisvogel was the son of Sarah's aunt's second husband. Convoluted, I know, but it made him a step-cousin of my partner. I wasn't sure what, if anything, old Ronny could be to Christy.

'He's being detained pretrial without bail, sharing a cell with this career drug dealer,' Christy said, holding her chin—minimalist at best—high. 'But Ronny's innocent, and I'm going to help him prove it. I've been on the computer all morning, Googling "surviving prison" and "innocence projects", and just a boodle of other fascinating stuff.' Ahh, mystery solved. Ronny was Christy's new hobby.

I looked at Sarah. 'You have tried to talk some sense into this young woman?'

'Please,' Sarah said, transforming the word into a defeated groan. 'Just look at her. She's probably already learned how to saw through iron bars and tie non-slip knots into sheets.'

'Don't be silly,' Christy said. 'Even a helicopter escape is nearly impossible nowadays.' Nearly. Even tanned and classifiable as a 'good crazy', our neighbor was an odd duck. Hair pulled back tightly, fresh-scrubbed face with no make-up at all, laser green eyes, but eyelashes and brows so light they didn't accent her one outstanding attribute. And then there were the gloves. Christy was rubbing antibacterial cleaner from a small vial into them.

'Helicopter?' I asked.

'Shh,' Sarah hissed. 'Do *not* ask. The woman is probably building one from a kit in her garage.'

'But why Ronny?' I whispered back to Sarah.

'Birds of a feather,' she whispered back. 'Or hypoallergenic down-substitute. Are you going to finish pouring my coffee?' I did and slid the cup toward her.

'What can I get you?' I asked Christy.

'Decaf, please. In a to-go cup.'

'Don't trust our dishwasher?' Sarah asked.

'I don't trust anybody's dishwasher,' Christy confirmed. She was pulling a small orange canister from her bag. I assumed it was some sort of artificial sweetener until she popped the top and removed what looked like the strips I'd used to test the chemical levels in Ted's and my pre-divorce swimming pool.

I poured Columbian decaf into her cup and Christy swiftly darted one end of the strip into the coffee, like a hummingbird at a feeder.

'OK, I'll bite. Just *what* are you doing now?' I asked.

'Testing for caffeine.' She continued to delicately hold the tester vertically in the cup.

'It *is* decaf.' I pointed at the pot I'd poured the coffee from.

'See? It has an orange handle so nobody gets confused.'

'I'm sure you're right, Maggy, but I can't take a chance. I'm very sensitive to caffeine. Makes me nervous, you know?' Sarah made a choking noise, and I was right there with her.

If this was Christy *relaxed*, no sane person would want to see her jazzed.

'How long do you need to keep that thing in there,' a man who looked like a reporter asked curiously.

'Thirty seconds,' Christy said. 'For absolute accuracy, anyway.'

'Your coffee will get cold,' a woman in line growled impatiently.

'Hot coffee is dangerous,' Christy said. 'Don't you know that a burn to the roof of your mouth is just an invitation for all kinds of unwelcome bacteria to take root?' Talk about annoying organisms. And here she was planted in front of my window.

'Sarah, could you help Christy to a table?' I said.

Sarah obligingly took her own coffee and Christy's, so she could gather up her test kit and handbag. As they moved away, I heard Sarah say, 'Oh, yeah? Just like a petri dish, huh?' Lovely. I turned to the next person in line. 'I'm sorry. Now what can I get you?' The man who stepped up to the counter was probably a print reporter, since he had a notebook in one hand and wasn't dressed for the camera. Too bad. The guy, around forty, was better looking than ninety per cent of our local on-air talent, male or female.

'First of all, I'd love a cup of coffee,' he said, with a slow grin meant to ingratiate. 'I think I heard you had La Minita?'

'Small, medium or large?' I asked.

'Large,' he answered with a wink. I wasn't sure if he was talking about the coffee or his stir stick. What I did suspect, though, was that the slick patter was meant to befriend me in order to get information.

The fact I knew nothing made it easy to banter back. 'I bet.' I poured him the La Minita. 'Anything else?'

He slid a ten-dollar bill toward me, but kept his hand on it. 'Some information, maybe?'

'For a ten? Your newspaper's got to provide you a bigger budget.'

'My charm and looks are supposed to make up the difference.'

'Good luck with that,' I said, taking the ten and handing him five back.

He looked down at it. 'Five dollars for a cup of coffee?'

'Plus tax and gratuity. Uncle Sam's got a deficit and—God bless—you're a good tipper.' He nodded once and stuck the five in his pocket.

'Well done,' the woman behind him said to me. Now *she* looked ready to do a stand-up on the evening news.

Lacquered hair, solid-colored sweater in a flattering blue, cute little hat for exterior live-remotes.

She nudged the print reporter aside and lowered her voice.

'Do you know where I can find Kevin Williams from Williams Props and Staging?'

'Why?' Sarah, having safely seated Christy and her caffeine-o-meter, had returned and even ventured to the 'working' side of our counter.

The woman in front of us replied, 'Williams is JoLynne Penn-Williams' husband. We'd like to get his reaction to his wife's death.' Assuming Kevin knew. Which, come to think of it, *should* have been Brewster Hampton's stated reason for looking for the props man: to tell Kevin he was a widower.

'But nobody seems to know where he is.'

'I do,' Christy said from her table. She was shaking her caffeine stick like it was an oral thermometer and seemed oblivious to us.

'Ignore her,' Sarah said. 'She's on a day pass from the loony bin.'

One glance at the yellow rubber gloves seemed to convince the hat lady. 'So, when was the last time either of you saw him?'

'Listen, sweetie,' Sarah said. 'If we're going to answer questions, they'll be from the police and, so far, they haven't asked.'

'They will,' offered the print reporter, inching back to eavesdrop.

'I know something,' Christy said again.

'That's good, dear,' I said in a sing-song voice. 'I'll be there in a second, so you can tell me all about the nasty caffeine.' I turned back to the woman in front of me. 'Aside from Tweety-Bird's hallucinations, do you want anything else? And if you're thinking of bribing us, you'd better be packing more than a ten.'

Sarah looked offended. 'A *ten*? Somebody tried to buy our souls for a measly ten bucks?'

'Minus his cup of coffee.' I was keeping an eye on Christy.

'Sarah, can you handle this?'

'Sure.' I waved at Art Jenada, who was next in line, and crossed to Christy's table.

She was taking careful sips of what now had to be very safe, very lukewarm, coffee.

Slipping into the chair next to her, I whispered, 'So you know where Kevin is now?' If she did, I'd call Pavlik and tell him. Maybe it would shorten his day so he could get to my place sooner.

'Not right this moment, silly,' she said. 'I'm here, and he isn't.'

OK. 'Then where? And when?'

Christy said, 'A Williams truck passed me on Brookhill Road when I was driving the opposite direction to go see Ronny.' Opposite direction. The Brookhills County Jail, where Ronny was being held until trial, was west of us. That meant Kevin had to be going east.

'I wonder if he had to run over to the Milwaukee train station.' Williams Props and Staging was handling the set-up for both the Brookhills and big city dedications. Anita probably had sent Kevin scurrying back to make sure *her* event was going swimmingly.

Meanwhile, ours literally had come crashing down—

unbeknownst to Kevin until the train or the news, in whichever order, reached him.

'And you're sure it was Kevin driving?'

'No,' Christy said, placing her cup carefully on the table.

'You really should listen better, Maggy. I said I saw the truck. I have no idea whether Kevin Williams was driving it. I don't think I've ever even met the man.'

Well, that was a big help. 'What time would this have been?'

'About eight or so? Visiting hours start at eight thirty in the morning on Wednesdays, and I wanted to be first in line.'

I shuddered just imagining the scene: 'Yoo-hoo? I've got dibs on prisoner number 18398476!' I started to stand, but realized it was a little rude to pump Christy for information and then just bolt. 'So, how was your visit with Ronny?'

At the mention of his name, Christy's almost-chin went up again. 'I'm sorry, Maggy. He asked me not to say anything to you.'

'But telling Sarah was just fine?'

'She's family to Ronny.' Given how he treated family, I was more than happy to be the odd woman out. Outside their bloodline, that is.

'Christy, I don't want to upset you, but Ronny is—'

She held up her palm to me. 'I don't want to hear anything—'

'I'm telling you this for your own good. And Sarah— Ronny's "family"—will tell you the same. Stay away from him. He's a nutcase loser.' I'd had my say, but Christy was right about not hearing anything. She'd stuck an index finger in each ear like a four-year-old who didn't want her older sister to burst the Easter Bunny bubble.

Blocking out information you don't want to hear doesn't work. I have recent and relevant personal experience. But neither does trying to penetrate the blockade.

So, I got up.

The coffee line had dwindled, maybe because Sarah had been quietly efficient or maybe because the customers had given up hope and bailed out to find an upper elsewhere.

'Where'd everybody go?' I asked.

Sarah, who was pushing buttons on the cash register, didn't look up. 'The county courthouse. Guess there's some news.'

'Already?' I went to the big track-side window and looked out. Sure enough, only a single uniformed officer remained, standing guard over the deflated cup, now finally cordoned off. The black lettering on the yellow plastic tape strung between the two balloon bouquets didn't read a vigilant 'CAUTION' but instead, an ominous 'POLICE LINE—DO NOT CROSS'.

The officer, though not the one I'd seen earlier, looked equally bored. There must be an awful lot of standing and waiting in cop-dom. Maybe that's where the expression 'flatfoot' comes from.

About to turn back, my attention was drawn to a truck coming down Junction Road, the two-lane street in front of the depot.

From a distance, it looked like Kevin's vehicle, the one that had been parked adjacent to the stage and that I figured Christy had seen heading downtown.

If it was Kevin, did he know about JoLynne? And if not, should I be the one to tell him?

Before I had a chance to answer those questions, the truck braked and turned in next to our building. I left my window and went out the front door and down the steps.

When I reached the truck, I crouched down to get a look at the driver through the tinted passenger side glass. Tall, but not as broad as Kevin.

The silhouetted figure inside the truck saw me looking. I waved. He gave a finger-wave back, vaguely familiar.

I gestured for him to come out.

He pointed to himself, as if saying, 'Who, me?'

'Yes, you,' I called back. The guy and I must have met, given the grief he was handing me.

But when the door finally swung open, out came a Nordic-looking blonde stranger.

'Hello,' I said, walking around the truck to him. 'Do you work for Williams Staging?'

'Yah. I am Ragnar Norstaadt. I come to do pick up. And you are?' Charmed is what I was. My grandparents had been born in Norway, making all Scandinavian accents subliminally attractive to me.

'Maggy Thorsen,' I said, extending my hand. 'I own Uncommon Grounds, inside. But I don't think I saw you here earlier.'

'It is good to meet you, Maggy Thorsen,' said Ragnar, taking my hand in his. He had a smidge of white shaving cream clinging just south of his right ear.

I was dying to wipe it off. Or run my fingers through the curly blonde hair springing out from under the 'Williams Staging' cap. I settled for the more universal greeting and shook.

'Kevin ask me to tell you that he is very sorry,' Ragnar continued as we walked up to the depot's front porch, 'but he will not today return here. He is…detained.'

Detained? 'By the police?'

'Please?' Ragnar looked puzzled.

'You said that Kevin wouldn't be here? That he is…'

'Detained.' Seeing that I didn't understand, Ragnar seemed to search for an alternate word. 'Busy is better, maybe?'

'Yes,' I said, feeling silly for jumping to conclusions. Detained. I had been hanging around cops and coroners way too much. Though that did remind me. 'I assume Kevin knows about his wife?'

'That she is late?' Ragnar asked.

Late. Who knew that so many perfectly serviceable English words could result in such ambiguities?

'Late?' I repeated, feeling my way. 'You mean as in…'

'Dead,' he said solemnly. 'Mrs Kevin, she is dead.'

'Yes. I am so sorry,' I said. 'Have they told Kevin how JoLynne died?'

Ragnar seemed surprised. 'It is here.' We'd reached the porch.

'Around back, but—'

'She was in the, how you say…' Ragnar held out his left hand, palm up, to form a bowl, then used the right hand to indicate holding a handle.

I could feel my eyes narrow. The pinky sticking out. The loose-fingered wave. The blonde curls that could be pulled back into a braid. It finally came together.

'Cup,' I supplied. I reached over and swiped at the 'shaving cream' on his neck. 'Face paint,' I said, holding up my finger for him to see. 'You're the mime.'

'But, yes.' Ragnar looked so innocent. 'You did not know?'

'No, I did not.' I was still ticked about his spitting out my imaginary coffee, but given the circumstances, it would have been pretty petty of me to bring it up.

'I am very sorry,' Ragnar said. 'But I must remain on character when performing.'

'In character.' But I got the point. Mickey Mouse and Cinderella couldn't very well go out drinking together after a hard day's work in the theme park.

'So, are you an actor?' I asked.

Ragnar nodded eagerly. 'I am, yah. But acting does not pay so well the bills.' Especially this far from the legitimate stage in New York and the sound stage in Los Angeles. Though our northern climate probably made him feel right at home.

'You work for Kevin, then?'

'It is a good putting together. Clients sometime need performer and, when I am not that, I can help the display work with Kevin.' He pointed to the white-clothed table from which Tien had served coffee. The eight-foot table had been pushed up against the building, empty except for a cluster of Mylar 'Celebrate!' balloons tethered to a clear round bowl filled with pink and white quartz for ballast.

'Pretty,' I said. 'There are two more on the stage.'

'Thank you. The police say I must leave those for now.' Ragnar thumped the balloons with his thumb and middle finger.

'I must have this bowl, but you keep the balloons. They are good still.'

'No, thank you.' The metallic floaty things lasted forever. When my son was little, I'd resorted to skewering 'Barney' balloons with a letter opener after Eric was in bed, so I could finally get rid of the dang things.

As Ragnar took the bowl to the truck, balloons trailing, I, in turn, trailed after them.

'I know you talked to Kevin,' I said. 'Did he say whether JoLynne had been sick or anything?'

'Sick?' Ragnar carefully put the breakable bowl on the passenger seat, pushing down the balloons like a deputy guiding the head of a bad guy into a police cruiser.

'Yes. I'm wondering why a healthy young woman would die so suddenly.' And without dignity. In a giant coffee cup.

'Kevin tell me only JoLynne is killed.' Ragnar closed the passenger door and now moved on to the rows of folding chairs in front of the stage. The cop-as-sentry gave a nod to let him know he could clear them but was still being watched.

I lowered my voice so the officer couldn't hear. 'Ragnar, killed, as in "murdered"?'

'Kill, murder—is all the same, yah?'

'Yah,' I replied, my own Norwegian coming back to me.

'And yah, not.' I collapsed a chair and put it on the pile Ragnar had started. 'Killed could also mean accident.'

'I do not know,' Ragnar said, picking up the stack. 'All they say is Mrs Kevin was…' He lifted his burden into the back of the pick-up and looked around to see if anyone else was within hearing range.

I did, too. Nobody.

Ragnar Norstaadt lowered his voice anyway. 'Mrs Kevin was stuffercated.'

FIVE

IN NORMAL TOWNS, the fact that the south-west side of our building was a crime scene would ward people off. In Brookhills, though, notoriety served as a door-buster special.

By noon the tidal wave that had receded when the press left had been rehydrated by locals. It was now about three in the afternoon, however, and the trickle was down far enough for me to send Amy for milk, cream and other staples we were running low on.

I drew the line at asking her to also pick up nibbles for Frank and a light bulb for my porch.

'It might be good for business,' I said to Sarah, who was back to poking at the cash register like it was going to bite her, 'but it's too bad tragedy brings out the ambulance chasers.' I looked at octogenarian Sophie Daystrom, our sole customer at the moment. 'Present company excepted.'

'Oh, fudge, Maggy,' Sophie said. 'I chase ambulances with the best of 'em.'

'Fudge?' Sarah echoed. 'That's not up to your usual swearing standards.'

Sophie shrugged. 'Henry is giving me shit…sorry, *crap* over what *he* calls profanity. So, I'm trying to clean up my act.' I didn't think Henry, Sophie's current old-goy boy-toy, meant she should turn to a thesaurus in search of synonyms for excrement. Henry was a true gentleman and, much as I loved Sophie, the old bird admittedly had a mouth on her.

Even as I had the thought, a staccato birdsong pierced the room, sending Sophie frantically digging through her handbag.

Finally, a cell phone found, button punched, and screen studied. 'Hmm.'

'Aren't you going to answer it?' I asked.

'It's a tweet,' Sarah said.

'What do you mean?'

'The bird call? Tweet? Get it?'

For the second time today, I didn't. 'Sure.'

'You like it?' Sophie was pushing buttons as she spoke.

'That ringtone was as close to a "tweet" as I could find without actually having to pay extra.' Ahh. The birdsong must be Sophie's ringtone for Twitter updates. I didn't know much, but I did know that Eric always seemed to know things before I did. Hell, before the TV news did. Downside? Rumors could spread like wildfire.

'So, what's the news?' I asked Sophie, pouring coffee into a ceramic Uncommon Grounds white and blue cup. No matching saucer, but aside from that, it was a small-scale model of the one in which JoLynne Penn-Williams had been found. I hoped no death-junkies noticed, or they'd start filching the things for souvenirs.

But Sophie warded me off the pour, pointing at our to-go cups. 'Put it in one of those,' she said. 'There's been a "sheriff sighting".'

I reached for a to-go, but held up. '*My* sheriff?' It might seem presumptuous, but Pavlik and I had, after all, been together for nearly eighteen months now.

'Yes, "your" sheriff,' Sophie said, scoring a cup from the top of the stack herself and holding it out for me to fill.

'But why would you want to follow Pavlik?' And was he on Twitter?

'Same reason we track you,' she said. 'Things happen wherever Maggy Thorsen goes.' Wait a minute. I was on Twitter?

'Your life is like an old-time radio serial.' Sophie gestured toward the pot with her cup. 'We can't wait for the next episode.' And who was 'we'?

'But I'm not on Twitter.' At least I didn't think so.

'You don't have to be.' Sarah took the carafe away from me and filled Sophie's waiting cup. 'People just use the network to report where they see you.'

'I'm here.' This senior stalking was creeping me out.

'I know,' Sophie said. 'I've already reported it.' With a shiver, I glanced toward the big front window just in time to glimpse a woman with steel-gray hair peer through the glass. When she saw me looking at her, she ducked sideways and disappeared with a dull thud.

'Oh, dear,' Sophie said, grabbing a cover for her cup and hurrying to the door. 'Teresa has toppled again. I keep telling her that she should bring her walker instead of a cane on stake-outs. More stability, of course.'

Stake-outs. 'Of course,' I repeated woodenly.

I turned to Sarah as the door closed behind Sophie. 'What was that all about?'

'The senior book club. They read a novel about this detective agency and decided to try it themselves.'

'Using Twitter?' And twitting me? And Pavlik?

Sarah shrugged. 'What can I say? The geezers in residence at Brookhills Manor are more technologically advanced than we are. Rodney Houston "friended" me on Facebook the other day. Said he's "in an open relationship" and wants to hook up.'

My head began to spin. 'Rodney has *got* to be eighty-five.'

'But not dead, apparently.'

'Apparently,' I said, feeling a little sheepish. 'And so long as people like Sophie and Henry and Rodney keep busy and occupy their minds, they'll stay sharp. Vibrant.'

'No,' Sarah said. 'I meant literally. Rodney's not dead. The *Brookhills Observer* accidentally ran an obit on him last week. Complete with "X's" for where his age should go when he finally does kick.'

'Rodney must've had a pretty impressive life for the paper to have a death notice already written and waiting.' That kind of pre-planning at media outlets was usually restricted to public figures or celebrities.

'Nah, Caron is writing them for everyone in town.' Sarah pulled a napkin toward her and made a note on it. 'I have to remember to let her know when I win the train contest.'

'*If* you win…' Wait a minute. 'Caron?' Caron Egan was my former partner in Uncommon Grounds. Not the deceased one, but the woman who pulled the plug on our partnership because of 'employment stress', as she put it. 'Caron is working again? For Kate at that rag?'

'Don't trundle your undies into a bundle,' Sarah said. 'She's just working at the *Observer* part-time. I think Kate needs the help because of the moonlighting she herself's doing for cable news.' Caron and I had met years ago in the marketing department of First National. Luckily for Caron, that was pre-Anita Hampton. At the time, Caron wrote advertising copy and I'd managed special events. When she married her lawyer-husband Bernie, and I got hitched to his college room-mate, Ted, the four of us became 'couple friends'.

The relationship with Caron had survived my divorce, our partnership and that partnership breaking up. She and I remained tight, but… 'This is the first I've heard that Caron hadn't adjusted very well to the "life of leisure".'

'Maybe she needs a new challenge,' Sarah said.

'Writing obits?' And before people died?

'You're right.' A dry reply. 'Pales in comparison to pouring coffee.' I could debate Sarah on the subject. Expound on the challenges of running a small business. Extol the rewards of financial self-sufficiency.

Nah.

My new partner was looking a little hurt. 'Why do you care, Maggy? It's Caron's life.'

'You're right,' I said, sensing Sarah was looking for reassurance. I rested a palm on her shoulder. 'And things have worked out for the best. I could never top you as a partner.' Sarah looked at my hand.

I removed it and cleared my throat. 'Anyway, things were so busy when I came back in that I didn't get a chance to tell you: JoLynne stuffer…I mean, *suffocated*.'

'That was quick. How'd you find out?'

'One of Kevin's guys. Apparently his boss told him.'

'If I was the deceased's husband,' Sarah said, 'I'd stop talking and start running.'

'Why?'

'Why not?' Sarah picked up a dish towel and started to wipe the counter. 'Rebecca maintains her sister is—

OK, was, but always had been—a slut. Maybe Kevin got tired of it.'

'Aren't you making a lot of assumptions?' I asked. 'We don't even know JoLynne was murdered.' Though that determination sure would be easier on our umbrella insurance policy. At least, I didn't think you could be held liable for Person A murdering Person B. Unless, of course, Person B died because of your negligence. Like not having the damn inflatables roped off...

'*Not* murder? Please.' Sarah snorted. 'What was it then, suicide? JoLynne presses a pillow over her face and then cannon-balls into a giant coffee cup?'

'I concede that suicide is a stretch. But it could have been an accident.'

'You mean like she *fell* into the cup and hit her head, had a seizure and choked on her tongue?' Sarah was a tough audience.

'Not "falling",' I said. 'That might mean we didn't take reasonable precautions. Like not putting a fence around your swimming pool.'

'Well,' Sarah seemed unconcerned, 'that'd be Kevin's problem, right? He's the contractor.' She had gone back to her wiping, doing a yeoman's job of rearranging the bacteria. I pulled a spray bottle of disinfectant from under the sink.

My partner accepted it with a long-suffering look and started over on the thick granite counters. The serving windows of Uncommon Grounds were formerly the ticket windows of the historical depot. 'Formerly', because the travel-by-rail process was now completely computerized. Stick your charge card in the kiosk on the corner of our porch, choose a route and out comes your train ticket.

Stepping back, Sarah surveyed her work. 'What I want to know is why JoLynne was up there in the first place.' With a glance at me, Sarah sprayed and wiped the same surface area again.

'Got me.' I pointed. 'You missed a spot.' Wordlessly, though rather stiffly, my partner handed me the towel and the bottle. Sometimes, even Sarah Kingston doesn't trust herself to speak.

The day continued in like manner. That is, Sarah did something, I corrected it—only to make her better, of course—and she left me to do the task myself.

Finally, I got smart and asked Amy, who'd returned from the grocery store, to deal with Sarah and the customers, so I could go back to the office. I was riffling through the papers on my desk, in search of the bill for the damn cup, when Tien stuck her head in the doorway.

'You're back,' I said, finding the invoice I was looking for.

$953, including tax. Kevin had thrown in the saucer for free—I'd been fully prepared to go saucerless, in order to keep the tab under a grand.

Tien smiled brightly, lifting the loaded plastic grocery bags she held in each hand. 'Got all my supplies and I'm itching to cook.'

'Whatever you do, don't show Amy those plastic bags. She hounded me about our old foam cups, so we switched to cardboard.' The cups were more expensive and less insulating, but they qualified as eco-friendly. The landfills and our 'progeny' would thank me, Amy had said.

'Oh, I know.' Tien set down one hand's worth of bags and pulled out a folded-up tote. 'She's already given me a "reusable".' She shook the cream-colored fabric to open it up.

'Uncommon Grounds' in dark blue letters on the front of it, matching navy handles.

Tien swiveled her wrist like a baton-twirler to turn the bag around. A picture of the earth adorned the back.

Huh. 'Nice.'

'*Really* nice,' Tien agreed, stashing it and picking up her groceries. 'And brilliant convergence, too. Grounds/ Earth? You're a genius, Maggy.' Was I? Because if I'd ordered the reusable tote bags, I'd misplaced the memory, not so unusual these days. But when had I done it? And from what supplier?

Like I said, Huh.

Tien continued into the kitchen and I abandoned the bills to return to our service counter. Though I'd heard a number of customers coming in and out, thanks to the sleigh bells that hung from our front door, no one was there at the time.

I looked at the clock. Six twenty.

Amy and Sarah were standing at the espresso machine, my partner tamping finely ground powder into a portafilter, a small metal basket, handle attached.

Sarah frowned. 'Now what, Amy?'

'You twist it on…here.' Our barista was pointing to one of two fittings on the machine.

Sarah looked at her.

Amy smiled. 'Like this.' She took an empty portafilter, held it up to the fitting and then twisted to engage it.

'Ah.' Sarah followed suit. 'That was easy. Next step?' She threw me a look that said, 'Now *here's* a natural teacher.'

'OK. Cup below the spout.' Amy pointed at a miniature metal pitcher and Sarah placed it under the portafilter's basket.

'Just push the button.' Uncertainty crossed Sarah's face, but she complied.

'And voila!' Amy's big hoop earrings swung as she nodded in approval.

'Is the milk already steamed?' I asked. Usually we poured milk into a full-size version of the metal pitcher and frothed the liquid so it could rest as the espresso was brewed. That way you didn't get a cupful of milk-flavored hot air that would dissipate the moment you left the shop, leaving you with half a drink.

'Maggy, this is a system of building blocks.' A warning expression on Amy's face. 'Today we learned how to make espresso, right?'

But Sarah, seemingly oblivious to my critique, was busily focused on pouring her 'baby' into a tiny porcelain cup. 'Uhhuh.'

'Tomorrow,' Amy continued, 'I'll show Sarah what else she can do using the espresso.' If Sarah didn't wipe the Cheshire Cat grin from her lips, *I'd show her what to do with it.*

As my partner moved away to get a matching, miniature saucer, I turned to Amy. 'Don't tell me. You were a kindergarten teacher?'

Before answering, she checked Sarah's position. 'Preschool. You wouldn't believe how often it comes in handy.'

I nodded at our cash register. 'Think you can run me through Money and Change 101?'

Amy appeared puzzled. 'But the installer showed us, remember?'

'Yes, only I've pretty much forgotten everything

he said.' I opened the drawer under the register and rifled through. 'I don't even know where we keep our list of codes.'

'Right here.' Amy slid the card out from below the register itself.

'Genius,' I said. Which reminded me. 'Hey, when did I order the Uncommon Grounds tote bags?'

'You didn't. I did.'

'But I'm the boss.' I glanced quickly at Sarah who was now sitting, sipping her carefully-constructed espresso. 'OK, *we're* the boss. But you still should run these things past one of us.'

'You were busy.' Amy pointed at the bag displayed on the wall. 'We've already sold nearly a dozen.'

Well, that was good. 'But still…'

'You like them, right?'

'Of course.'

'Anything you'd change? We can do that next order.'

'Nothing, but…' Oh, the hell with it. The bags were great and so was Amy.

Before I could tell her so, though, the floor trembled, the air rumbled and then came a distant whistle.

The Death Train Returneth.

SIX

'I DON'T KNOW why you're calling it that,' Pavlik said. 'Unlike the last incident, this train didn't actually kill anyone.'

'Other than our business, potentially. Not a single person got off when it made its return run tonight.'

'You know as well as I do that the commuter line wasn't running a regular schedule today. Tomorrow will be better.'

'It better be,' I grumbled. 'And I still like my nickname better than the train's official one.' Pavlik had arrived at my house around eight with a pizza. The box was on the kitchen table, my sheepdog Frank positioned on the floor next to Pavlik, waiting for his piece of the pie. As high as the beast's head reached, he might as well have been in a chair like we were.

'Chin off the table, Frank,' I ordered.

'You don't like the name of the train or you don't like the fact that Sarah won the contest?' Pavlik tossed the sheepdog a frisbee of pepperoni.

Perfect. If Frank wriggled his way into my bed, I'd be greeted by a canine depth-charge when I rippled the covers.

'Both,' I conceded. 'My heartache began the moment I caught the scroll-line under the news. It's probably already been added to her obit.'

Pavlik seemed shocked. 'Sarah's obituary?'

'Long story, but not a big deal,' I said. 'My point is, I'll likely be Sarah's next call, so she can crow.' A sideways glance at Pavlik. 'Assuming the news has reached her, of course.'

'Sarah'd be told before it was released to the media, wouldn't she?'

I shrugged. 'JoLynne Penn-Williams was running the competition. With her gone so suddenly, who knows what might have slipped through the cracks?' I let it hang there, but Pavlik didn't comment.

'I understand the cause of JoLynne's death came back,' I tried. 'That was fast.'

'The *preliminary* cause of death,' our sheriff corrected. Frank was on his haunches begging and when Pavlik turned his head, he came face to muzzle with my shaggy dog.

My beau fanned the air between them. 'I think Frank could use some mouthwash. Industrial-strength.'

'I tried brushing his teeth last week. *Not* a happy experience for either of us.' A mournful howl as confirmation.

I wanted to corroborate Ragnar's story. 'So, what *is* the preliminary cause of death?'

'Asphyxiation.'

'Is that the same thing as suffocation?'

'Asphyxia is simply not getting enough oxygen to sustain life. Suffocation can be a cause of asphyxiation. Because there are no apparent signs of ligatures, bruising around the neck or hanging, it looks like suffocation. Maybe even choking on a piece of food, though Doc didn't find anything obstructing Ms Penn-Williams' airway.'

'An asthma attack, then?' *I'll take 'Natural Causes' for $500, Alex.*

Pavlik fed Frank a chunk of mushroom, mozzarella cheese yo-yoing from it. 'You've gotten all you're going to get from me tonight, Maggy.' Well, that was no fun. I was about to ask if he'd brought the handcuffs when my cell rang. By the time I dug through my bag and came up with it, all I had was a voicemail. Which was OK. I usually preferred those to talking with actual people.

Hi. How are you? Good. And you? Great thanks. How about the family? And on, and on, and...

Then I saw the missed call came from my partner's home phone. 'That was Sarah,' I told Pavlik. 'Do you mind if I listen to her message?'

'Not at all,' he said, a hint of 'smirk' tickling the corners of his lips.

I pushed 'SEND', waited and then punched in my code. Finally Sarah's recorded voice came on the line: 'Told you so, told you so! *My* "To 'L' and Back" is the Grand Prize winner. Hah!' End of message.

'Sarah knows.'

'So I suspected. And heard. Why does she even bother using the phone? We probably could've heard her through an open window.' Sarah's house lay a mile away from mine, but still an apt comment. 'I wish I could figure out how to turn down the voice volume on my cell. I don't mind your listening in, but not necessarily the rest of the world.'

'I don't like that, either. I can show you the adjustment sometime.' A pause. 'You going to call her back?'

'Nope. Sarah will lord it over me tomorrow ad nauseam. Her gloating will give us something to share if business is slow again.'

'One thing I didn't hear. Did Sarah say if it was Anita Hampton who notified her?'

'No. Why?'

'Just wondering if she's taken over Ms Penn-Williams' duties.'

'Maybe temporarily, but with Brewster being the Brookhills County Exec, I doubt Anita would be allowed to work long-term for her own husband. By the way—' I reached across the table and ran my palm over Pavlik's beard stubble—'Anita was getting mighty friendly on that stage this morning. She better not let Brewster catch her flirting.'

'Friendly?' Pavlik looked surprised. Didn't stop him from adding onions to the toxic soup steeping in Frank's stomach.

'With who?'

'Whom,' I corrected automatically.

Now Pavlik gave me a look with no surprise in it at all.

'Sorry,' I said. 'But the "to whom" is you. She was rubbing your arm.'

'Why bring it up?' Pavlik pushed back a bit from the table, a grin on his face. 'Are you jealous?'

'Of course not.' At least I didn't think I was. Until now. Shit. Should I be?

'Good.' Pavlik reached over to lay his right hand on mine, which, in turn, had hold of a triangle of pizza. 'Because I'm not interested in Anita. I'm interested in you.'

'I like that.' I gazed down at the pizza, my first slice trapped under our hands. Much as I loved the reassurance, I was hungry and the pizza supply was rapidly dwindling. 'Anita and Brewster make quite the power couple.'

'They do, indeed,' Pavlik said, leaving his right paw on mine, but picking up a piece of pizza with his left. 'Though I'm not sure what the attraction is.'

I tried to slide my hand back a little. 'Besides him being handsome and powerful?'

'No, I meant what's the attraction for Brewster. You used to work with Anita, right?'

'*For* her,' I corrected.

'I'm not sure there's a difference. She treats everybody like minions. And it's starting to rub off on Brewster.'

I traced my thumbnail along the side of his hand. 'Have you needed to work with her?' I asked.

'Not much, though that may change.' Pavlik took another bite. 'The two county execs just announced an initiative that would have involved both JoLynne Penn-Williams and Anita Hampton.'

'What kind of initiative?'

'Drugs. We're focusing primarily on heroin and cocaine in the city and marijuana and crystal meth in the countryside. That's what the regional DEA conference the last two days was all about.' Take *that*, Sarah. A regional meeting with the Drug Enforcement Agency of the federal government, not an assignation.

'Aren't all four of those drugs more urban problems, though?' This was staid 'exurbia', after all.

Another bite. 'You'd be surprised, Maggy. As my counterpart in Milwaukee keeps reminding me, Brookhills has its share of drug action. It's just more invisible here in the 'burbs—easier to keep under wraps. For example, a meth lab in the city is easier to find than one hidden in the hinterlands. Properties are larger, houses farther apart, so we're not as aware of what people around us are doing.'

My neighbors seemed plenty well-informed, but then Frank was hard to miss. 'Was Walensky there, too?' Milwaukee County Sheriff Kenneth Walensky and Pavlik had been in the same department in Chicago. Apparently it wasn't a mutually enjoyable experience.

'Unfortunately.' Pavlik thought for a moment. 'Maggy, a question?'

'Sure.' I wasn't sure I was prepared for the role reversal.

'About JoLynne Penn-Williams.' Pavlik tossed his crust to Frank, who caught and swallowed it with one flick of the head. 'She was in events and marketing, like you were. How well did you know her?'

'Not well, and mostly through Rebecca. Our paths didn't cross professionally, because JoLynne moved to Milwaukee just as I was leaving marketing behind.' Along with my specious marriage, my spacious house and any financial security I'd probably ever know. *Not* that I was bitter.

'But *you* must have known her,' I continued. 'When I was managing events, any time public lands or streets were involved, we contacted the police and sheriff's departments.'

'You'd think so, wouldn't you?' Now he was taking a swig of wine, also lefty.

I looked at my glass, just out of reach.

'Not to speak ill of the dead,' he continued, 'but I'm told Ms Penn-Williams didn't accomplish much in the position. Now Anita Hampton, whatever you and I may think of her, gets things done. She's proactive. When Wynona and I had dinner with her and Brewster—'

I pulled my hand back. 'You had…dinner?' The Brookhills county executive and sheriff, dining with the Milwaukee county executive and marketing executive. I was getting a twinge of something I didn't like. Something green, perhaps fueled by my conversation with Sarah this morning. 'Were you all planning some event?'

'Event? No, this was purely social.' Pavlik picked up the wine bottle and poured Cabernet first into my glass and then into his. 'Wynona and I went out a few times.' I remembered Sarah's comments about Pavlik and Wynona Counsel acting friendly.

'So, when was this?'

'I met her just after I moved up here—last spring?' He was holding a piece of sausage over Frank's nose. 'In fact, I'm sure it was then, because we went to the museum's May Fund-raiser.'

'But you and I were dating in May.' My voice sounded small, even to me.

Pavlik looked up, his blue eyes startled. 'Well, yes. But we didn't see much of each other as I recall.'

'Because I was busy. Because you were busy.' With *her*?

It was like he'd read my mind. 'Maggy, I never said I wasn't dating other people.'

People? As in the plural? 'You never said you were.'

'You didn't ask.'

'You didn't tell.' Pizza forgotten, I stood up. 'And you knew I wasn't seeing anyone else.' Pavlik came out of his chair, too, and around the table to me.

'Listen,' he said, 'I'm not sure what to say. All I can

tell you is that Wynona and I did go out for a while last year.'

'Why'd you stop?' I was hoping for one of those 'because I knew it was you I loved'.

Yeah, yeah. I know. Not only a hopeless romantic, but a hapless one as well.

'She dumped me.' I didn't know if his answer made me feel jealous or just plain stupid. I'd come very close to telling Pavlik I loved him a couple of months back. Thank God...well, the idea had scared me silly.

'So, if Wynona hadn't "dumped" you, would you still be together?'

He held his hands up in the way that just screams: *what do you want from me?* 'We weren't "together", Maggy. I only saw her from time to time.'

'Well, then, what about us?' I asked. 'Are we "together" or just "seeing each other from time to time"?'

He put his hands on my shoulders and looked me straight in the eyes. 'You tell me.'

All I could do was answer honestly. 'I don't know.'

Pavlik kissed me on the forehead. 'Me neither. But I'd like the opportunity to find out.'

SEVEN

'Now what exactly did he mean by that?' I demanded.

Sarah's head was in our bakery case, so 'wmm-mmwf-ot' was her entire reply.

'I mean, if the word "relationship" had been floated out by yours truly, what would Pavlik have said?'

'Mwwmufml.'

'Does it feel like the two of us are a couple? Yeah, at least to me. His deputies haze him about our seeing each other. That seems a good sign.'

'Frcigdskshrtmimo.'

'Sarah, enough. In recognizable English, please.'

She pulled out of the glass-fronted case. 'I said, for God's sake, Maggy, stop acting like you're in high school. Next thing you'll be driving by his house ten times a night or calling his friends to see what—if any-thing—he's saying about you.'

'Please. We're well into a new millennium. There has to be a better way by now. And besides—' I pushed the brew button on our coffee urn—'I was married for nearly twenty years and dated Ted from college onward. Outside of him, I'm a social virgin.'

'Pot?'

'Just once.'

'No, you idiot.' Sarah pointed to the brewer, now making spitting noises. 'I mean, aren't you going to put a pot under that?'

'Oh.' I slid a carafe below the filter basket just in time to catch the coffee. All cylinders in Maggy's engine just weren't firing this morning.

The bells on the front door tinkled as Amy entered.

'It's starting to rain out there,' she said, doffing a poncho. Under it, she wore a white Uncommon Grounds T-shirt featuring a sleek, silver espresso machine.

'Wow. Nice shirt,' I said. 'But…where'd you get it?'

'I ordered a bunch of them.' She pulled two more just like it out of her Uncommon Grounds tote.

'Cool.' Sarah took one, stripped to her—God save us all—red lace bra and slipped it on.

I studied the shirt. 'You know, the espresso machine looks kind of like a locomotive.'

'Clever, huh? A friend at the university came up with this design.' Amy retreated into our office to drop off her stuff.

'Should we keep letting her do that?' I whispered to Sarah.

'Do what?' More the stage whisper in a Shakespearean play.

'Shh.' I put a finger up to my lips. 'Should we allow Amy to order things without our permission?'

'Have you seen a bill?'

'Well, no.'

'Are they good purchases?'

'Well, yeah.'

'Then I say more power to her. We could use a little image-spiffing around here.' Sarah had a point. It was a shame to open a brand new location and wear our tacky old T-shirts. 'Hey, maybe if the customers want them, we can even sell a few, like the bags.'

'That's the spirit.' Sarah smacked me between my shoulder blades.

Since my friend had been diagnosed bipolar, I'd come to regard any un-Sarah-like moods with suspicion. You know, things like chipper or even…hearty.

Before I could give the subject more thought, Amy rejoined us, tying on an apron. 'Did you hear the news? They say somebody smothered JoLynne and dumped her in our coffee cup.' Homicide, confirmed. So why was Pavlik so close-mouthed last night?

'But why?' I asked. 'Attempted robbery?'

'Supposedly they found JoLynne's purse under her body.'

'Nothing taken?' Sarah asked. She had moved from the bakery case to the cooler, pricing the sandwiches and salads Tien had made. I had to hand it to my new partner. She was definitely a self-starter. Assuming this also wasn't the start of a manic phase.

Amy shook her head and it took me a second to realize she was answering Sarah's question about Jo's handbag, rather than any concern about my partner's mental status. Nothing had been stolen, so robbery wasn't the motive. What did that leave? Lust? Jealousy?

The front door opened with another jangle. 'Still closed,' the three of us said in blind unison.

'I'm so sorry.' Christy stood at the door. She had on a yellow rubber raincoat and matching boots and gloves. Her hood was up, only her face showing, and water glistened from every article of clothing she wore. 'I could just really use a cup of coffee for my drive.'

'Not a problem, Christy,' I said, the pot I'd started now full. I snagged a to-go cup off the stack and began pouring.

'Want me to leave room for cream?' She shook her head, so I topped off the drink and capped off the cup. 'No charge.'

'Don't be silly.' Christy had picked up her coffee and was struggling to get out her purse, apparently slung over her shoulder before she donned the slicker.

'First one's on us,' I said. 'Come back. Often.'

'Thank you so much, Maggy. I needed a little pick-me-up before seeing Ronny again.'

I glanced up at our Brookhills clock. 'It's not even six thirty. Does the prison have visiting hours this early?'

'Jail. Ronny's still in pretrial confinement.' Christy's face flamed. 'And I'm going to get ready first. The tanning salon on Civic opens early so people can stop by for a session before work.' She gestured me closer and whispered, 'Ronny likes it when I have a tan.' I didn't want to imagine what the two loonies—the one homicidal, the other holistic—might be doing together.

'Those tanning beds aren't good for you.'

'Ooh, I would never actually *lie* in one of those filthy things, even with my clothes on,' Christy said. 'I get a spray tan.' I was going to ask her how she could be sure the nozzle was clean, but I didn't want to sour her morning.

Christy exited with a wave, passing another neighbor.

'Rebecca,' I greeted JoLynne's younger sister. 'I'm so sorry about what happened.' Rebecca's eyes were red, and her hair plastered down from the rain, but other than that she projected normally.

'Don't be sorry,' she said. 'JoLynne brought this on herself. Rehab, my ass. The only good to come of that was her meeting Kevin in Chicago. I knew something self-destructive was bound to happen.' If Rebecca had actually foreseen her sister's bizarre death, I could use the surviving sibling's help picking lottery numbers.

'What do you mean?' I asked as the bells jingled again and in came Michael, Rebecca's biz-dom partner.

She ignored him. 'I knew JoLynne's lifestyle would kill her eventually. She was an all-purpose addict. Alcohol, sex, drugs, you name it.'

'Now, Becc—' Michael started.

I'd have told him to save his breath, but if the stud hadn't figured that out already, he was beyond salvaging by me.

'*Re*becca,' she snapped. 'And what do you know about my sister, Michael? You didn't see her two years ago. "Pretty, little JoLynne"—' quotation marks in the air from the grieving sister's index and middle fingers— 'home from Chicago. Broke, and broken.'

'Becca,' Michael said again. You had to admire the man for being stubborn as a badger. He knew the nickname irritated his principal squeeze, but he wasn't going to back off using it.

'JoLynne came back clean. She'd been in rehab and started over.'

'More like tarted over.'

'You can't keep blaming her for the past. There was nothing—' he looked at us for emphasis, if not support—'*nothing* more important to Jo than her future.'

Rebecca seethed. 'And when did she tell you that, Michael? Pillow talk?' Enough. The woman was going to scare away our customers.

'C'mon, Rebecca,' I said, 'cool down. You don't want to make a fool of yourself.'

'*Me* make a fool of *my*self?' Rebecca turned on me. 'You're the fool. Or,' a sly smile, 'don't you know?'

Know? 'Know what?'

'You think you have the perfect "relationship", right?' More punctuation marks in the air. Then she threw a disdainful look at Michael. 'Well, I did, too.'

'No relationship is perfect,' I said slowly. I didn't like where Rebecca was going with this. 'And mine is none of your business.'

'Fine,' she said, yanking the door open and sending the bells crashing against it. 'Then I won't tell you.' Sheesh. Talk about your mood swings. Maybe it was Rebecca I should be worried about. Not that I gave a rat's ass.

'Tell me what?'

'*Tell* you,' she said mimicking my tone, 'that my Michael and some guy she worked with evidently weren't enough for the little slut. JoLynne was also banging your Sheriff Jake like a drum.' Rebecca wheeled and stalked out, leaving the door open behind her.

I followed her into the rain like she had me on a tractor beam. 'What do you mean? Where? When?'

'Where? Here.' Rebecca kept going.

'That's impossible. Pavlik has only been in Brookhills a year and a half. Back in Chicago, maybe, but—' She finally stopped and turned again. Now water streamed from her hair, mascara turning even *her* beautiful face into a pulsating mask.

'You really don't know, do you? You poor, moonstruck little twit. No, not in Chicago. And not last year. Not even last *month*. JoLynne told me about Sheriff Jake the day before she died.'

EIGHT

'UH, FORGIVE ME for noticing, but why did Rebecca come in here to start with?' Sarah asked as I re-entered the shop. 'She didn't even get any coffee.'

No, the surviving sister seemed satisfied with simply ruining my life.

Was Pavlik having an affair with JoLynne Penn-Williams? He hadn't said there was anyone after Wynona. Except me, of course. Then again, as Pavlik would repeat 'you didn't ask.'

Great. Just what I needed: a 'relationship' built on Twenty Questions.

Is this woman concurrent or sequential? Serious or casual? Bigger than a bread box?

Fit into a coffee cup?

Bad taste, I know, but beyond that, a broader consideration. Should Pavlik be investigating the murder of a married woman he'd been 'dating'?

'Maggy?' JoLynne had clued Rebecca about her affair with Pavlik. The next day, the 'cluer' is dead. Coincidence?

God, angry or not, I hoped so.

Maybe JoLynne's husband Kevin somehow discovered she'd been unfaithful, then killed her. Much as I liked the man, I preferred he be the murderer. Pavlik might be a two-timer, but he was *my* two-timer. And if *any*one was going to 'send him away,' it was...

'Maggy! Are you OK?' Michael Inkel was staring at me, Sarah now nowhere to be seen. I had stopped, dripping, just inside the door, chin on chest, thinking. Or trying to think. Maybe Rebecca was a nutcase. After all, she didn't like Michael hanging around me and I, for one, had utterly no interest in him. Maybe Rebecca thought every woman was loose and every man—or, at least, *her* man—a perpetual target.

'Do you want a towel?' he asked.

I ignored the offer. 'Is Rebecca right? Did you sleep with her sister?' Michael started to shake his head in the negative.

I lowered my voice a couple of notches below hysterical.

'It's important, Michael. Whatever you tell me will go no further, but I have to know.' An inner struggle reached his face. That was my answer, but I needed more. And Michael didn't want to say the words.

'Just nod, then. Did you have an affair—or even just a one-night stand—with JoLynne?' And, finally, Michael Inkel nodded.

But he didn't buy coffee before leaving, either.

'Incredible,' Sarah said, coming back into the shop proper from our storeroom. 'What do people think, they just come in here to act out? Do we do that at their stores?'

'Yes,' I said absently. I was still trying to get my head around this jolt of fresh gossip. To understand. Rebecca had been right about Michael. That meant she wasn't completely delusional. Her sister is…was 'sleeping around'. And JoLynne had said one of her 'circle' was Pavlik.

Boy, did I know how to pick 'em.

'True.' But Sarah was agreeing with whatever I'd just said, not thought. 'Though what's there to buy? Piano lessons from Christy? Catering from Art? Advertising from Rebecca and Michael?'

'Advertising, definitely.' This answer came from a different quarter. At some point, Amy had begun prepping the espresso machine. 'We should be publicizing our new location.' I might be dripping wet and devastated by what I'd just learned, but I couldn't let anyone think I'd fallen down on my job.

'I *did* publicize it. The grand opening, the newspaper stories.'

'You mean this one?' Sarah tossed a copy of the daily *CitySentinel* to me. The issue was folded to a photo of JoLynne's body, taken by someone neither as sensitive nor considerate as Jerome. The paper did have the decency to blur her face, but the caption read: 'Freak coffeehouse death mars Milwaukee–Brookhills commuter-rail dedication.'

'They could at least have mentioned which "freak"ing coffeehouse,' I muttered, taking a stack of napkins to blot off the rain on my face.

Sarah and Amy must have heard some of Rebecca's pronouncement, but—maybe by mutual agreement—they didn't bring it up. Which was good, because I didn't intend to, either, for the time being. First I wanted to crawl into a hole—aka, my house—and think.

'Here we are.' Amy pointed to the fabric partially obscuring JoLynne's leg. The Uncommon Grounds logo was clearly visible. It was even being held upright by the raised edge of the saucer, the only part of the whole thing that still had air in it.

Including JoLynne, as it turned out.

'And that's not all,' Sarah said, grabbing the paper away from me and flipping to an inside page. 'Look at this.' I did. A photo of Sarah accompanied an article headlined, '"From L & Back" says it all for local woman.'

No wonder my partner was in a good mood. 'By the time I listened to your message, it was too late to return the call. I'm so happy for you.'

'Sure you are.' Sarah thrust the paper back at me. 'Read it and weep.' Knowing that she would value my perceived envy over my professed congratulations, I didn't argue and took the paper.

The story went on to explain—for a very long three paragraphs—exactly what 'all' its headline signified, pretty much as Sarah had waxed eloquent with me. The last, blessedly succinct, sentence reported that the train would be known as 'The L' for short.

Thank the Lord. 'Did they interview you?'

'Nope, they just used the information on the entry form. I sent the photo, too.' Sarah was turning over the 'CLOSED' sign on the door, something we should have done three noncustomers ago. 'To be fair, though, there really wasn't time for the *CitySentinel* to do an interview after Anita Hampton telephoned last night to tell me I'd won.' So Pavlik was right: Anita was picking up the slack left by JoLynne's untimely death.

Before I could comment, the morning rush started in earnest. And I do mean 'rush'.

At the old Uncommon Grounds, most of our early customers were commuters, too, but they were commuting in their own cars. They came in small, manageable waves, drivers seeming to leave for work on the hour, half-hour or quarter-hour. (Had anyone thought that maybe backing out of their driveways at 7:23 instead of 7:30 might cede them a lead on the pack?) The small 'waves' were nothing, though, in comparison to the tsunami that hit us fifteen minutes before the first of the two scheduled trains arrived at 6:50 a.m.

'Holy shit,' said Sarah as a parade of cars passed our windows and descended into the big commuter parking lot.

'Do we have enough to feed and water this herd?'

'Not every head of steer will come in,' I said. 'Some of them will go right to the boarding platform.' I might have been right, but all I could see were the people coming in our door, folding umbrellas and stamping their wet feet on our wooden floor.

Since Amy was still the only one who really knew how to run the cash register, she handled the order window and Tien's baked goods. I took the espresso machines and specialty drinks, with Sarah on the express coffee window.

We'd added the express window so the 'I'll have a medium, black' crowd, didn't have to wait behind the 'triple-shot, extra large, non-fat, no-foam latte' cultists. Still training on the espresso machine, Sarah was the ideal person to serve folks who wanted regular old coffee instead of the more time-consuming specialty drinks. Her 'take it and get out' attitude probably didn't hurt, either.

Our system, though admittedly overtaxed, proved to be a good one. At first, the two lines were fairly equal, but as boarding time grew short, people migrated to the express line and I moved off the espresso machine to keep old-fashioned coffee brewing.

'Whew,' Amy said as the second train finally departed at 7:45 a.m. 'This was the morning from hell.'

'L,' Sarah corrected. 'We need more staff. And machines, both coffee-makers and espresso.'

'We sure did today, but this was our first experience with the train's regular schedule.' For the fourth time in ninety minutes, I was filling up the creamer on the condiment cart by the door. Good thing I'd sent Amy to the store yesterday.

'What if this morning's early shift was an aberration?'

'Or morbid curiosity.' Amy, who was mopping up the puddles on our planked floor, gestured toward the window.

'When do you suppose they'll take that down?' She was referring to the stage, now empty except for torn remnants of police tape skittering across. Both the rain and our cup/saucer were gone, the former heading east on to Lake Michigan and the latter likely hauled off by the crime-scene unit some time after we'd left the prior day.

'I'll call Kevin.' I tossed the empty half-and-half carton into the wastebasket under the sink. 'They probably don't know the police have cleared out.'

'Sheriff's team,' Sarah corrected. I'd noticed she was doing a lot of that, probably fueled by her win in the train-naming contest. 'And Kevin Williams himself may not be there. From what Anita Hampton told me last night, he's your boyfriend's prime suspect.' Well, lah-de-dah. And how exactly could Anita know that?

'Really? The only thing Pavlik said to me was that JoLynne died by asphyxiation.'

'Don't they always suspect the husband first?' Amy

asked. Or the wife's lover. But I didn't want to think about that.

Or start a debate over it.

Sarah seemed to be counting the empty brewing pots lined up on the counter. 'Anita said the county guys know it was murder and Pavlik is focusing on Kevin. Is there something I should do with these?'

'Wash them,' I said.

'How?'

I pointed at the sink. 'Hot water, soap.'

'Or you can use the dishwasher,' Amy said gently. 'Here, I'll show you.' Thankfully, Amy had patience, because I certainly didn't. At least not today. It wasn't even Sarah's fault. We should have trained her on all the equipment ahead of Dedication Day. Problem was, the last of the paraphernalia hadn't been installed before Monday and we'd opened on Wednesday.

Amy, though terrific, still had just two hands. Even when Sarah got up to speed, the three of us wouldn't be able to handle long-term the magnitude and urgency of the crowd we'd had this morning. 'I've got a train to catch' wasn't just blowing smoke in this case.

Would the commuters keep patronizing our shop long-term? I couldn't predict. But I did know we had a very defined—and narrow—window of opportunity to prove we could serve our customers efficiently enough to assure them they'd make their trains. If we failed at that, it wouldn't be long before our 'to-go' cups would be replaced by ones from Dunkin' Donuts and Mickey D's.

Amy seemed to read my mind. 'It'd be awkward to hire someone only to lay them off if things quieted down. Do you think Tien would consider helping us out as a stopgap in the morning?'

'Not a bad idea.' Sarah pushed the 'wash' button and, with a pat on the dishwasher's stainless steel head, stepped back proudly. 'We'd need her for only a couple hours.' The dishwasher sounded less like a cat purring in appreciation than one hawking up a hairball, as in 'ker-chuk, ker-chuk'.

Sarah might be on the high side regarding our need for Tien. It was more like an hour and a quarter, from 6:30 to about 7:45, when the second train left. Seventy-five really hectic minutes, though an extra pair of hands could make all the difference.

'Tien arrives here at closing time to do her baking, so she's not in the way during business hours,' I reminded them. 'I can't very well expect her to come back.'

'Maybe she'd be willing to work midnight to eight?' Amy asked.

'I don't know, but I can ask.' I wasn't looking forward to it.

'It's not such a bad shift,' Amy went on, 'at least compared with what Tien is already doing. If she didn't start work until midnight, she could still go out to dinner or see a movie beforehand. As it is, she'll have no time for any social life.' Only someone who *has* a social life would conceive of such things. I came close to asking Amy to call Tien, but as a partner, it was my responsibility. Or Sarah's.

The latter, pots now in the dishwasher, had picked up the frothing pitcher and was gazing into it like milk was a foreign substance. My partner had enough on her proverbial plate.

'Amy, if you show Sarah how to froth milk, I'll go

phone Tien right now.' And I did just that. Awakening her, of course.

'I am so sorry, Tien.' I glanced at the clock. Eight fifteen. The calm between the commuters and the soccer moms who, I hoped, would drop their kids off at school and continue on to Uncommon Grounds. 'I didn't even think of what time it must be.'

'Not a problem, Maggy.' Even half asleep, the woman was perky. 'How's it going so far?'

'Well, that's what I'm calling about.'

'Uh-oh. Was something wrong with my food?' I should have realized that Tien Romano, as conscientious as she was, would fear I was calling to complain about something.

'Just the opposite. Your pastries and sandwiches were a huge hit,' I said honestly. 'We even ran out of coffee cake.'

'Oh, dear. I knew I should have made two.'

'No, no, no,' I said sternly, '*you* are perfect. Your *food* is perfect. I am the screw-up who didn't realize we'd be bombarded this morning.'

'Really? There was a crowd?' Tien's voice was sunny again.

'Crowd? The line went out the door. We literally could not keep up.'

'That's wonderful!'

'Wonderful, yes. But—' worming into my reason for calling—'it's a problem, too.'

'A problem?'

'A "good" problem, Tien. We had a ton of customers, only we couldn't serve them all before each train left.'

'Oh.' A thoughtful silence.

I joined her in it, and then: 'I just don't know if this

gold rush will last. The novelty of the train may wear off.' Or the novelty of the murder at its dedication.

Another silence. 'You know, if you wanted me to, I could schedule my work in the kitchen so I can stay later into the morning and help you out.'

'Really?' I was almost ashamed of myself. *Almost*. 'Tien, I couldn't ask you to do that.'

'You're not asking me. I'm offering.'

OK. Now I *was* ashamed of myself. 'Honestly, if you can do that, I would be really grateful. And I promise that it won't be for long. Once we get a gauge on things, we'll have a better idea how to staff.'

'Don't be silly, Maggy. I really enjoyed working the counter yesterday. It made me realize how much I miss the store.' Tien and her father Luc Romano had owned An's Foods, the market around the corner from the original Uncommon Grounds. When the plaza that both operations rented in had collapsed, the father/daughter team decided not to reopen in another location. Luc had wanted his beautiful daughter to have a life outside managing a family store. Tien, in turn, said her father needed to stand somewhere other than behind a butcher counter.

Both of them thought they were giving the other what he or she wanted, but it had turned out like 'The Gift of the Magi' with shopping carts. Luc and Tien each had sacrificed what one loved most for the other. Sticking point: they both loved the same thing, the market that bore the name of Tien's deceased Vietnamese mother.

'In fact,' Tien continued, 'if we need more help, I bet my father would be happy to pitch in occasionally. I know he misses the socialization our market gave him, too.'

'And we'd be happy to have Luc,' I said. I hadn't thought about a male barista, shame on me. 'Isn't he enjoying retirement, though?'

'Of course not,' Tien said flatly. 'You know how he can be. But I'm working on him to get out more.'

'You know, that might be a side benefit of shifting your hours.' I was now drawing on what Amy had told me. 'You'd be able to go out to dinner, enjoy the night life.'

'Date, you mean.' She laughed. 'Did you talk to my dad first?'

'No.'

'Good, then you've been spared his "next generation" spiel.' Tien was trying to act perturbed, but she seemed more amused than irritated.

'Luc wants grandchildren, I take it?'

'Of course.' I could picture Tien throwing her hands in the air. If she wasn't holding the receiver in one.

'After all,' she continued, 'everyone *else* has them.' Not me. Not yet. And, when your only offspring is a gay male, maybe never. But that was OK with me, if it was OK with Eric.

'Sounds like peer pressure.'

'That's what I told him. All those "if everyone jumped off a building, would you do it?" lectures are coming back to haunt him.' Then her voice changed. 'Umm. Not that having kids is like jumping off a cliff, of course.'

Yeah. Like Tien had to worry about offending me. 'At three a.m., with a colicky baby and a job to leave for in three more hours, it sure can feel that way.'

She laughed. 'So, how's this? I won't show up before closing tonight. I'll arrive more like midnight or

one a.m. and get my baking done, put together sandwiches and maybe make soup. Then I'll be able to help
after you get in at six.'

'I can't tell you how much I appreciate this, Tien.'

'Maggy, it'll be fun.' I hung up the phone thinking I
didn't deserve her. Before I could start pondering less
pleasant things I also didn't deserve, I heard a commotion out front.

Enter the soccer moms.

At the original Uncommon Grounds, the group had
staked out their favorite tables, even their favorite seats
around same. On this occasion, though—the soccer
moms' first visit to our new location—you'd think we'd
just shanghaied them to another planet.

Ten minutes, minimum, for the ladies to decide on
a table. And I thought they'd never find the condiment
cart and napkins.

'Maggy, just lovely,' one of them said, as she went
to open the door to finally leave. Since Caron had, in
the first incarnation of Uncommon Grounds, a better
memory for names than me, I'd never bothered to dif-
ferentiate among 'the moms'. The whole group knew
me, though.

This mom dropped her voice. 'I thought we'd be here
yesterday, but with all the unpleasantness…' Hands held
out and a shrug.

Yes. Death could be so…inconvenient. Especially
for the dead guy. Or gal, in this case.

'Well, I'm glad you made it this morning,' I said,
genuinely meaning it, despite the fact that I sometimes
(OK, often) make fun of their foibles. The group had
sought us out in our new location, and I really was very

grateful. 'Thanks so much.' I went to close the door behind her, but it was pulled out of my hands.

'Sorry, Maggy,' Jerome said.

He wasn't carrying his camera today, but he did arrive with Kate McNamara, more's the pity.

'C'mon in,' I said, circling back to my post behind
the service window. 'What would you like?'

'Answers.' Kate slapped a five on the counter.

I pushed it back. 'I refused to be bought for a ten
yesterday.'

'This is for the coffee.' She shoved it again. 'I don't
pay for information.'

'Kate has journalistic ethics,' Jerome said.

'And,' Sarah whispered in my ear, 'no slush fund for
informants, I'll bet.'

'OK,' I said to Kate. 'Let's start with the coffee and
forget about the answers.' And, please, God, everything
else that had happened over the last two days—at least
until I could get home for a decent glass of wine, a good
think, and a better cry. 'Jerome? What can I get you?'

'Coffee. Black.'

'Really? When did you start drinking the stuff
straight?'

The hard-bitten videographer waggled his head. 'All
right, I'm outed. Iced mocha, extra whipped cream.'

'Cherry?' He looked at Kate, who rolled her eyes,
before he said, 'Sure.' I'd plop on two.

'And you?'

'Coffee. Black.' Kate threw Jerome a withering look.
Sarah reached for the pot on a bottom burner of the coffee brewer, but I redirected her to one on top.

Again she whispered in my ear, 'But should we use
that? Hasn't it been sitting too long?'

'Of course. And who else would we serve it to?' I slid the inky brew over to Kate. As I feared, instead of carrying it to a table, she stayed put.

'Your sheriff took Kevin Williams in for questioning.'

My sheriff. I didn't bother to correct her or, for that matter, rein in my growing anger at Pavlik. Mad, I could still function. Sad, I'd curl up in the fetal position under a table.

'So they're sure JoLynne's death wasn't an accident?' I knew the answer unofficially, but I wanted to hear it from Kate.

'An accident?' I'd never seen anybody physically project the word 'dumbfounded' before. It seemed a little over the top.

But, then, so was Kate. 'You're the one who had that inflated monstrosity built. The sides were like four-feet tall.'

'Five, if you count the saucer,' I corrected.

Kate was trying to look patient. 'So *five* feet, even better. It's not like she just "oopsied" and fell in.'

'Told you.' This from Sarah passing behind me as she went to empty the dishwasher.

I said, 'Maybe JoLynne first climbed up so she could see into the cup and…slipped?'

'Funny. The sheriff doesn't think a five-foot two-inch woman in a pencil skirt and strappy high heels could have climbed a five-foot high—' Kate checked her notes—'"convex surface"—that means a curved out one.' She showed me a supercilious smile.

'I know what it means, Kate.'

'Splendid. And here I thought your former partner was the wordsmith.' At this rate, in a minute, Ms Mc-

Namara was going to be 'former'—as in formerly able to stand erect. 'OK, so JoLynne didn't clamber in on her own. Could she have had help?'

'Or a ladder.' Sarah again, now moving the other way.

'Good guess,' Kate said. 'But there was no ladder in reach.' The smile had gone from supercilious to deprecating.

Had Kate been practicing in the mirror? What was next? Envy? Lust? Despair?

Life is short, and it was time for me to cut through the crap. 'Then what *do* the authorities think happened?'

'Murder, plain and simple. Someone smothered her and hid her body in your screwy cup.'

'Why?'

'Apparently JoLynne was having an affair with someone in county government. Her husband probably found out.' Sarah dropped the handful of clean spoons she'd been using to restock the condiment cart. To her credit, she picked them up and kept her mouth shut.

'Who?' My question came out more like a croak.

I got 'contempt' from Kate on this one. 'Kevin Williams, of course.'

'Thanks, but I meant who was JoLynne having an affair with?' I didn't want to ask the question and I sure as hell didn't want the answer. My hands were sweating and the top of my head tingling.

'With *whom*.' I vowed never to correct Pavlik's English again. *Assuming* I ever talked to him.

'Fine,' I said through clenched teeth. 'With *whom* was JoLynne having an affair?'

'Oh, that.' Kate flapped her hand, like it was inconsequential. 'No one knows. Or maybe they're just not talking. If the person is important enough, there could even be a cover-up.' From her tone, I could tell Kate hoped so, just as I did. My reason was that whatever was going on between Pavlik and me, I didn't like to think of him publicly embarrassed. Or run out of town on a rail. Tarred and feathered...

I had a hunch, though, that Kate McNamara actually, genuinely, wanted the opportunity to dig out the truth.

Jerome, who had been quiet so far, wiped whipped cream off his lip. 'Kate's a great investigative reporter. She'll find out what really happened.' That's what I was afraid of. I needed to hear what the woman already knew.

Maybe throw out some alternative scenarios, keep her busy.

'Could JoLynne's body have been in the cup *before* it was inflated?' Jerome's brow furrowed.

'Still wouldn't clear Williams,' Kate said. 'He inflated the thing. Who knows what—or who—was in it?'

'I do.' Jerome turned to face Kate. 'You told me to get there early and film background stuff. I taped Kevin and one of his guys filling the cup.' Which, presumably, didn't contain JoLynne's body or Jerome would have seen it.

'So where's that leave us?' I asked.

Impatience was now Kate's emotion of choice. 'Just what I said, weren't you listening? Someone killed JoLynne Penn-Williams and dumped her body into your precious balloon after it was inflated.'

'It's not—' I interrupted myself because a thought suddenly struck me. Turning to Sarah, I said, 'We were on the porch with a clear view of the cup, right?'

She slid the dropped spoons back into the dishwasher's utensil basket. 'Right.'

'We stayed until after the thing fell, but what time did we get there?'

'Seven fifteen,' Amy contributed, coming from the back.

'I saw you pass by the side window—' a gesture toward the tracks— 'as I was filling the second thermal pot of coffee for Tien to take outside.'

'And when did they inflate the cup?' I asked Jerome.

'I'm not sure.' He seemed distracted by Amy's appearance, both in the sense of her joining us and her looks.

Cougar Kate growled at him. 'Jerome?'

He blinked. 'Uh, sorry. Maybe a little before six a.m.?'

'Isn't there a time stamp or something on your tape?' I asked as he continued to stare at our barista. Amy might be pierced, dyed and tattooed, but under it all she was a mighty attractive girl.

Jerome colored up. 'Oh, sure. I can check the counter on my camera, but I'm pretty sure it was about then. Still dark, with that white cup the only thing filmable until County Exec Hampton arrived around the same time to take the train to Milwaukee.' He shrugged. 'Since the engineer was making the run just to take him down and have the train in place for the Milwaukee celebration, even that wasn't very visual.'

Brewster? Not visual? 'Was his wife Anita leading him?'

Jerome shook his head. 'She came later. In fact, almost missed her ride. I remember because I got a nice long shot of the locomotive and cars heading off into the sunrise.'

Anita was probably off somewhere primping. Or sharpening her talons. 'And what time is sunrise these days? Six fifteen?'

'Roughly,' said Jerome.

I turned back to Kate. 'Well, there's your timeline. JoLynne could have been put in the cup between six a.m. and when Sarah and I arrived at seven fifteen.'

The reporter's eyes darted left-right-left, then her mouth dropped open. 'You're right.'

'Of course she is,' Sarah said. 'We've gotten good at this detection stuff.'

We? 'Now go tell the sheriff,' I suggested.

'Sheriff?' Kate virtually spat out the word. 'Don't be silly. I'm taking this to my station. I could get lead story, with a page one follow-up in the *CitySentinel*.'

'But shouldn't Maggy get contributing credit?' asked Jerome.

I waved him off. 'Whatever helps solve the case is fine with me. I don't need—or want—any more publicity from a homicide.' And I was being truthful, so far as it went. But my unstated motivation was to have Kate fixate on JoLynne's murderer, rather than the dead woman's paramour.

Because, I feared, the victim's lover was also mine.

NINE

WHEN THEY SAY love hurts, they ain't kidding.

'Damn.' I was grasping the handle of what used to be a glass coffee carafe, blood dripping from a cut on my right thumb.

'What did you do?' Amy searched for a towel in the drawer next to the sink.

We were reaching the end of a day that felt longer than the prior, dead-body one. Soccer moms, the lunch-bunch, even a sprinkling of seniors and home-office types looking for someone, *any*one, to talk to. All our usuals had come and gone, bless them, leaving us with just the returning commuter trains left. One at 5:30 and one at 6:30. And they couldn't arrive a moment too soon.

'Maggy broke a carafe,' Sarah said, gesturing to the shards on the floor. 'Another one.'

'Another one?' Carefully, Amy traded the towel for the handle, about all that remained of the pot. 'We have the clumsies today, don't we?' Clumsies. The pre-school teacher coming into play again.

'Clumsies is right,' Sarah said. She was watching my blood drip on to the glass. 'You don't see me dropping any carafes.'

'I didn't drop the thing,' I protested. 'The bottom fell out on its own.'

'After you banged that carafe against the brewer, probably cracking—'

'They should be sturdier than that,' I grumbled, going to the sink to run water over my cut.

'You might get away with hitting the brewer's metal corner once, maybe even twice. But you were at least grazing it every time you put a carafe up there.' By 'up there' Sarah meant the top of our tall brewer. The piece of equipment had three heating elements. One below, where you brewed the coffee, and two on top, so you could keep the filled pots warm, while you were brewing a replacement.

'It's too high.' Oww. The water rushed over the cut, circling pink around the stainless-steel tub before draining out. *Psycho* in a slop sink.

'You're too *short*,' Sarah countered. 'You should let someone who can reach the carafes and brewers move them.' She meant herself and, when I glanced over my shoulder, I realized my partner was preening—proud of mastering the process. The hell of it? She had. Sarah was even using the right technical jargon, like 'brewers' for the machines and 'carafes' for the glass pots.

'OK,' I said, turning off the water with my left hand. I picked up the towel to dry my thumb. 'You're right.'

Amy was already standing ready with a Band-Aid. 'Do you think you need stitches?' she asked, ministering to me.

'Nope,' I said, wiggling the finger. 'It'll be fine.'

'Good,' Sarah said. 'Because I hear a train coming. You stay at the espresso machine, where you can't break anything.' I let her have the jibe, though given my preoccupation that afternoon, I probably shouldn't be trusted with the frothing wand either, lest I scald myself or somebody else with the steam.

Amy took her position at the cash register, Sarah at the express line and me, as ordered, at the espresso machine. As we did, we could see the train slide to a stop through our side window.

A second later, the train doors opened and out poured a jumble of people and newspapers, tote bags and brief-cases. Chattering student-types had backpacks slung over their shoulders. As the doors slid closed, we braced ourselves for the onslaught.

Finally, we unclenched.

'What happened?' Sarah asked. 'Where'd they all go?' I pointed out the front window. A parade of cars was exiting the parking lot, heading either south into Brookhills proper or north into lake country.

In other words, straight home.

'Maybe they don't know we're open,' Amy said, coming out from behind her counter to look through the panes.

'Our huge "Now Open!" banner flapping against the side of the building isn't enough of an eye-catcher?' I said.

'You know what I mean,' Amy said, turning around. 'They know we're open for business, but they don't know what hours. The original Uncommon Grounds closed at six.' She was right, of course.

And I knew what was going to be the next word out of her mouth. So I said it first: 'Advertising.'

'What a wonderful idea, Maggy!' The former pre-school teacher's tone was along the lines of, *See, Kelsey? You* can *make wee-wee!*

Hoping to head off the clapping of hands and awarding of a gold star, I said, 'Amy, I think you have a good handle on what—'

'Might be the only handle still intact in this place,' Sarah muttered. She was surveying her domain, which included a slightly diminished inventory of carafes.

'We need,' I continued, focusing on our barista while ignoring my partner. 'Would you put together some ideas for signage and ad copy?' 'Of course,' Amy said, delightedly. 'And I can work with Rebecca on the design.'

Better Amy than me, but I needed to rein the enthusiastic young women in a scosh. 'Sarah and I will need to look at what you come up with, and then you can get quotes from Penn and Ink.'

'Gotcha,' Amy said, her face still glowing with pleasure. Sarah had been rummaging in the drawers. Now she held up a tape dispenser and the back of a menu with large hand-lettering in black Magic Marker. 'Open until 7 p.m.' Moving toward our door, Sarah said, 'In the meantime...' My partner's sign didn't help much, but at least a couple of people from the second train glanced into our windows as they drove away.

I did likewise, as I left for home about an hour later.

It really had been a good start. We were just facing a steep learning curve. How to serve commuters: timing, staffing, inventory.

And perishables.

Poor Tien. In addition to her successful luncheon sandwiches and breakfast pastries, she'd packaged two entrées—meatloaf with mashed potatoes and roast chicken over rice—for people to take home for dinner. Soup, too.

She'd had two customers, at least. Frank and me.

The meatloaf for the big loafer and the chicken for…
yeah, the chicken.

What was I being chicken about, you ask?

Well, Fear One: I'd spent most of the day trying *not*
to think about Pavlik and JoLynne. Rather unsuccess-
fully, given the broken pots—sorry, carafes.

And if I wasn't chicken, I'd pick up the phone and
ask Pavlik, straight out.

Fear Two: I didn't want to hear the answer I felt
I'd get. And, once I got it, Fear Three kicked in: what
would I do about it?

If Pavlik had been having an affair with JoLynne,
a married woman and a homicide victim, he certainly
shouldn't be investigating his lover's murder.

It had to be unethical, right? Like insider trading or
performing brain surgery on a family member.

I could see why Pavlik suspected Kevin Williams.
The sheriff knew that Kevin had a reason for killing
JoLynne. Problem was, that reason was Pavlik himself.

Also, as we'd discussed earlier at Uncommon
Grounds, the police always focus first on the surviving spouse. If Pavlik didn't bring Kevin in for questioning, he'd look careless. Beyond careless.

But our sheriff also had to be hesitant about raising the possibility that JoLynne was unfaithful to her
husband. Unless Pavlik was certain Kevin didn't know
who it was.

Or, who *they* were.

Because while the husband might be the number one
suspect, the lover(s) would run a close second. I didn't
think for a moment that Pavlik was a killer…

No, I *knew* he wasn't a killer. Assuming I 'knew' him at all. Which I wasn't so sure of anymore.

I decided not to think about it. More proof I was chicken. A raucous barking pulled me from my metaphysical trance, if all the crap spinning through my brain merited such a highfalutin' term.

I was sitting in the dark, my Ford Escape now parked in the driveway. On the seat beside me, two dinners. Inside my house, one hungry sheepdog.

If it had been a long day for me, it had been equally long for Frank. Even longer, since he'd have been counting the sands of time in doggy years and didn't have death and betrayal to distract him.

I climbed out of the car and went around to its passenger side. As I did, Frank's barking reached fever pitch.

'I'm coming.' I opened the Escape's door and took out the two, plastic-covered containers. I balanced one of them on the other as I swung the door closed and pressed 'LOCK' on the key fob.

Cursing myself for not remembering to pick up a replacement for the burnt-out light bulb over the side door, I made my way there more by memory than vision. I had one foot on the bottom step of the porch stairs when a form materialized, looming above me.

'I've been waiting for you.' That's when I lost my dinner—or dinners—literally. With my thumb stiff and throbbing under Amy's Band-Aid, meat loaf went one way, chicken the other.

The human stayed put as Pavlik stepped out of the shadows.

'Sorry,' he said, coming down the stairs and giving

my forehead a quick kiss. 'I didn't mean to scare you.'
Pavlik wrapped me up in his arms. 'Hey, you're shaking.' I tried to relax against the buttery leather of his
jacket—the jacket I loved so. I'd kidded Pavlik that it
and I were going to run away together. Now I could only
think about how many other women had been pressed
against that leather. And wonder how many of them
had said they'd loved it.

And him.

Damn right, I was shaking. How in the world do you
go from—at least *practically*—loving a man to fearing he might be a killer? And all in twenty-four hours?

I didn't know. But maybe, after things resolved themselves, I could write a book about what to do if your
husband cheats and then your lover does the same. I'd
call it *The Idiot's Guide to Being an Idiot*.

I stepped back. 'Not your fault. I should have put
a new bulb in the porch light. You just startled me.' I
leaned down to pick up one of the food containers. The
meat loaf. Still intact.

The roast chicken hadn't been as lucky, but that is
the way of chickens. They gets what they deserves.

My sheepdog had resumed his barking. 'I need to let
Frank out,' I told Pavlik, 'but we can't let him eat the
chicken.' Pavlik nodded. He, too, had a dog—Muffin,
the toothless pit bull—and knew that splintered poul-
try bones could be deadly.

I unlocked the door and opened it wide, stepping
aside so Frank wouldn't bowl me over as he came bar-
reling out. I'd have thought the captivating aroma of our
dinners would distract him from his primary objective,
but I was wrong.

He ran immediately up to his sheriff friend for a scratch. As Pavlik obliged, Frank let loose like a fire hose.

Pavlik did a quickstep sideways, lest his shoes be doused.

'I appreciate the multitasking, but you're a male,' he told Frank. 'You're supposed to lift your leg.'

'Just be grateful he didn't take you for a tree,' I said, all the while wondering how the surface exchanges could seem so normal?

But maybe 'normal' was the way to go for now. 'Have you eaten?' I pointed down at the chicken and rice spread far and wide. 'That was supposed to be mine, but I still have Frank's meat loaf.' I held up the container. 'We can split it.' Like a ballistic boomerang, Frank was at my side, sniffing Tien's Delight.

'He doesn't look like he wants to share,' Pavlik said, turning around to pick up a bag from the porch's shadow. 'But I did bring Chinese.' Then a bottle. 'And Shiraz.'

'Wow,' I said. 'Unexpected pleasures. What's the occasion?'

'The quick end of a potentially messy case. Late this afternoon, we arrested Kevin Williams for the murder of his wife.'

TEN

Oh, boy. *Now* what's a poor girl do?

'Come in and I'll get out the plates and silverware,' I said as heartily as my troubled soul could manage.

Raising my thumb, I hitch-hiked it toward the kitchen counter.

'I cut myself at work. Could you chop up Frank's meat loaf so he doesn't swallow it whole?' I began chattering trivially about Chinese food, English sheepdogs and Australian wine. A very different conversation, however, was clattering around my mind: *'...I'm told Ms Penn-Williams didn't accomplish much in the position.'* Exactly which 'position' were you talking about, Pavlik? Missionary? Doggy-style?

'I never said I wasn't dating other people.' People? As in multiples?

'You never said you were.'

'You didn't ask.'

'Shiraz with our Chinese?' I asked out loud. 'I have white chilled, if you'd prefer?'

Pavlik came up behind me at the kitchen counter and circled his hands around my waist. 'The Shiraz. I know it's your favorite,' he said into my hair. 'With pretty much any food.' So intimate, and yet...

'You like reds, too,' I said, 'so that's fine. Great.' I was trying to be cheery, upbeat—natural, even—as

I slid out of his embrace on the pretext of getting the corkscrew from the drawer next to the sink.

Pavlik cocked his head, his blue eyes darkening as he studied my face. 'Maggy, what's wrong?'

Hmm. Maybe cheery and upbeat didn't reflect my natural state any more than it did Sarah's. 'Nothing. Why do you ask?'

'Well, I know that you were worried about Uncommon Grounds being liable in some way for JoLynne's death. I thought you'd be happy to know the shop was off the hook.'

And you? Should I be happy you're off the hook, too?

I handed him the corkscrew. 'Of course, I am. But I like Kevin Williams, and he and JoLynne seemed to be happy.'

'You'd be surprised.' Pavlik levered the cork out of the bottle.

'No one knows what really goes on in somebody else's house.'

Or head.

'So, what about Kevin and JoLynne? What was happening in their house?'

Pavlik shrugged. 'Professional jealousy is my guess. No matter what Kevin tried to believe, he never got past being the construction worker from Chicago who still worked with his hands.'

'That's it?' I turned, holding the cardboard container of moo-shu pork. 'If you're right, there should be an epidemic of husbands killing their wives. And vice versa. You must have some more evidence beyond an inferiority complex.' Going to set the moo-shu and a plastic tray of dumplings on the table, I heard Pavlik clear his throat. I waved him and the wine over to the table and sat down. 'So give.'

Pavlik seemed understandably reluctant. 'I've already told you plenty, Maggy. I—'

'It'll all be public record.' I had a brainstorm. 'Not to mention TV news. I hear Kate McNamara scored some sort of investigative coup.'

The sheriff had been about to pour wine into my glass, then paused. 'What kind of "coup"?'

Popping the clear top off the plastic tray, I scooped out a dumpling for each of us. 'Not sure. She just seemed to think it was important. Something about timing, maybe?'

Pavlik visibly relaxed and finished pouring. 'Well, that's easy enough to reconstruct. We have a tape from the television station showing the cup being blown up—'

'Please, "inflated"!' I had enough problems.

'Inflated just before six a.m., no corpse evident. Eight a.m. out tumbles JoLynne.' JoLynne. Not 'the victim' or 'the deceased', nor even 'Ms Penn-Williams', as earlier. No, instead Pavlik, the ultimate law-enforcement professional, broke protocol to use the first name of a murdered woman he claimed not to know.

Bullshit. In fact, I wouldn't be surprised if JoLynne had taken a sudden trip to Chicago earlier this week, staying at the same hotel hosting Pavlik's DEA conference.

He'd finished his dumpling and moved to the mooshu, first spreading hoisin sauce on a pancake, and then adding shredded pork. 'Which means she was killed and dumped there in that two-hour period before she was found.' Before I could reply, 'my' sheriff lifted his wineglass. 'How about a toast? To the new Uncommon Grounds. Long may it brew.'

'I'll drink to that,' I said, clinking with him. I took a sip of the Shiraz and carefully placed my glass back on the table.

'I assume Kevin doesn't have an alibi for that time period?'

'Parts yes and parts no, from what we can tell so far.' He was looking at my fried dumpling, lust in his eyes and a fork in his hand. 'Are you going to eat that?'

'Yup.' I speared the thing. The guy had taken my post-divorce innocence. He sure as hell wasn't getting my dumpling, too. 'So by "parts yes and parts no", you mean Kevin's alibi has holes in it?'

Pavlik had returned to his moo-shu. 'He was supposedly setting up the staging and all. But according to my detectives' canvas at the scene, nobody saw him after about seven twenty.' Hmm. Sarah and I had been with Kevin part of that time.

Should I tell Pavlik?

Heck, why not? Maybe even push things a little further.

'I'm sorry to mess up your case,' I said, laying my hand on his this time, 'but Kevin was with Sarah and me between seven thirty and maybe seven forty-five. He went off in search of caution tape to cordon off the stairs and gallows, but Sarah and I were near the base of the cup from seven fifteen until it toppled. We'd have noticed anybody dumping JoLynne's body into it.'

'Gallows?'

I had Pavlik's attention now. 'It's what the staging guys call the raised structure they built for the cup.'

'Kevin Williams, too?' I seemed to be getting poor

Kevin in deeper, despite my good intentions. 'It's just an expression,' I said. 'You know, trade jargon?'

'We'll see.' Pavlik pulled his hand out from under mine to retrieve a notepad from his jeans pocket. I leaned forward, but couldn't quite make out what he was writing from across the table.

'Tough to read upside down, huh?' Pavlik said with a grin, as he slipped his notepad back into the pocket.

'Did you make a note about what I said?' I asked. 'So you can look into it?'

'Of course. We aren't trying to railroad anyone. The TV footage is time-stamped and more accurate than your—' he looked up at me apologetically—'or anyone else's, memory could be. Thing is, it would have taken somebody only five minutes to suffocate JoLynne and hoist her pretty petite body over the cup's side.' Again with 'JoLynne'. And was there a comma hanging in the air between 'pretty' and 'petite'?

That-a-way, Maggy. Be jealous of a corpse. *I*, at least, still had a lifetime to lose those five extra pounds. Which is probably about how long it would take me.

I kept my tone level. 'That "somebody" you're talking about being Kevin.'

'Our current theory.' Theory? They'd arrested the man.

'The sides of that cup and saucer were five-feet high,' I reminded Pavlik.

'But made like a kid's swimming pool. Once he had her on the edge, he'd just have to roll her over. Remember, Kevin's a big guy and, like I said, JoLynne was tiny.' Well, he should know. I made it look like I was contemplating something.

'What?' Pavlik asked as he began assembling another moo-shu burrito.

'Oh, I was just thinking that Kate should probably concentrate on her other theory.'

He grinned. 'And what's our intrepid reporter's "other theory"?'

I smiled sweetly, taking in the blue eyes for what I feared would be the last time. 'She thinks JoLynne was having an affair. Or even, affairs. Plural.'

Pavlik left shortly after that. No, that's an understatement. He shoveled his moo-shu and chugged his Shiraz, all the time being careful not to denigrate the idea.

If: *'Well, Maggy, there's certainly precedent for that kind of motive.'* And: *'I suppose Kevin could have found out something and confronted JoLynne.'* But: *'Why wouldn't Kevin tell me about* any *affair involving his wife if he knew?'* Indeed, why wouldn't he? Unless Kevin also knew he was sitting across the table from the man who was banging his spouse.

'Probably didn't want to provide you with a motive for him to kill JoLynne,' I suggested mildly as I followed Pavlik to the door after our hastily concluded dinner.

'Sorry, I have to run,' he said, stepping out on the porch.

'Only I've got a ton of paperwork to do.'

'Not to worry.' Pavlik kissed me quickly and I handed him his jacket, giving it one last feel.

Which turned into one last feeling.

The three of us—Pavlik, the coat, and me—were done.

ELEVEN

I SLEPT SOUNDLY that Thursday night. Granted, the remainder of the Shiraz I'd downed might have played a role.

If I'd needed confirmation of Pavlik's affair with JoLynne, his behavior had provided it. He'd bolted from my house as fast as decently possible, though I didn't think 'decent' would be a word I'd use in describing him again.

I felt so stupid. I thought those eyes burned bright and blue only for me.

Stupid, stupid, stupid.

'Maybe I read too much into what he said, Frank.' It was just before five a.m. and I was lying on my back in bed, waiting for the alarm clock to beep and send me off to the morning shift at Uncommon Grounds. The sheepdog's gigantic head was on my stomach and I played absently with his tousled hair as I stared up at the ceiling. Believe me, I saw the irony.

'I guess I wanted to believe Pavlik loved us.' Frank opened one eye.

'OK,' I admitted. 'He probably does love you.' If throwing an increasingly slimy tennis ball time after time wasn't love, then I didn't know what could be.

Which maybe I…didn't? I hadn't told Pavlik I loved him. Partly because I wanted him to say it first, but also because I wasn't sure. I mean, I thought I'd loved Ted, too, but it had been disturbingly easy to transform that feeling into contempt and, later, even pity.

'If it's love, shouldn't we be talking about forever?' I asked Frank. 'No matter what the other person does?' The stump of a tail thumped the comforter twice. I didn't know if that meant he'd love me forever or he thought I was a patsy.

'I love Eric that way—through thick and thin. But maybe it's different.' Frank rolled over on his back, nearly clouting me with one uncoordinated foreleg, but still managing to keep his head on my stomach.

'I mean, maybe we're just muddling the semantics. Maybe "love", when it refers to your child, is a wholly different animal.' Frank flopped his head sideways to look at me.

'Sorry, not *your* kind of animal. Amend that to "emotion".' Frank showed his approval by wriggling, though it also was the signal he wanted a belly-rub.

I obliged. 'Anyway. I was saying that for your children you feel all kinds of innate emotions—from nurturing to fierce protectiveness. Like a mama lion.' That earned me another look.

'Or mama sheepdog,' I conceded. 'But maybe there should be a different word for what we feel toward a spouse or a lover. In addition to lust, of course.' Frank unleashed a groan of delight, which I had to admit creeped me out a bit. The beeping of the alarm clock forestalled further conversation. It was for the best, anyway. Pillow talk with a sheepdog is probably right up there with hearing voices.

The alarm cued Frank that his belly-rub was at an end. He rolled back over on to his stomach, giving me just enough time to slither out from under.

'Hope I didn't disturb you.' I clicked off the alarm.

The dog's sigh as he settled back down, this time with his head on my pillow, said it all. Yes, I had disturbed him, but he was willing to forgive and forget.

If only people were so easy.

It was still dark when I arrived at Uncommon Grounds a little before six. I left my Escape in the depot's rear parking lot and walked up its driveway and around to the front entrance. As I mounted the porch steps I thought I could see the sky lightening slightly toward the east. That would have cheered me up if the days weren't already getting shorter as winter approached.

And in Wisconsin, it could be a very long winter. This past one, the first snow appeared in November and the last didn't melt until May. An oddity for the area, but a disaster for my prior business location.

Which led me to the door of the new Uncommon Grounds. I turned the key and stepped into the dark shop, bells ajingling.

'Morning,' a cheery voice called from in back.

Tien Romano stuck her head out of the kitchen. 'I have coffee brewed and the sticky buns just came out of the oven. Got time for one?' God, yes.

'You are a wonder, Tien,' I said as I joined her in our kitchen. The place smelled wonderful. Caramelized sugar and butter and pecans, all brought lovingly together in a little mound of perfection called a sticky bun.

Tien removed a pan from the oven and slid a knife around the edges. As I poured both of us cups of coffee, I watched her, in one smooth motion, invert the pan so what had been the top of the swirled rolls was now the bottom, resting on waxed paper.

With two taps and a little shake, Tien lifted the pan straight up and off the buns slowly, allowing the nuts and home-made caramel—that had been nesting comfortably on the buttered bottom of the pan—to cascade over the rolls, bathing them in syrupy sinfulness.

'I think I just had an orgasm,' I said.

Tien laughed. 'They are enticing, aren't they?'

'Enticing?' I said, holding out a paper plate. 'With the store smelling this good, customers will never want to leave.' Hell, I might never leave.

Using a pancake turner, so she wouldn't lose any of the 'sticky', Tien slid a bun on to my plate. I set it down and passed her another.

We repaired cozily to one of the deuce, or two-seater, tables, rolls and coffees in front of us. I raised my cup. 'To Tien. Thank you so much for rearranging your schedule to stay and help us. You've truly brightened my day.' I took a sip, then picked up my fork to start eating. It was only then that I realized Tien was looking at me with concern.

'Are you OK, Maggy?'

'Fine.' I forked a piece of bun and put it in my mouth, closing my eyes in ecstasy. If Tien made these every day, I'd never lose those five pounds. A sacrifice I was willing to make. 'Why do you ask?'

Tien was holding her coffee cup in two hands and now she looked down into it. 'Well…'

'You know something I don't?' I asked the question, but I was hoping her answer would be 'no'.

And it was. She returned her cup to the table and looked up. 'I don't want to intrude, Maggy, but I heard about the confrontation with Rebecca yesterday and what she said about her sister…'

'And Pavlik,' I supplied. I shouldn't have been surprised that it was getting around, at least within our own, small circle. Sarah, Amy and Michael had all heard Rebecca say JoLynne and my sheriff were…

'Yes, Pavlik.' Tien began extending a hand to pat mine, but the latter was busy delivering sticky bun to my mouth. I always envied people who *couldn't* eat when stressed. 'I wanted to make sure you were all right. I know how close you've been to him.'

'Not as close as you—or I, it appears—thought.'

Tien stopped my hand. 'Men are different, Maggy.' Oh, puh-leeze. Not a 'they have their needs' sermon. Especially from someone who had even less experience with multiples of the opposite sex than I did.

'I appreciate the concern, Tien, but—' I raised my fork. Tien actually took it away from me.

'But, nothing. I know that I've not been married, as you have, and I also haven't dated much, what with running the store and all. I have, however, spent pretty much my whole life in a man's world—my father's.' I dearly hoped she wasn't going to tell me something I *really* didn't want to hear.

I opened my mouth for a reason unclear to me. I wasn't going to interrogate Tien, nor was I going to shovel in more food, thanks to her.

Nonetheless, she waved down any potential interruption.

'As I said, I don't know much about dating, marrying and loving a male partner. What I do know, though, is that men live very simple lives. Either you are a friend or an enemy. Nothing else counts. If you are a man's friend, it's for life, unless you really trash that relationship.

'Maggy, men are not wondering what you're thinking. They expect you to tell them anything important, and, if they independently want to know, they'll ask. They can't understand why we don't do the same. If you confide a problem, they will try to fix it. Analyze, rather than empathize. They don't see why we would *want* to "share" if we also didn't want their version of a solution.' I took a sip of my coffee. I was thinking back to when Eric entered high school. He'd had a terrible time getting to his locker and back to his classes in time, but couldn't carry all his books. God help him, should he need an interim bathroom stop.

I'd suggested he talk to his friends. Share his feelings with them.

Ted, on the other hand, sat down with our son and diagrammed the school building. They mapped out Eric's classes, his locker and, yes, even the bathrooms. Problem solved.

The 'guy' way.

'So what are you saying?' I asked. 'That if I had wanted Pavlik to be "exclusive" with me, I needed to spell it out for him?'

'My experience, limited as it is, answers yes.' Tien pulled apart her sticky bun. 'Men don't look ahead in relationships. They're not into fairy tales. They're not planning their next Saturday night, much less a June wedding. They're just…there.'

'I exist, therefore I am?'

'More like, they exist, therefore they're men.'

I laughed and reclaimed my fork. Then set it down. 'But Pavlik and…'

'JoLynne Penn-Williams?'

I nodded.

I couldn't, wouldn't say anything about Pavlik's

'dating' Wynona Counsel early in our relationship. Tien would think it wasn't relevant and she'd probably be right. Still, on the tail of that, the affair with JoLynne was just another nail in the coffin of trust.

Tien blushed a bit, tried to cover it by getting up for a carafe and pouring us more coffee.

'What?' I said, after she sat back down.

'I once had an affair with a married man.' Yeah, well, there was a lot of that going around. Still, Tien seemed like such an innocent, despite the fact she had to be well into her thirties by now. I didn't ask her with whom, or when, or why. I just waited.

She stirred her coffee. I was coveting her nearly untouched bun, but I kept my already-sticky fingers to themselves.

A glance at the Brookhills clock. Six fifteen. Amy and Sarah would arrive any minute. Actually, should be here already.

'Mistake?' Tien looked up from her reverie, almost startled. I realized then that the affair was—or at least had been—extremely important to her. Not something to belittle or criticize.

She gave me a… I don't know what kind of look it was. Forlorn? Brave? Wise beyond her years? Wise beyond *my* years?

'You know the opening lines in *A Tale of Two Cities*?' Tien asked, just a touch of damp luminosity shining from her hazel eyes. '"It was the best of times, it was the worst of times"? That pretty much sums up the way I felt.'

'You enjoyed the excitement?' I asked gently.

'And the attention.' She shrugged. 'Also, I can't deny

that I loved believing I could make him happy, when his wife couldn't. Stupid.'

'Join the ever-growing club,' I said.

'I was hoping for "happily ever after",' Tien said, with a shy grin, 'but all I got was "The End".'

'With him or you as the author?'

'Me.' Now she picked at her sticky bun. 'He was fine with going on as we were. I don't think his wife even cared. They'd been following separate paths for years, staying together only for the sake of their kids.' Or not. Funny how easily spotted bullshit is from a distance. Then you just go step in it anyway.

'I respected him for that,' Tien continued. 'But I'm thirty-three years old, Maggy. I haven't been engaged. I haven't been married. I haven't given birth to a baby. Heck, I've scarcely held somebody *else's* baby. I want it all.'

'Which you deserve.'

'I think so, too.' This was said with a little smile. 'But I guess the point of all this is that sometimes we make up fairy tales and cast ourselves in the starring roles.' Tien looked out the window to the noticeably brightening sky and then came back to me. 'Men aren't mind-readers.

'They also aren't Prince Charmings or whatever more we like to pretend about them. They're human, complicated and simple all at the same time. And if you really want to know what's running through a man's mind, you only need to ask.' Tien Romano stood up to clear the table. 'Because, unlike us women, chances are they'll actually tell you.' Out of the mouths of thirty-somethings.

Sarah Kingston and Amy Caprese arrived moments

later, swooning over the aromas still wafting into the air of Uncommon Grounds.

'Great idea to have Tien work mornings,' Sarah said. 'The baked goods are fresh and the place smells terrific. We should patent and package the scent.'

'You know, I didn't even ask what time she came in,' I said.

'Well, what *were* you doing?' my partner demanded. 'Not grinding beans, I see.'

'Eating sticky buns,' I retorted. 'And grind your own business.'

'Oh, a coffeehouse joke,' she said, opening a Lucite bin to scoop out the morning's 'featured' roast. 'How very, very droll of you, partner.' I got up to help. We usually ground three or four pounds ahead, so we could just dip into the tubs and fill the filters. Smaller quantities of finely ground dark-roasted beans were needed for espresso, since it was brewed one tiny cup, instead of one substantial carafe, at a time.

All four of us were in our positions and ready to serve when the commuters started to arrive for the 6:50 a.m. train.

Tien worked at the main window beside Amy, but instead of handling the cash register and calling out drink orders, Tien stayed on the food side. That way she could expound on the fresh breads and pastries and also hawk the lunch sandwiches and dinner entrées.

By the time 8 a.m. rolled around, we were feeling pretty good. Tired, too, but a 'satisfied' tired.

'Any more of those sticky buns around?' Sarah asked, dropping into a chair.

Amy, who was cleaning the glass top of the bakery case, peered in. 'Sorry. All headed for Milwaukee.'

'Aww, geez,' Sarah crabbed. 'I was really looking forward to one after we got rid of the riff-raff.' Otherwise known as our valued customers. 'What do you think? Was the crowd smaller or did we just handle them more efficiently?'

'Yes to both.' Amy had printed out the transactions so far today on to a cash-register receipt. 'We had ten fewer customers, but toted twelve per cent more revenue.'

'Yes!' I said, jumping up and punching the air. Everybody else just looked at me.

'Don't you see what this means?' I asked. 'We're on the right track.' Groans all around at my painful pun.

Undeterred, Maggy drove on. 'Having Tien here works beautifully. She's helping us out on the serving end and that provides the opportunity to promote her food.'

'How do you feel about that, Tien?' Sarah called to the other woman, who was back in the kitchen. 'What time did you start?'

'I got here about one, I guess,' she said, coming around the corner with a plate.

'A.m.?' from Sarah. 'That qualifies as the shift from hell. You can't continue for any length of—' Tien set the plate down in front of her.

Sarah practically inhaled the sticky bun. There was only the sound of chewing and swallowing, punctuated by the occasional burp and sigh.

It was like being home with Frank.

When my partner finished, she sat back. 'Tien, you must never leave us.'

'I won't,' Tien said, taking the plate. 'But if you want fresh rolls, you need to get here at six, like Maggy did.

I can't promise I'll be able to save you one like I did today.' Genius. The woman was a genius.

'And you truly don't mind the hours?' I asked.

'Actually, I *like* the hours,' our baker-extraordinaire answered, as the bells on the front door jangled. 'I probably wouldn't if I was going to bed and then getting up at midnight or one, but I'll go home now, and get my eight hours, and I'll be fine.'

'Like a morning news anchor.' Kate McNamara had just entered. The woman had the ears—or radar capability—of a vampire bat. And a personality to complete the package.

'Have you ever been an anchor, Kate?' Amy asked, moving to the cash register.

I knew the answer, but I was waiting for Kate's version.

'I was behind the desk for a short period a few years ago, before I became publisher of the *Observer*,' she said stiffly. 'I found anchoring very limiting. I much prefer running the paper and reporting from the field occasionally for cable news. Reading from a teleprompter on a daily basis is vastly overrated.' Especially if your share of the viewing audience was vastly underrated.

Still, I had to hand it to Kate. As evasions go, not a bad one. She smiled icily in my direction, like she was daring me to differ.

I didn't. It wasn't worth my time to mention that Kate sucked big-time in the studio, and—gosh, it was so long ago, I could scarcely remember—something further had resulted in her demotion to standing in blinding blizzards and covering pie-eating contests at county fairs. Humiliated, she'd quit, bought the weekly Brookhills paper and made herself both its editor and publisher.

Jerome came banging in, today laden with camera, wires and equipment case.

'Geez, Kate,' I said, going to help him. 'Couldn't you have carried something?'

'That's OK, Maggy,' Jerome said, setting the camera down on a table and the rest of his gear on the floor. 'We came separately.' Jerome wasn't quite looking at me as he said it. He did slide a glance toward Amy at the cash register.

The implication didn't go unnoticed by Kate. 'Jerome, I need you to set up. And *now*.'

'New assignment?' I asked. I was at the point that I just wanted to wash my hands of her old assignment, that being JoLynne's death and everything related to it. Including Pavlik.

Fat chance.

'Actually,' Kate said, seeming a whole lot more eager to talk about it than Jerome, 'it's the second part of the original assignment. The other shoe dropping, if you will.' She signaled Jerome and he reluctantly hoisted the camera on to his shoulder.

'What shoe is that?' I was backing away. A happy Kate meant pestilence and famine were on their way, with locusts to follow—all during a solar eclipse to round out the plagues. Reflexively, I glanced out the window.

'I'd guess size ten, ten-and-a-half,' Kate said. 'But you'd probably know better, Maggy.' Jerome turned on the camera light and leveled it at Kate. Somehow a clip-on microphone had blossomed on her lapel and now she brandished a hand-held one as well.

'We are in Uncommon Grounds, relocated to Brookhills Junction after, some of you may remember, a freak May snowstorm leveled its original home in Benson Plaza. When that storm cleared, it left bodies behind—murder victims. It seems, more freakably, the bloody legacy has followed this shop here. Charming to look at, though, isn't it?' She swept her arm toward the ticket/service windows and Amy dove to the floor as Jerome's camera followed. Myself, I was still stuck on 'freakably'.

'That charm, however, belies the horrendous crime that took place just two days ago. A young woman, as-phyxiated and then discarded like a human stir-stick in a prop meant for the grand opening of this establish-ment at the dedication of "The L", the new Brookhills-to-Milwaukee commuter line.' Sarah slid behind Kate, one hand forming a capital 'L' and the other pointing to herself. Then she smiled and waved.

Over her shoulder, the reporter tossed Sarah an an-noyed look and shifted slightly toward me. The lesser of two evils?

'The prop in question was a giant, inflatable coffee cup, commissioned by shop co-owner Maggy Thorsen. But that's not the strangest thing about this case.' She pivoted and thrust the hand-held mic in my face. 'Is it, Maggy?' I'm sure my eyes went wide, but I remained calm, relying on my public relations training. I'd done way too many interviews to let this banshee rattle me.

'I really don't know, Kate,' I replied truthfully. I'd pretty much missed everything following 'human stir-stick'.

'Then I'll tell you.' A stern expression, now returned to the camera lens. 'In fact, I'll tell all of you. After JoLynne Penn-Williams, Brookhills' event manager, was found murdered, Sheriff Jake Pavlik detained her husband, Kevin Williams, owner of Williams Props and Staging.

'No one except the sheriff, apparently, knew the motive of Williams' alleged crime. No one, that is, until reports began to surface that JoLynne Penn-Williams had been having an extramarital affair. An affair with a man high-up in our own Brookhills County government.' Kate whirled and again stuck her microphone toward my mouth.

If the reporter was trying to get a 'surprise!' moment out of me, she failed. After all, I already knew about Pavlik and JoLynne. And I certainly wasn't going to comment on it for the noonday news.

I said, 'Really?' Kate stared at me, apparently trying to decide whether to push it. I'd bested her before and I'd bested better than her as well. And she knew it.

To her damage-control credit, Kate accurately weighed the percentages and again turned to the camera. 'Yes, Maggy Thorsen. *Really.*' She moved dramatically toward the lens. Jerome back-pedaled, until his back was literally against a wall. With luck, Kate might show up on the screen as nothing more than a nose surrounded by freckles.

'But the real shocker,' Kate continued as I walked away, 'learned by this reporter just moments ago, is that the questioner will be answering some questions himself.' I froze.

'Our sources tell us that the Milwaukee County Sheriff's Department has taken over the Penn-Williams murder case. And Brookhills Sheriff Jake Pavlik is now considered "a person of interest" in its investigation.'

TWELVE

AT THE MENTION of Jake's name, I swung around to see Kate gesturing wildly for her assistant to turn his camera on me.

Jerome, bless him, was still tight on Kate, hopefully focused close enough now to count enlarged skin pores.

As for me, I took off for our kitchen, through its store room and into the office beyond. There, I pushed the button lock on the door and swung it closed, none too quietly.

Collapsing into our office chair, I folded my arms on its desk and rested my chin on top of them, a la nap time in kindergarten.

I felt about as lost, too. (Kindergarten had been a tough year for me. All that paste. The orange construction paper. And those crayons? Brrr.) I lifted my face. I could see the back parking lot through the window above the desk. There had to be twenty or thirty cars in it.

I counted them, anyway. Just as I reached the end of the second row, another vehicle pulled in and parked in the first. I started over.

'What, you're counting cars now?' I jumped and the chair swiveled.

'How'd you get in? I locked—' Sarah punched in the lock button on the knob and closed the door. The button popped back out.

'Gotta secure this baby *after* you close the door.'

'Oh.' I resumed my position and the parallel contemplation of the parking lot. The driver's door of the new entry, a white Lexus, was standing open. Nobody had emerged so far as I could tell.

'Kate still here?' I asked.

'I can't heeear you,' Sarah sing-songed. 'If you have something to say, sit up straight.' Geez. I *was* back in kindergarten. But, as in that class, I did as I was told.

'Now repeat what you said,' Miss Sarah demanded.

Through clenched teeth: 'I asked if Kate was still in the store.'

'Nah,' Sarah said, uncoiling into the side chair. 'I kicked her tight ass out.' Great.

'Jerome capture the moment on tape?'

'Sadly, no.' Sarah shrugged. 'Jerome was too busy chatting up Amy. And did Katie Cougar ever love that.' I still couldn't picture Kate with Jerome. But I'd been naive about so many people.

'What's Anita Hampton doing here?' Sarah asked, indicating the woman who had finally climbed out of the Lexus. Anita was on her cell phone. 'Maybe she has my award.'

'*Maybe* she's just stopping for coffee.' I changed the subject to something more important. My life. 'Pavlik's in trouble.'

'Pavlik's a sleaze.' Sarah was watching Anita disappear around the corner. 'He was cheating on you, you forget?'

Suddenly, I found myself defending him. 'To be honest, he and I never talked about being exclusive. I guess I just figured Pavlik wasn't dating anyone else, because I wasn't.'

'"Dating"?' Sarah repeated. 'Quaint euphemism for committing adultery with another man's wife.'

'This is Brookhills,' I said. 'We survive on our quaint euphemisms.'

'Sooo?' Sarah, leadingly.

'Sooo…' I was trying to follow. 'We're deluding ourselves. Living in Peyton Place while pretending it's Sunnybrook Farm.'

'No, you idiot. I meant, sooo did you see Pavlik last night and confront him with what Rebecca said? Ask him if it was true?' If Sarah called me an idiot one more time, I was going to smack her.

And of course I didn't ask Pavlik. That would have made too much sense. 'No. But I did tell him Kate suspected that JoLynne was having an affair with someone in the county government.'

'Nice move. What did our sheriff say?'

'He took off like a scalded cat.'

'Did he now?' Sarah said, contemplating. 'Guess Kate should be glad she isn't at the bottom of Lake Michigan, wearing concrete galoshes.'

Involuntarily, a hand went to my mouth. 'Please tell me you don't believe Pavlik would kill someone.'

'Please tell me you haven't thought about it,' Sarah mimicked me.

A moment of silence as she rose from the side chair. Then: 'My opinion, Maggy? Pavlik is certainly capable of killing someone.' Sarah palmed the doorknob. 'But do I believe that he would physically hurt you or Kate? Or kill JoLynne Penn-Williams? Not for a minute.' Sarah opened the door, then turned back to me. 'And no matter how emotionally hurt you are, you don't believe it either.' She waved a hand to indicate I should leave first.

'Now, get your mopey butt out there to help. It's nearly Tennis Barbies time and, besides, Anita might be here to see me.' In truth, it was still a good half-hour until the Tennis Barbies would finish their matches, air-kiss the opposing team, and get their color-coordinated selves over here. The store was empty. No sign of even Anita Hampton. Amy was at the cash register, breaking open sleeves of coins and putting them in the cash drawer.

I didn't see Tien. She must have called it a day— or night—and headed home. I hoped our shift-savior would sleep well. Tien had certainly earned it.

'Did Anita come in?' Sarah asked Amy.

'Anita who?'

'Hampton. Brewster's wife. And the events person for Milwaukee.' It didn't seem to come up on Amy's rec-ollection screen, so I elaborated. 'Tall and slim? Dresses well, with dark hair?'

'Ohh, that PR woman?' Amy wrinkled her nose. 'She's not "slim", she's downright skinny. I saw her hustle past. I wanted to toss her a muffin, flesh the beanpole out a little.' Look who was talking. Amy didn't have a pound of fat on her. The signpost was calling the rail anorexic.

Or something like that.

'Anita has lost a few pounds lately,' I said, 'but the woman never stops moving.' It takes a lot of energy to be a pain in the ass, with the added unfair benefit of the effort reducing the ass of the pain involved.

Sarah was pouring herself a cup of coffee, seeming to have lost interest in Anita now that she hadn't come into the shop, trophy in hand, for an awards presenta-tion. By comparison, I was curious to know where the woman had gone.

'I'll be outside.' I pulled open the front door. 'Back in time for the tennis team.' Amy waved me along and I stepped on to our wrap-around porch. For sentimental reasons we'd retained the one piece of furniture that had been there when we took over, a battered rocker-recliner patched with duct tape. We'd also moved in lovely white café tables with matching chairs, even a couple of wicker love seats.

Guess where people always chose to sit?

Right the first time. And that banged-up chair, rusty hinges and all, admittedly did envelop you when you sank into it.

It was there that I found Anita Hampton, duly enveloped and snoring.

'Anita?' I pulled a seat away from the nearest table and dropped my rump on to it, facing her. 'Anita?' This time nudging her recliner with my foot.

Eyelids fluttered. 'Where...?'

'You seem to have zonked on the porch of Uncommon Grounds. Are you OK?' My former boss jolted awake and darted her feet into Manolo pumps. God forbid Anita should be caught out of uniform.

'I did have trouble falling asleep last night,' she admitted, levering the chair up. 'And then I awoke early. I was hoping to catch Kevin Williams breaking down your stage. He's not answering his phone and he still needs to finish downtown. We have another Milwaukee event scheduled there this weekend.'

'But isn't Kevin still—' how to put it—'a guest of the sheriff's department?'

'Oh, Maggy, I'm so sorry, I thought you knew. Kevin was cleared and released early this morning.' Anita leaned forward and patted my hand. 'You *do* know who they're looking at now, don't you, dear?' Her tone was meant to show concern for a former co-worker in a difficult time.

Underline 'show' as opposed to 'feel'.

'I do.' Rather than give Anita information, it'd be dandy if I could pry some out of her. 'But wasn't the alleged affair—' the last word stuck in my throat— 'thought to be *Kevin's* motive for killing JoLynne?'

'Originally, I believe you're right. But witnesses saw Kevin from the time the balloon was inflated until poor Jo's body was found.' And damned if I wasn't one of those witnesses. Great for Kevin, not so much for Pavlik, now probably the sole suspect.

Before I could pose another question, Anita pushed herself up and out of the chair. Her hands bore telltale filaments from the deteriorating Naugahyde.

'Clap them together like blackboard erasers,' I suggested.

'And don't forget to brush off your clothes.' Hey, comfort and heritage come with a price.

Anita, always the go-getter, managed somehow to clap and brush at the same time. Then she pointed. 'Finally.' I turned to see Kevin's truck approaching. As it passed, I could just make out the burly silhouette of Kevin in the driver's seat.

'Oh, good,' I said, starting down the porch stairs behind Anita. 'I need to talk to him, too.' Anita held up a hand, stopping me. 'In order to save time for both of us, I suggest that I have my discussion with Kevin first.' I started to protest, but she kept right on talking. 'Then I will send Kevin to see you. That way you'll be able to be in your store.' She nodded toward a clique of seven or eight women dressed in tennis togs, just turn-

ing the corner. While Sarah was better suited to interact
with the ladies who do tennis—she'd actually been one
(though, granted, only for a couple of weeks)—Anita
was, for once, right: I really should get in there to help.

Besides, I'd prefer to speak with Kevin privately,
anyway.

'That sounds…' I started, and then realized that
Anita was nowhere to be seen. 'Fine.'

'You're talking to yourself, Maggy,' one of the tennis players said, as they charged up the steps, sweeping
me inside with them.

'I always do that,' a squat woman offered.

'That's because no one else will.' This from a fif-
tyish blonde.

'Says you.' An elbow to the ribs, delivered by the
squat woman.

'Tough morning on the courts?' I asked, holding the
door for them. Usually the ladies of tennis were com-
panionable. Until someone left. *Then* the pack would
rip the departed apart.

'This is Buster Chops Day,' the blonde volunteered,
slurring the phrase. 'First annual.'

'Bust *your* chops,' the silver-haired lady corrected.
'It means the hell with the air-kissing, you bitches.'
She slapped her hand over her mouth in horror and
then giggled.

Sounded like they'd done more busting open of the
Grey Goose than chops. Bloody Marys all around. 'And
what does Bust Your Chops Day involve?'

'You know, like the guys,' the blonde said. 'We've
been scratching our balls and swearing all morning. I
sort of like it.'

'I've watched a lot of men's tennis,' I said. 'But I

don't recall any ball scratching. A fair amount of adjusting, front and back, but—'

'Not those balls.' Silver Hair, seemingly the ringleader, set her tennis bag on the chair and, after pulling out sweatbands and a sun visor, hand sanitizer and a box of tissues, she finally came up with a canister.

'Hold out your hand,' she commanded.

Yeah, like I was that stupid. I had two older brothers and I'd fallen for all of their tricks. The offer of ABC gum which, when plunked into my eager four-year-old hand, turned out to stand for 'Already Been Chewed'. For God's sake, I was so young, I couldn't even spell. It took me until first grade to get the joke.

Then there was Cowboys, the card game that consisted of throwing the cards all over the room and yelling 'round 'em up' to the gullible victim.

My brothers were evil geniuses. Whoopie cushions and plastic vomit were child's play to them. Fake dog poop? They had the real thing.

'C'mon, it won't hurt you.' I studied Silver Hair for ill intent. The top was already off the can, so a paper snake couldn't leap out at me.

I sighed and held out my hand. Silver Hair rolled a ball from the can into my palm.

'Feels like a real ball,' I said.

'Scratch it to be sure,' someone yelled. Sheesh.

I did a quick calculation. Eight customers, three times a week, buying pricey specialty drinks. 'OK, I get it. I'll scratch your ball.' Managing a weak smile, I did so, then handed the ball back.

Silver Hair examined it. 'Seemed a lot funnier on the court.'

'I think we could all use some coffee, don't you,

Maggy?' Amy, who'd come out to man the window, said with a wink.

'You bet. Coffee all around.'

'On the house?' someone asked.

'Hell, no,' I said loudly. 'This is Bust-Your-Chops Day. Pay for your own damn caffeine.' A good-natured cheer went up.

Kevin Williams came in just as the last of the rowdy tennis group left. Let's hope the blonde Barbie was right about the 'annual' part and that B-Y-C Day didn't come but once a year.

Still, the commotion had served as a welcomed distraction. I'd barely thought about Pavlik, but on seeing Kevin, everything came flooding back.

The props man looked awful. Still thighs the size of tree trunks and biceps like tree limbs, but this tree was hurting.

All I could think of was a weeping willow.

'Why don't you tell me what you'd like to drink, Kevin, and we'll take them in back.' The store wasn't busy, but I didn't want anyone, even Sarah and Amy, to be able to overhear us.

'A cup of black sounds good.' He leaned his elbows on the counter. 'What a difference a day or two makes, huh? Wednesday at dawn, everything was fine. Now it's all—'

'Excuse me.' Anita was holding the door open, sleigh bells banging against the glass. 'Kevin, you can reach me at home tomorrow if need be.'

He raised his bear paw of a hand. 'Sorry about getting our signals crossed, but we'll take care of it.'

'I know you will.' She gave me a self-satisfied smile. 'And now that the police are gone, Maggy, I'm sure

Kevin will take care of your breakdown as soon as he resolves my issue. Right, Kevin?' Anita Hampton didn't wait for an answer, instead disappearing with the incongruously cheery jingle-jangle of the sleigh bells.

"'"ere she drove out of sight",' Kevin recited. '"Happy Christmas to all, and to all a goodnight!"'

'I'd love to stuff *her* up a chimney,' I said under my breath.

'Christmas *is* coming,' Kevin muttered right back.

Our eyes met and we both laughed. He shrugged. 'Anita's a good customer of mine. Things are tough these days, so you do what's necessary.' Amen. Like hosting Tennis Barbies Gone Wild.

I hadn't realized that Kevin's company was having trouble, though, other than the pilfering of materials he'd told us about. Now to make matters worse, he'd be minus both JoLynne and her outside salary.

'Ready?' I said, handing him his coffee and picking up my iced latte.

'Sure, but instead of sitting in your office or something, can we go out to the boarding platform? I'm still trying to figure this thing.'

'Of course.' We took our drinks to a trackside door, the one by…

I gestured to where the machine had been. 'Did the police take your air pump?'

'My compressor? Yeah. And the inflatables themselves, of course.' He swung the door open and we stepped out, settling ourselves on the edge of the planking, legs dangling.

The stage was cleared off, but Kevin's men hadn't gotten much further on the breakdown before he'd pulled them away to do Anita's bidding.

Kevin was staring at the spot his wife's body had hit. He might look like a big muscle-bound lug, but he had the most beautiful, golden-brown eyes. And now there were tears in them. 'I'll have all this crap out of here tomorrow. My guys had to leave off on the gallows and go downtown.'

'Anita. Got it.' I wanted to talk to him about Pavlik and JoLynne, but I needed to ease into it. 'Any idea what event she's having?'

Kevin looked up, surprised. 'Don't know. All Anita said was she needed the train dedication stuff cleared out.'

'She probably made it up.' He looked sideways at me. 'So I'd do what she wanted?' A moment of cogitation. 'That Anita, she's a piece of work.'

'Don't I know it. I used to work with her.'

'So I heard. You're a better man than I am, Gunga Din.' A weak grin.

'I thought Anita might mellow when she got married.'

'I'm sure the pants in the family hang from her closet pole. That Brewster, he bends with the wind.' He seemed to remember himself. 'Sorry, I don't mean to be bad-mouthing clients.'

I rearranged my butt on the hard boards and stuck out my hand. 'Nothing we say goes beyond here. Deal?' He looked at my palm, then took my hand.

'Deal.'

'By the way, I met your mime.' Kevin chuckled. 'Ragnar? What'd you think?'

'Adorable. That hair? That accent? I can almost forgive him for being a mime.'

'How did you make him?' Kevin asked.

'A smudge of make-*up*,' I said, pointing to the part

of my neck that corresponded with Ragnar's dab of face paint. 'And certain mannerisms.'

'I hope everybody's eyes aren't as sharp as yours. I told Ragnar to keep his secret life as a mime under wraps.' I laughed. 'A hidden closet with a lone red-and-white striped shirt and short pants awaiting the next assignment? A phone booth for the quick change?'

'Yeah, only it's an imaginary phone booth, which can cause problems,' Kevin said, his lips between a grin and a grimace.

'Charges of…indecent mimicry?'

Kevin hesitated, then got it. 'Exactly.' I liked the man and it was good to see him animated, but the time had come to steer the discussion toward my agenda.

'I understand the sheriff talked with you.'

'Nice way of putting it.' His face was flushed. 'All the time he's asking me if I was jealous or if Jo had been unfaithful, I have no idea the guy who's asking the questions is the one who already knows the answers.'

'Did you suspect?' We were still sitting side by side, faces forward, not looking at each other.

'About the affair? No.' A pause. 'You?'

'No.'

'You and the sheriff were—what, engaged or something?'

'No, just dating.' Seeing each other. Not even sure it was a relationship. 'It's a lot harder for you.' Duh. Of course it's harder for him. Not only did Kevin's wife cheat on him, but she's dead. And, oh yeah, the police thought—hell, might still think—he killed her.

Kevin glanced quickly at me and then away. 'If you trust someone and they betray that trust…well, nothing's harder than that.' Amen.

'So now the authorities are questioning Pavlik,' I said. 'Does that mean they've cleared you?' It should have been an awkward question to handle, but, somehow, it didn't seem to be.

'For now.' Kevin's big shoulders went up and down.

'Between the background film the television crews have—the B-roll I think it's called—and me seeing and talking to people, the cops can't find a time that I could have killed Jo and gotten her into the cup without somebody seeing something.'

'That's a relief.' I knew I was saying it weakly, but I meant it. Nothing could bring JoLynne back or change what she and Pavlik had done, but the last thing I wanted was for Kevin to be falsely accused of her killing. 'I've been told the cause of death was asphyxiation. Do you know anything more than that?' Also, an apparently awkward question, but again it didn't feel that way.

'She was—' he swallowed hard—'burked.' The word sounded like 'burped' and I knew it couldn't be that.

'I'm sorry, Kevin. But…?'

'B-u-r-k. I'd never heard of it either.' He was staring off in the distance, almost reciting. 'The cops told me it's when you hold someone's nose and mouth closed until they suffocate.' Awful. The murderer could be looking right into the victim's eyes as life began to fade from them.

'But JoLynne would have struggled.' A barely noticeable shake of the head, then almost a spasm.

'Not if you're sitting on the person's chest, arms pinned under your knees.'

'JoLynne was so little, I guess it wouldn't have to be someone very big.' God help me, I was thinking of

Pavlik at almost six feet. Or Kevin, himself, a giant of a man. Or even...

'If you do it right, they tell me, anyone can...' Do it right. When the act itself was so wrong.

'Do you think Pavlik killed JoLynne?'

'Not for me to say.' A shrug. 'She's gone. Nothing will change that.' A silence, then: 'Do you?'

'Do I what?'

'Think the sheriff did it?' I started to shake my head automatically, but after the way Kevin had opened up to me, I owed it to him to really consider his question. Not to mention my owing Pavlik as well.

No matter what kind of sugar-coating you layered on, 'my' sheriff knew that I cared about him. Yet, instead of being with me as much as his demanding job would allow, he'd started an affair with a married woman.

That did not mean he was a killer.

Yet, like Sarah, I believed Pavlik would kill. He'd take a life to protect me. Or to protect someone else. He would kill to defend his country—or his county— and the people in it. Pavlik would use deadly force to stop an armed bad guy.

My lover might even kill in anger. Or for revenge.

But Pavlik could *not* sit on a woman's chest, pinch her nose closed, place a hand over her mouth and watch the light drain from her terrified eyes.

That he could never do.

'No.' I turned to Kevin. 'No. Pavlik did not kill JoLynne.'

THIRTEEN

MY ANSWER DID, however, pretty much kill the conversation. And if that weren't enough, Sarah arrived to put a second bullet in its head.

'I've been looking for you everywhere,' she said, standing on the gravel below where Kevin and I were seated. 'Are you going to stay out here all day? Tomorrow's Saturday and you're off. We have to talk about scheduling.' Then, as an afterthought to Kevin: 'Sorry.'

'That's OK.' He hopped off the train platform. 'I have to get going anyway. Ragnar's car is in the repair shop, and I said I'd pick him up around noon.'

'Noon?' I asked. 'It's not that late, is it?'

'Nah, but he lives out in the boonies. Pain in the butt, only we need him.'

'Ragnar is one of Kevin's guys, Sarah. He also—'

'I'm sure he's fascinating.' My. Weren't we in a snit all of a sudden?

'OK, I'm coming in.' I brushed off my bum and turned to the props man. 'It was good talking to you, Kevin. Let me know if there's anything I can do.'

'Same here, Maggy. Thanks.'

Sarah waited for Kevin to drive away before asking, 'Does he know about his wife and Pavlik?'

'Ohhh, yeah.'

'Must have been a sprightly discussion out here.' Sarah inspected me. 'Are you all right?'

'Of course.'

'Of course?'

'Yes.' I led the way around the corner to the front entrance.

'It's not like being cheated on is exactly new to me.'

'Ahh, that's a good sign,' Sarah said, climbing the steps after me. 'You're blaming Pavlik and your ex rather than yourself. And about time, too.'

I stopped at the door. 'I wasn't blaming myself.'

A rude noise. 'Like hell you weren't. It's what you always do.' She put her palms together and laid them aside one cheek, a la Pauline, the damsel perennially in peril. 'Oh, woe is me. What could I have done to make my husband of twenty years run off with his bimboid hygienist?'

'First off, Rachel wasn't a bimboid.' A slut, sure, but a rich one with more brains than my ex-husband.

'Secondly, you barely knew me back then. You can't have any idea how I reacted.'

'I do, too.' Sarah opened the door to usher me into our shop. 'To know you is…well, to know you.' I could feel my fingers curl involuntarily.

'Oh, dear,' a voice behind us said. 'Isn't that just the most irritating thing someone can possibly say?' I pivoted, running into Sarah who was still holding the door open for me.

She let go, the automatic closer taking over.

A hand caught the door before it could shut itself. A yellow-gloved hand. 'I'm so sorry,' Christy said. 'I didn't mean to eavesdrop.'

'Then don't,' Sarah said. 'Maggy, will you please go in?'

But Christy was still talking. 'It's just that people

have said that about me and Ronny, and he hasn't even gone to trial yet.' She followed us over the threshold. 'They'll say, "I *know* you, Christy. You'll never be happy with a felon." Or "I *know* you, Christy. You won't be able to set so much as a foot in that filthy jail." Just goes to show.' The piano teacher stood in the middle of our coffeehouse, feet wide, yellow fists planted defiantly on her hips, like a superhero. 'No one really knows you. Except…*you*.' A smattering of applause from the peanut gallery, which consisted of Jerome and Amy, seated at a table together by the window. Jerome had left the shop with Kate earlier, but apparently wended his way back.

Christy blushed in response. 'Sorry. I guess I get so, so…'

'Passionate,' Amy said, rising to wait on her. 'Passion's a good thing.'

Christy looked like she was going to cry. 'It's just that I'm not used to, to…'

'Touching human flesh?' Sarah said in my ear. 'I wonder if Cousin Ronny and Christy are…conjugating.' As in conjugal visits. I smacked my partner in the shoulder.

'That's mean.' And none of Sarah's business, either. Besides, Courageous Christy was too busy fighting grime, if not crime, to have a personal life. Maybe she should dump Ronny and hook up with Ragnar. They could share an invisible phone booth.

All right, a very *clean* invisible phone booth.

I waved Amy back to her table. 'I've got this.' I pushed through the swinging door into the service area behind the windows.

'I've been waiting for you.'

'Holy shit, Pavlik,' I said, hand on my heart, check-ing to be sure it was still beating. 'Are you going to make a habit of scaring the hell out of me?' He didn't look much like a sheriff in his jeans and a black, long-sleeved Harley-Davidson 'Fat Boys Rule' T-shirt. I was surprised I hadn't heard him vroom up on his motor-cycle, but I'd been otherwise engaged.

Pavlik held up a hand. 'Sorry.' Yeah, everybody was sorry today.

I went to the service windows and stuck my head through one. 'Christy, can I get you something?'

'Not this second, Maggy.' The piano teacher was sitting with Amy and Jerome at their table, deep in conversation.

For her part, Sarah had disappeared. I had a feel-ing I now knew why she'd been so eager to get me to come inside.

I turned to Pavlik, hovering by the sink. 'I assume Sarah smuggled you past our airtight security?'

Pavlik looked hurt. 'I walked through the front door.'

'So why are you hiding in here?'

'I wanted to talk to you and Sarah thought it would be better—'

'Gotcha.' I leaned against the door jamb to the kitchen, facing him. 'I understand there's been a twist in your case.'

'I wasn't having an affair with JoLynne, Maggy.' Pavlik's eyes, which I'd come to believe reflected his moods, were basic gray. No sparkling blue floaters, like when he was teasing me and happy, or brooding charcoal embers, like when he was angry. In short, they told me nothing.

I tried to pull in a deep breath, but it was like a

sledgehammer had collapsed a lung. 'Are you a suspect in her murder?'

'No,' he said, reaching for me.

I slid to the side, away from him.

Pavlik dropped his hand. 'I mean, at least I don't think so. Not seriously.'

'You don't *think* so?' Directing the subject to him, keeping the 'us' of it all at bay for the time being. 'I understand they bounced you off the investigation.'

'Standard procedure.' His jaw was set. 'The Milwaukee County Department is taking over.' Sheriff Walensky—not someone I'd expect to have Pavlik's back. Except maybe to stick a knife in it.

'I don't think you killed her.'

Pavlik closed his eyes. When he opened them again, they were nearly black. 'Thank you.' Ironic? Facetious? Sarcastic, even? After nearly a year and a half of intimacy, all of a sudden I couldn't read him anymore.

Christy was right. We don't know people. How could we possibly?

'Is there something I can do to help?' I meant it as a genuine offer.

'You can believe me.' A vein in his temple was throbbing.

'I told you I did.'

'I mean about the affair.'

I wanted to. 'You had one with Wynona Counsel you didn't tell me about. They move in the same circles.'

'So you think I was doing all of them? Maggy, you overestimate me.' A flash of the old Pavlik.

'You didn't tell me about Wynona.'

'I did when you asked.' I shook my head, fighting

the impulse to capitulate. 'That's a cop-out and you know it.'

'You're right.' I waited.

Pavlik studied the floor before finally meeting my eyes again. 'I was dating Wynona before you and I met. And when we *did* meet, you were entangled in a case I was investigating. It would have been unethical for us to become involved with each other.'

'I agree.' I was trying not to yield any ground, nor soften my tone of voice or body language.

Pavlik sighed. 'The two of you...overlapped about six months.' Overlapped. Like a tag team.

'You said Wynona dumped you?'

'She confronted me. Said she could tell I was seeing someone else.'

'What did you do?'

Pavlik looked me straight in the eye. For what that was worth anymore. 'I told Wynona she was right. I was seeing someone else and I intended to continue.' Willpower fading, I could feel myself wanting to believe. Pavlik put his hands on my shoulders. 'I didn't lie to Wynona and I didn't lie to you about her. Maybe I should have disclosed that relationship upfront, but... have you told me everything you did in the months before we got together? Or soon after?' Of course not. But old movies, red wine and take-out food weren't exactly sizzling nights on the town.

'No,' I said, figuring I'd let his imagination chew on that.

'You said you'd never met JoLynne. Is that true? Scout's honor?'

'Scout's honor.' A little shake at my shoulders. 'I need you to believe me.'

'I need that, too.' I thought for a second. 'But why would Rebecca lie about the affair? Or, alternatively, why would JoLynne lie to Rebecca about it?'

'I wish I knew.' Pavlik pulled me into his arms and kissed the top of my head.

'Uh-uh,' I said. 'Not good enough.'

'Not...?' I pulled his head down to mine so that our lips aligned. Damn, but the man could kiss.

'Where is he?' a demanding voice from out front.

Pavlik and I broke apart, looking around frantically like two guilty teenagers.

'We know he came in here!' A second woman's voice thundered. Definitely different from the first, but similar at the same time.

As in old.

I signaled for Pavlik to go into the storeroom and moved stealthily to the service window. Staying to one side of the opening, I peeked out.

And was proved right. Milling around was a troop of nine or ten women, all of them upwards of eighty and all of them armed with...cell phones.

Sarah was standing her ground bravely. 'Who are you talking about?'

'The sheriff.' Now this voice I knew. Sophie Daystrom pushed her way to the front of the pack and held up her phone.

'He was spotted by CuteGal, who reported to the rest of us on Twitter.' I saw Amy, still at the table with Jerome and Christy, pull her phone out of her apron pocket. Calling for reinforcements? Maybe, but who? And from where?

The last thing we needed was the police showing up.

For all I knew, Pavlik *was* a fugitive. He hadn't quite said that, but then, as my law-enforcement lover was wont to remind me, I hadn't asked, either.

I stepped around the corner to face down the Twitterazzi.

'What's going on here?' Most of the group backed off a little, but Sophie stayed where she was. 'We have reports the sheriff is here, Maggy. Don't deny it.' Her cell phone was raised up as a second advocate. 'We have eyes everywhere.' Then Sophie's phone rang.

Within three seconds, the rest of the phones had followed suit.

Flip-phones flipping all around us. A great example of higher technology falling into the wrong hands.

'Schultz's Market,' a woman in a pink bike helmet yelled.

'C'mon, that's Brookhill Road.' And then they were gone.

An eerie silence settled inside. Outside cars came roaring to life, punctuated by the sputtering sound of a single Vespa being kick-started.

Christy rushed to the window. 'Gone. Nobody in sight.'

'What happened?' Sarah asked. Jerome and Amy were giggling.

'What's so funny?' I asked, going over to them.

Amy held up her phone. Its small screen read 'Pavlik at Schulz. Now.'

'He's…?' I consciously avoided looking back toward where Pavlik was. Or, at least, where I'd left him.

Amy escalated from giggles to a deep, musical laugh. Unable to talk, she gestured that Jerome take over.

'Amy tweeted them,' he said, a proud smile on his face.

'Tweeted them?'

'With a Pavlik spotting,' Amy finally managed. She took back her phone. 'I can do one for you, too, if you'd like.'

'Only if you can transport me fifty miles from here with that thing,' I said. 'But, thank you. That was a brilliant diversion.'

'Brilliant?' Sarah said, commandeering the cell. 'It's beyond brilliant. We can keep those old birds scurrying all over town, run them into the ground.'

'Now, Sarah. Be nice.' I turned to Amy. 'And for your reward, why don't you take off?'

'You're letting her leave early?' Sarah seemed shocked. Or maybe jealous.

'Sure. She'll be back to open with you in the morning. You and I can hold the fort for the rest of the afternoon.' My partner seemed less certain.

'I can help,' Christy said, raising her hand.

'You?' Sarah started. 'That's ri—'

'Really generous, Christy,' I said quickly. Sarah sent me a dirty look.

'Now you…' I stopped myself before I finished with 'two kids run along', like some inter-meddling spinster.

'Two kids run along?' Christy said, pulling off her gloves.

'What are you doing?' Sarah asked suspiciously of Christy as Amy and Jerome broke for the door.

'Going to wash my hands, of course.' Christy pulled a new pair of gloves from her pocket.

'You're washing your hands before you put on…?' Sarah was floundering beyond her depth as I ducked into the back.

'All clear,' I called to Pavlik as I passed through the kitchen and into the store room. 'Can you believe they're tracking you—us, really—on Twitter?' No answer.

I looked around. No Pavlik, either.

FOURTEEN

I RETURNED TO the front of Uncommon Grounds after checking in closets and behind doors. By the time I got to our refrigerator, I was feeling foolish, so I skipped that.

The sheriff had likely left via the kitchen door into the hallway and then on to the boarding platform, while I was keeping the elderly players from Team Pavlik occupied. Good plan. I just hoped he hadn't stopped at Schultz's Market to get something for dinner.

'Lose something?' Sarah asked.

'Just the usual,' I answered. 'What's she doing?' Christy was on her hands and knees next to our condiment cart.

'Scrubbing the wheels. She said they were, and I quote, "a disgrace".'

'That cart is brand new,' I pointed out. 'We've used it for all of three days.'

'Three days too many, evidently.' Sarah was watching the process, arms folded. 'Think maybe Christy'll wash the floors, too?'

'I think she'll clean anything that can't move away from her.' Which might explain the woman's fascination with Ronny Eisvogel.

As if on cue, Christy straightened up, toothbrush in hand.

'These wheels are lint magnets over the carpeted area. You really should watch that.'

What can be said, except: 'Thank you.'

'You're welcome.' Christy moved on to the next caster on the cart.

'So I'm assuming Pavlik is gone?' Sarah asked. I nodded meaningfully at Christy.

'She can't hear us,' Sarah said. 'She's in the zone. A bomb could go off under the espresso machine, and Christy wouldn't miss a stroke. Just mop up the blood splatter and move on.'

'Pavlik must have pulled the ripcord when I went out front.'

'He's a smart guy, probably cell-monitoring the biddies following him on Twitter. That way he knows where not to be.'

I didn't understand much about the technology, but I got the gist of what Sarah was saying. 'Maybe I should do the same. They're keeping track of me, too.'

'You? I can understand Pavlik—he's hot. But why would anybody be interested in *you*?'

I tried to rise above Sarah's slight. 'According to Sophie, they don't want to miss the next time I trip over a body.'

'Those old Twiddies start after you, just lead them in circles. One's bound to drop eventually and there'll be their corpse. Instant gratification.'

'Nice image.' I looked at the Brookhills clock on the wall. Nearly four p.m. 'Here's an idea. Why don't you and I leave Christy to her cleaning so we can gather some goodies for people to sample when they get off the train?'

'Won't help much if they don't come in.'

'So, let's go to them. We'll cut up sandwiches and anything else that lends itself—'

'Tien made focaccia.'

'Perfect.'

'Hmm. Maybe the reverse of what we set up on the front porch for Dedication Day? A table on the back platform they'll be forced to pass on their way to the parking lot?' Sarah was clearly warming to the idea.

As I led the way toward the kitchen, I saw Christy cleaning the crack between the baseboard and the floor with a table knife. And not one of ours. Apparently Yellow Gloves came equipped with her own cleaning supplies.

'She doesn't have to do that,' I said, starting over to her.

Sarah grabbed my arm. 'Have you lost your mind? Leave her alone in here for an hour and the place'll be spotless.'

'It already *is* spotless.' I kicked a coffee bean under the counter, but the thing ricocheted and came tumbling back out.

'Don't move,' Christy's voice said. She was advancing on me with the knife.

Granted, it may be just flatware, but it was still a blade. And Christy *was* a tad crazy.

I stepped back. *Crunch.*

'I *told* you not to move.' For the second time that afternoon, Christy looked like she was going to cry. 'It's so much easier to pick up a whole coffee bean than the remains of a crushed one.' Looking down, I saw her point. The bean—French Roast, by its color—was pretty much pulverized.

'Not a big deal,' I said. 'Let me vacuum the—'

'Don't touch it,' Christy ordered.

Her tone reminded me of Brewster Hampton, when Art Jenada had approached JoLynne's body. Except then, of course, it had been 'her' rather than 'it'. Even after someone's dead, we don't seem to feel comfortable referring to his or her corpse as 'it'. Plus, Brewster didn't know JoLynne was dead. No one did.

Except, presumably, the killer.

Christy was using an antiseptic wipe to gather up the fragments of bean. '...and just blow the dirt around. Like taking a bath and then wallowing in your own filth.' She shuddered.

I looked at Sarah.

'A soliloquy on vacuum cleaners, I think.' She shrugged.

'Shall we leave her to it?' You betcha. 'Christy, yell if anyone comes in.'

But she was still going on. '...and feather dusters. Besides the fact you're sending the dust airborne to land somewhere else, who knows where those birds were mucking around? Or what they were doing there?'

'OK. Well, thanks.' I looked at Sarah. 'Let's get the hell out of Dodge.'

'Speaking of Dodge,' Sarah said, following me into the kitchen, 'you didn't tell me about your visit with our sheriff.'

'No, I didn't.' I unwrapped the focaccia. Tien had topped the flat oven-baked bread with caramelized onions and roasted red peppers. 'This looks delicious.'

Sarah snorted. 'Just an anemic pizza with a fancy name. Which reminds me. Why don't you come over tonight and we'll order one. A real pizza, I mean. Give us a chance to talk.'

I looked at her suspiciously. 'You want to pump your business partner for information. I'm telling you right now, I don't know anything.'

'But maybe I do,' Sarah said cryptically.

I knew she was baiting me, but a girl still has to eat. 'I'll come over, but only if we order something else. I just had pizza with Pavlik.'

'Speaking of whom—'

'Later. Maybe. Now help me cut these.' By five o'clock we had the plates of focaccia ready, along with triangle sandwiches of chicken salad and roast beef.

'I don't know why you insist on trimming off the crusts,' Sarah grumbled as she swept the offending bread borders into a trash basket.

'Because the sandwiches look symmetrical. And more appetizing.' I put the last triangle nose-up on the serving platter and stood back to admire our handiwork. 'Now, how's that?'

'Fabulous. Until somebody plucks one off the platter. Then your perfect lines of finger food will domino down, and this plate'll look the same way it would have if you'd let me do the arranging.' I ignored her and took off my apron. 'Help me move a table from the store room into the parking lot.'

'That's all you think I'm good for,' Sarah groused. 'Heavy lifting.'

'Not all.' I motioned her to the other end of the six-foot folding table. 'If you're good, I'll let you spread the tablecloth over this.' With the table on its long edge, legs still folded, Sarah maneuvered her end out of the store room and into the space by the sink. From there, I led the way, backwards, through the kitchen, into the hallway and out the rear door, following the same route the 'Flight of the Pavlik' must have taken.

We had just cleared the doorway when Sarah dropped her end. 'God damn it. You scared the hell out of me.'

'But I didn't do anything.' I set down my end but rested a hand on it to keep the table steady. 'In fact, you almost made me drop the thing on my toes.'

'Not you, you idiot.' She pointed. 'Him.' Again with the idiot, but I turned. Ragnar. In full mime mode.

'Afternoon,' I said.

He waved, waggling his fingers the way he had while sitting in Kevin's staging truck.

'What's he doing here?' Sarah looked no happier to see the mime now than she had during his debut two days before.

And here I'd thought she'd been warming to him. 'He works for—' Ragnar put his finger vertically to his lips. Apparently, I was supposed to shush. Then he moved his hand back and forth between us.

'Just you and me, huh?' I said, realizing he didn't want to break character. I couldn't speak for his other work, but—and this was *really* reluctant praise—Ragnar was a damned good mime.

He nodded and pointed at the table and then himself.

'Thanks, but I think we can handle it,' I said, picking up my end again and waggling it, so Sarah would take hers.

She got the hint and lifted. 'I didn't know you spoke "mime".'

'There's a lot of things about me you don't know anything about, Sarah,' I quoted. Then: 'Things you wouldn't understand.' Ragnar chuckled. Mimes aren't supposed to chuckle. He held his thumb and index finger about an inch apart to indicate something small.

'PeeWee?' I knew where he was going, but thought it might be fun getting there. Especially with Sarah trailing cluelessly behind us.

Next, Ragnar spaced his hands far apart.

'Large?' Sarah ventured half-heartedly, still holding up her end of the table.

'Big,' I corrected.

I assume she threw me a dirty look, as Ragnar put his hand up as if to shade his eyes and scan the horizon eagerly.

'You're looking for 'adventure,' I guessed. 'As in, *PeeWee's Big Adventure*.'

Ragnar applauded, any sound completely muffled by his white gloves.

I turned to Sarah. 'That's the movie that the line of dialogue, "there's a lot of things you don't know", came from.'

'Oh, goody. Now will you stop playing with the mime and raise your end?' Sarah said. 'This table is heavy.'

'All right, all right.' I continued backing up until we reached a patch of boarding platform near the stairs leading to the parking lot.

Sarah and I rested the table on its edge and Sarah turned to Ragnar, who had followed us out.

'You!' She waved her hands like he was a pest to be shooed away from a picnic. 'Go. You'll scare our customers.' Sarah turned away to unfold the legs on her side of the table. When she straightened back up, the mime's nose and hers were so close they touched.

Speaking for Ragnar, I said, 'Boo!' Another sour

look from Sarah. The mime and I might be pushing our luck.

I pulled out the legs on my end and we set the table upright.

'Is Kevin with you?' I asked Ragnar, remembering the props man had said he would be giving his employee a lift.

The mime shook his head and pointed at the staging truck. Then his hands moved like he was holding a steering wheel.

'You drove,' I said, nodding. 'Are you going to start work here?' I meant instead of Milwaukee, where I assumed the rest of the crew was.

'A mime?' Sarah asked. 'We don't need no stinkin' mimes.' Her turn for imitations.

Ragnar raised one impossibly white finger, seemed to ponder for a moment, and then searched through his pocket, coming up with a cigarette lighter.

He flicked it to get a flame and then pantomimed that he was riding a horse.

'*Blazing Saddles*,' I said, impressed. 'Exactly.' I turned to Sarah. '*Blazing Saddles* used a misquote— or a consolidation, really—of the original lines from *The Treasure of the Sierra Madre*.' Sarah looked at me blankly.

'You know what I'm talking about,' I persisted. 'The line in the original movie was "We don't need no badges. I don't have to show you any stinkin' badges!" In *Blazing Saddles* it morphed into "Badges? We don't need no stinkin' badges", so that's what everyone remembers. Sort of like *Casablanca*'s "Play it again—"'

'"Sam",' Sarah supplied, looking venomous. 'I know. You've told me a million times. Bogie really doesn't say that anywhere in the movie. But maybe if you had a life…' The mime was wagging a finger at her, a scolding expression on his mobile face.

'He says—'

'Enough!' Sarah exploded. 'You two are sawing through my last nerve.'

I turned to Ragnar apologetically. 'You'd better go, before she decks the both of us.' The mime rubbed both fists into his eyes, like he was grinding away tears. Starting to leave, blonde braid waggling, he passed the steps of the stage and hesitated. Turning back, he held his left hand out, palm up and rounded like a bowl. With his right, he seemed to be grasping a line coming from the top.

'Your balloons?' I guessed. 'They were already taken down. Yesterday morning, I think.' He paused then nodded, slowly and sadly, tracing a tear down his cheek. Finally, twirling an imaginary walking stick, he waddled away like Charlie Chaplin.

FIFTEEN

SARAH AND I had managed to get all the finger food to our table before the first train slid to a stop at Brookhills Junction. The focaccia and sandwiches were a hit. In fact, we were cleaned out before the second train was in sight, so we called it a day and headed to Sarah's house, me making a quick stop home to let Frank out. I might be hungry, but I was well aware of Frank's priorities. Eat. Sleep. Poop. Rinse and repeat.

'I thought Christy was going to brain you over taking that toothbrush away and telling her to go home,' Sarah said, coming back into the living room after calling in our order.

'I know.' I was in my favorite reclining corner of her sectional couch, feet up. 'You were answering the phone at the time, I think, but the only way I got Christy to leave was to tell her she could come back tomorrow, cleaning implements awaiting.'

'What else did the girl need to do with that toothbrush anyway?' Sarah settled into the opposite corner, also a recliner, and up went her feet, too. 'After her meticulous attention to the casters on our condiment cart, I mean.'

'Clean the grout in the bathroom. I tried to explain the tile had just been *re*-grouted, but she ignored me.'

'What a headcase,' Sarah said. 'No wonder Christy gets along with my cousin Ronny.'

'Well, if Christy thinks our new brand new coffeehouse is dirty, how can she walk into that cruddy jail without going comatose?'

'Think they strip-search her? Confiscate her toothbrush and table knife?' I laughed. God, after the days we'd had, it felt great to relax.

'Want some wine?' Sarah asked. 'I have a nice Cab if you're going red or Sauvignon Blanc if you're doing white for a change.'

'The white,' I said. 'I don't like it as much, so I'll only have a glass.' Or two.

'It's in the fridge.'

'You're going to make me get my own wine? Some hostess you are.' I levered myself out of the recliner.

'I ordered the food. What do you want from me?'

'Are the kids coming home for dinner?' I asked from the kitchen.

Sarah was the guardian of two teenagers, the children of my former partner, Patricia. The one who died the day we opened the original Uncommon Grounds. Sarah had been Patricia's best friend.

'Sam's at college, did you forget?'

I reappeared, bottle and corkscrew in hand. 'I did, honestly. Time sure has flown.'

'You're telling me. And Courtney has her driver's license.'

Yikes. 'Is she out cruising now?' I looked through the window and into the darkness.

'I don't let her drive at night yet, and the law forbids friends in the car. So, I dropped Courtney and her posse off at the mall and she'll call when they need a lift home. Probably won't be until eleven, or even after. The bunch of them are catching a late movie.' I'd forgotten. Friday night was date night.

I held up the bottle of wine and looked at my date. 'Are you joining me?'

'Nope. Doesn't mix well with my medications.'

'I remember.' I put the bottle down and positioned the corkscrew above it. 'I was just checking to make sure you did.'

'Go ahead, though. Don't mind me.' Sarah was watching me with a smirk on her face.

'What?' I gave the corkscrew a twist. Nothing. Now I looked more closely at the bottle. 'When exactly were you going to tell me this was a twist-off?'

'Honestly? I thought you'd notice when there was no foil to slit and strip. Then I figured, hell, maybe Maggy's old-fashioned and wants to pop the bottle anyway, sniff the tin top and all.'

'Funny.' Sarah heaved herself up to get me a stemmed glass from the inverted rack over her wet bar. 'Here. Don't want you drinking straight from the bottle.'

'That happened only once,' I said, gladly taking the glass.

'And it was a joke.'

'Right.'

She watched me pour. 'Thinking of cutting back? Alcohol's not healthy, you know.' The only person more self-righteous than an ex-smoker is an ex-drinker, and Sarah was both. Unfortunately, she also was right.

I *had* been hitting the vino a little hard the last year or so. While a glass of red might be good for your heart, the whole bottle? Too much of a good thing.

I hadn't reached that stage yet, but, realizing I was edging up there, I'd consciously begun to rein myself in.

'As I said—' raising the glass—'the reason for my

choosing Sauvignon Blanc.' I took a sip and made a face. 'While it's perfect with food, the stuff is so bone dry that I'm not tempted to continue quaffing it after dinner.'

'Hey, whatever works.'

'I'll drink to that.' I raised my glass a little higher as a toast and then settled back into my corner. 'So, tell me your news.'

'What news?'

'Don't play stupid with me,' I said.

'Sorry,' she said apologetically. 'I'd forgotten how much better you are at it.'

'Yeah, yeah. Very funny. Now give.' Sarah crossed her arms stubbornly. 'Uh-unh. You first.'

'Me first on what?'

'Now who's playing stupid?'

'Like you said—' I put down my glass—'I'm good at it.' She just looked at me.

And me, back at her.

We had ourselves a stand-off.

Finally, I sighed. 'OK, I surrender. You want to know about Pavlik.' Sarah tried to lean forward, but was defeated by her recliner and the laws of physics. 'What did he say? Did he admit to the affair?'

'Your first priority is the affair? What about JoLynne's murder?'

Sarah waved my reaction aside. 'The murder I know he didn't commit. The affair, well, who knows? JoLynne was a very good-looking woman.'

'And I'm not?' Sarah eyed my comfy jeans, coffee-spotted Uncommon Grounds T-shirt and, propped up on the footrest, sneakers. Vented, over time, by holes at the soles.

'I clean up good,' I said defensively.

She said something under her breath. It sounded suspiciously like 'Not as good as JoLynne did.' I couldn't argue with Sarah's assessment. 'For your information, Pavlik did not have an affair with JoLynne.'

'Who says?'

'He does.'

'Well—' Sarah now leaned back, seeming unfulfilled without a cigarette to puff nor a drink to sip—'there you have it, then.'

I exploded. 'Why do you even ask me these things if you're going to pooh-pooh my answers?'

'You, I believe,' Sarah said. 'Him, ehhh, not so sure.'

'I thought you liked Pavlik.'

'I do. I just don't trust him.' Another snatch of something: '...all dogs.' Granted, Sarah had at least one bad relationship that I knew of under her own belt. As in, don't you just *hate* it when your new beau turns out to be a criminal?

Still, I thought she was overgeneralizing. 'Pavlik has admitted another relationship, so yeah, I believe him when he says he didn't do the dirty with JoLynne.' But my friend hadn't heard anything past the first phrase.

'See, Maggy? I told you.'

'Fine, believe what you want. But Pavlik was seeing this woman first, so she's the lover betrayed, not me.'

'Which makes *Maggy* the "other woman" this time.' Sarah seemed to be savoring the role reversal. 'Now that's an interesting turn of events. Were they in a committed relationship?' Committed? Right about now I was thinking one Maggy Thorsen should be 'committed' for opening her stupid mouth about Pavlik and Milwaukee County Executive Wynona Counsel. Thank God I hadn't named names.

'No,' I said simply, hoping that would end the discussion.

'According to your sheriff.' The doorbell rang and Sarah rose to answer it.

'What's biting you?' I called after her. 'A day or two ago, didn't my best friend tell me I should grow up? That naive no longer became me?'

From over a shoulder: 'My advice applied toward your playing he-loves-me, he-loves-me-not. This is the other side of that coin and you're still acting naive. *Maggy* has to protect herself, because nobody else will.' Sarah flung open the door.

'What?' I got to Sarah's foyer as fast as my feet would propel me.

The poor delivery guy, thank God, managed to stand his ground and keep his grip. He had our food. 'China Inn?' the young Asian man ventured hesitantly.

'Yes, thank you.' I swept Sarah out of her own doorway so I could take the corrugated slat of cartoned goodies. 'Pay the man.' Surprisingly, Sarah did and quietly followed the food and me to the kitchen table.

As I opened the containers, I realized that—contrary to what I'd told Sarah—it was Chinese, not pizza, that Pavlik and I had eaten the night before. Pizza was Wednesday night. Can't keep track of the take-out without a scorecard. Or, better yet, an annotated menu.

Happily, though, there were no repeats from the night before, except for fried dumplings which, as everybody knows, are staples.

'Good job ordering,' I said, standing back to survey the array of white boxes. 'Dumplings, egg rolls, Kung Pao chicken and...'

'Pork-fried rice. I had them add cashews.' Sarah knew I loved the nuts. Either she was being unusually kind or carefully priming my pump for even more information. *What* answers my friend hoped for, I didn't know. Sarah sure didn't seem pleased with what she'd gotten thus far.

We doled out plates and silverware, sinking a soup spoon into the contents of each little white carton. Then I went to retrieve my wine from the living room.

'I really appreciate your ordering the cashews,' I said, sitting down and claiming the fried rice as my first helping.

'Hey, I like them, too.' Sarah speared a dumpling and popped it in her mouth whole before setting down her fork.

I had the disquieting thought that the only difference between my friend and my sheepdog was the—occasional—involvement of utensils.

'So, *if* Pavlik is telling the truth,' Sarah said around the dumpling, 'then it must be Rebecca who lied.'

'Or JoLynne, lying to her.'

'Why would the recently deceased do that?'

I mulled the question as I sipped my wine. 'To hide an affair she was having with someone else?'

'Exactly,' Sarah said, mouth now full of a second dumpling. I tried not to look.

'Are you telling me you know who?'

'Wish I did.' Next up to Sarah's plate was an egg roll. 'You should eat the appetizers first, they're not good cold.'

'I like variety,' I said, adding Kung Pao Chicken to my plate.

'You and JoLynne both.'

I ignored that. 'You know what makes the most sense, don't you?'

'Maggy, I don't like playing guessing games any more than you do.'

'Rhetorical question.' I held up one finger. 'Who's the one affairee JoLynne wouldn't want Rebecca to know about?'

'You're doing it again,' Sarah griped. 'But I get your drift. JoLynne would tell her sister she was banging Pavlik to hide the fact she was already doing her future brother-in-law.'

I wouldn't have put it in those terms, perhaps, but, basically: 'Yes.' Then I did a double take. 'Rebecca and Michael are getting married?' Poor Michael. 'Wait a minute. How could you know that?'

'People do tell me things, you know.' No, I didn't. In fact, Sarah was the *last* person folks usually turned to with their secrets. Not because she would maliciously blab them, but rather because my friend just couldn't give a shit.

For me, though, Sarah was the perfect incarnation of a confessional experience. The warm confidentiality of a priest and the cool detachment of a psychiatrist. Now, if only she had a prescription pad.

I took another slug of wine. 'Who told you about the pending nuptials, Rebecca or Michael?'

'Neither.' A shrug. 'It was Mary, our librarian. With the town not opening the building before noon and cutting even *her* hours to save money, she's been working at the jewelry store part-time.' Things were very bad when the head book-guru was forced to moonlight. No wonder Mary had the time to attend the dedication on Wednesday.

I closed my eyes, searching for reliable, visual memories.

'I don't recall seeing an engagement ring on Rebecca's finger.'

'Maybe Michael hasn't given it to her yet.' I opened my eyes, only to see Sarah shoving the last of the egg roll into her mouth. Prelude devoured, she reached for the meal's main act.

I managed to snag two cashews off the top of the pork-fried rice as it zoomed past me. 'Knowing Rebecca, I'd expect she'd want to choose her own ring.'

'Me, too.' Sarah was digging around, cherry-picking pork morsels and nuts.

I paused, fork in mid-air. The cashew that I'd balanced carefully on top of rice and pork hit the table.

'What?' Sarah said, snatching the nut—mine, by all that was holy—and popping it on to her tongue.

I stuck the remaining forkful of food into my own mouth, lest it meet the fate of the cashew, and held up a finger as I chewed.

Lips closed. My mother taught me well.

Then, after I'd patted my mouth with a paper napkin: 'What if it wasn't an engagement ring for Rebecca?'

'Why else would Michael lay out that kind of money?' I raised my eyebrows to drive home the point. 'For JoLynne?'

'Maggy?' The tone used to explain the obvious to a slow learner. 'JoLynne is...*was* married. To Kevin, remember?' Sarah reached for my wineglass and took a sip.

'Hey,' I said. 'You're not supposed to have alcohol.'

'Just checking to see if you're right that Sauvignon Blanc's good with Chinese.' She made a face. 'Not.' The only clear drink Sarah truly enjoyed was vodka. And, yes, that includes water. Unless it was mixed with vodka.

'Good. Give it back.' I set my glass out of her reach. 'You're certain the purchase was an engagement ring?'

'A diamond ring, Mary said.'

'They set diamonds in other types of rings beyond engagement ones,' I pointed out. 'Maybe it's a cocktail ring for his mother.'

'What mother?'

'Do you know Michael's mother is dead?'

'No. You know she's not?'

This was getting us nowhere. 'All I'm saying is that maybe the ring was a gift for JoLynne and Rebecca found out.'

'How?'

'Mary told *you*, didn't she?' If you wanted to be specific, Mary didn't 'tell' anybody anything. She only asked, as in: *'I was going to the store?'*

'Your book is overdue?'

'Your cat just got run over by a semi?' Subtract twenty years of age and add a designer handbag, Mary'd be a valley girl. Kate must have had a picnic interviewing her at the dedication ceremony.

A thought that cheered me immensely.

Sarah was thinking, too. 'I just can't believe Mary would spill the beans to Rebecca. Especially if she thought Michael was planning a surprise.'

'Maybe she assumed he'd already proposed.'

'Without a ring to show his intended?' Sarah held up her hands to stave off further discussion. 'Regardless of how Rebecca *supposedly* found out that Michael had bought a ring he *perhaps* meant to give to someone else, what could she do about it?'

'Confront him.' I picked up the remaining egg roll and set it back down.

'Told you.' Sarah waved her fork at me. 'Gotta eat 'em while they're hot.' I hate it when she's right. Normally I'm eating with Frank and the food doesn't have a chance to get cold. The dinner conversation between the sheepdog and me amounts to chewing, swallowing and slobbering, accented with the occasional 'yum'. Sometimes Frank makes noises, too.

'Rebecca—' I picked up the cold egg roll and took a defiant bite from it—'is not afraid to start a row.' Sarah grabbed the roll out of my hand, wrapped it in a pink paper napkin and stuck the package in her microwave.

'To recap—' she pushed a button and turned—'Rebecca *may* have discovered that Michael bought a ring he *might*—or might *not*—have intended for JoLynne. Rebecca *perhaps* reams him out. What does he do, maybe confess?'

'Will you stop with all the "perhapses", "maybes" and "mights"? Of course, we're just theorizing. It comes with the territory.'

'*You're* theorizing. I'm making it up as I go.' The microwave beeped and Sarah removed the napkin-wrapped egg roll.

'Thank you,' I said as she plopped it on my plate. The thing was steaming now. 'But my answer to your question is, no. I don't think Michael told her the ring was for JoLynne. Rebecca must have suspected, though. There seems to be a long, convoluted history between the sisters.'

'Only, what, thirty years of sibling bickering?' Sarah pointed at the egg roll.

'Better eat that before it gets cold again.' I gingerly tried to unroll it from the napkin without searing any fingers. 'You know what I mean. Rebecca was jealous of her sister, maybe with good reason. If Michael and JoLynne were involved, Michael would have warned Jo if her sister suspected.' I knew the affair was fact because Michael had admitted it to me. I didn't tell Sarah that, though, figuring it wasn't crucial to our conjecture.

She said, 'So, JoLynne confided the supposed affair with Pavlik to Rebecca, to put her younger sister off the track.'

'Exactly. And, apparently, Rebecca believed her.' Sarah pointed toward my plate. 'There's a little bit stuck to it.' A little? The layer of napkin that had been closest to the egg roll seemed permanently bonded to it.

'And you, in turn, believed Rebecca.' Sarah pointed again.

'Try that edge. Once you get it started, the rest should come right off.' Spoken like a woman who had dealt with paper-encased food in the past.

I said, 'Only problem: the fact that Rebecca thought her sister was having an affair with Pavlik didn't seem to stop her from believing Michael was also in the mix. Remember how she carped at him?'

'And called her sibling a slut, I might add. Even after JoLynne's body was found.' I gave up on restoring my food and pushed the plate away.

'You know what this means, right?'

'That I ordered that egg roll and reheated it for you in vain?'

I looked at the soggy pink tube between us. 'Sad, but true. It's not what I was thinking, though.'

Sarah stood up, picked up my plate and rolled the shrouded egg roll into the garbage. 'Then I give up.'

'It means—' I picked up my glass, which contained a carefully preserved half-inch of Sauvignon Blanc—'that Rebecca Penn had a motive for killing her sister.'

Sarah turned. 'Well, that will be good for your sheriff.'

'Yup.' I took a self-satisfied sip. 'This will give him a viable suspect, now that Kevin has been cleared.' Assuming Pavlik listened to me. He sometimes pooh-poohed my theories for no reason beyond their being wildly imaginative.

'Actually,' Sarah said, 'it'll give *some*one another suspect. That was *my* piece of news.'

'Your news?'

I'd forgotten that while I'd told Sarah, at her request, about my conversation with our sheriff, she hadn't reciprocated. 'What, that Milwaukee County is taking over Pavlik's investigation into JoLynne's murder? I already know. You were there when Kate sprang it on me, remember? On camera, I might add.' Sarah stood over the sink, rinsing off my plate, then turned off the water and faced me.

'Yeah, I remember.' Almost apologetic. And Sarah was seldom apologetic. 'This is more recent, Maggy. I just found out on my drive home.'

Suddenly my second dinner of Chinese food in as many days wasn't sitting so lightly in my stomach. 'Found out what?'

Sarah wiped her hands on the thighs of her jeans. 'It's Pavlik. It looks like he's been arrested.'

SIXTEEN

'FOR MURDER?' I GASPED.

'No. A parking ticket. What do you *think* he was arrested for?' Sarah, having shifted from apologetic to sarcastic, compensated by filling my wineglass to the brim.

I ignored it. There had to be a mistake. Even if the investigators believed Rebecca about the affair, it was just hearsay, right? Besides, there couldn't be any real evidence against Pavlik.

Could there? 'Sarah, how do you know about the arrest?'

'Twitter. Apparently they were waiting for Pavlik at his house.' I assumed Sarah meant the authorities were waiting, not the old Twiddies, as my partner so disdainfully called them. Didn't stop her from *being* one.

But, hold on: 'This must have just happened. What about the "news" you were dangling like a carrot all afternoon?' I didn't even bother asking why she—having gotten the information en route to her house—had waited until after dinner to tell me. That was simply quintessential Sarah. After all, why ruin a good meal?

'I lied. I wanted information and figured you'd spill if you thought I knew something you didn't.'

'I *hate* your knowing things I don't know,' I muttered, still trying to get a handle on her 'news'.

'I know.' Sarah held my wine up to me. 'Hence the

lie.' This time I took the glass. I didn't drink from it, though.

'I should go home.'

'Why? So you can sulk?'

'I don't sulk,' I countered. 'I cogitate.'

'You wallow in your bed and talk to a dog.' Had me there.

'I do not.' Liar, liar, pants on fire.

'Stay here and discuss it,' Sarah urged. 'At least I can talk back.' Sarah's talking back was the problem. Frank seldom commented beyond a sage nod and the occasional fart as punctuation mark.

I stood up and put the overfilled wineglass on the kitchen counter. 'Thanks, but I really don't know what there is to say. I need more information and neither of us is going to get any tonight.'

'True.' Sarah had begun digging through a cabinet. 'But tomorrow's Saturday. What do you think you're going to find out on a weekend?'

'I don't know, but I'm off from Uncommon Grounds and I have to try. Maybe I'll visit Brewster and Anita Hampton at home. Brewster should have some sense of the facts.' Sarah turned with Cling Wrap in her hand. 'You're just going to pop in on our county executive and his lovely wife?'

'Why not?' I said defensively. 'I introduced them before they became who they are.'

'Right. Makes you practically family. Anita, Brew and you.' Sarah waved the yellow and red box at me. 'Want your wine saved?'

'In plastic wrap? What's wrong—run out of Baggies to pour it into?'

'I'll just stretch it over the top,' Sarah said, tearing

off a strip, 'so the wine is waiting for your next visit. Waste not, want not.'

I know when I'm being punished. 'Fine. I'll eat the egg roll next time, pink napkin and all.'

'Yes, you will,' my frugal friend said, sliding the wineglass into her fridge.

The next day, as Sarah had said, was Saturday, my least favorite day to work at Uncommon Grounds. Everyone was in a good mood—stopping by for coffee before going off to meet friends, shop or visit a museum or art fair.

They were happy.

And so I hated them. I wanted to be happy, too.

That's why I'd engineered Saturday as my traditional day away from the shop. I could be on a frolic of my own. No coffee smell permeating my hair, no signature T-shirt nor navy-blue apron.

Speaking of aprons, I was hoping my cell phone was in the pocket of one I'd hung from a wooden hook the night before.

If not, the thing could be anywhere, and I'd probably need it. I hadn't decided whether to call and give Anita and Brewster Hampton a heads-up on my coming by their place. My investigative instincts said no, but my manners shrank at that tactic. Drop in unannounced? Horrors.

Anyway, I still wanted the phone and I didn't half-mind visiting Uncommon Grounds when I, too, could be a woman of weekend leisure.

Sarah was behind the counter when I entered. Having left my car on the street in front rather than our parking lot out back, I was surprised there wasn't a single customer in the place.

'Uh-oh,' I said, after checking the stand-up tables around the corner. 'Where is everyone?'

'You think they'd be leaning over an elbow when they could be sitting on chairs three sizes too small for their butts? Or, speaking of sitting, did you check in the bathroom?' And top of the morning to you, as well.

'So, *no*body's been in?' I asked.

Sarah gestured at the Brookhills clock above her head. 'See that? Well, I opened at six, and now it's nine. Three hours and nothing with a pulse except Amy and you has come through that door.' Hearing our voices, Amy stuck her head out of the kitchen.

'It's perfectly understandable, you know. Until we build a reputation in this new location, people aren't going to think about coming here as a destination on their precious weekends.' She pointed across the quiet street outside our front window.

'Especially when none of the other businesses are open.' Admittedly, Rebecca and Michael's graphics and writing studio was closed on Saturdays and, even during the week, it wasn't the type of business that drew casual shoppers. Same with Art Jenada's catering operation and Christy's piano studio.

'We need something special to go in next door,' I said.

'Next door' was an abandoned florist shop. 'Women's clothing, maybe a kitchen gadget store or gourmet spice emporium.'

'One store isn't going to make a difference,' Sarah said.

'We need all our low-traffic neighbors across the street to move out, so some high-end shops can replace them.'

'Speaking of neighbors.' I looked around. 'The place looks great. Did Christy come back this morning?'

'Nope,' Sarah said. 'If this is what Ms Clean considers a half-finished job, I'm afraid she'll scrub the paint off the walls if I let her back in.'

'You turned her away?'

'Sarah wouldn't even let her get her toothbrush,' Amy tattled.

Poor Christy. But I had no idea where I'd put the thing anyway.

I went to the back hooks and felt through apron pockets until I found my cell phone. As I came back out, I held it up.

'I just stopped by to get this. Is there anything else I can do?' I figured it was the perfect time to make the offer. No customers and the place was spotless.

'Take my place,' Sarah said, untying her apron.

'Sorry.' I was backing toward the door. 'I'd really like to, but I have to go see Brewster.'

'But you said you wanted to help,' Sarah protested.

'I lied.' I disappeared out the door.

As I made my way down the sidewalk, I could hear hammering, so I followed the direction of the sound.

As I rounded the corner bordering the train tracks, the hammering was joined by a power drill, its whine a little off-key.

Ragnar Norstaadt was working on the stage with the drill, backing out screws toward removing the plywood panels that formed the floor. I waited until he paused to pluck out the screws he'd just loosened.

'Ragnar,' I called.

'Good morning, Maggy Thorsen,' he said, standing up and brushing off his hands.

'Good morning.' It wasn't, of course, but no one wants to hear 'Crappy morning' or even 'So-so morning'.

'You look for Kevin?' Ragnar asked, approaching the edge of the stage. 'He must take a meeting this morning and cannot join us until after we lunch.'

'Assuming you're not already done by then.' I waved my hand toward a Williams Staging guy that I didn't know, who was dismantling the gallows where the cup and saucer had stood. Another worker was busy loading Ragnar's detached plywood panels into the back of a stenciled van. 'You're making great progress.'

'Ahh,' he said, hopping down so we were on the same level, 'it is what you call the optical illusion, yah? After the top decking is gone, our hard work begins.'

'But you'll be done today?'

'True, Maggy Thorsen. We will not be back.' His blue, blue eyes met and held mine.

Sigh.

Was it wrong of me—main squeeze in the slammer—to be sorry that Ragnar wouldn't be coming 'round my shop no more, no more'?

Of course it was. And I was deeply ashamed of myself. Though Pavlik's 'overlapping' of Wynona Counsel and me took away a bit of that guilty sting.

Two wrongs might not make a right, but they sure could feel good.

Or would. If I did. But I wouldn't.

With an effort I pried my eyes away from Ragnar's and stuck out my hand. 'Well, thank you for everything.' He pulled off his work gloves and took my hand, turning it palm up. 'I feel our life paths will cross again, Maggy Thorsen. Very soon, I think.' He didn't let go.

All of a sudden, I had a devil on each shoulder, both of them leaning forward, hissing, 'Go for it, Maggy. What can you *possibly* have to lose?' To my eternal credit, I shushed the evil—yet remarkably cogent—fiends.

'That sounds wonderful,' I said, giving Ragnar's hand a quick shake before I pulled mine away. 'But right now I need to go see my, ummm…boyfriend. The sheriff, you know.' I dug my toe into the dirt and twisted it.

'The Pavlik of Brookhills?' Ragnar drew himself to full height. 'But he is jailed.' I knew that.

'How did you find out?' I was expecting Twitter or Facebook or some such thing.

'The news that is on my television this morning. I watch before I come to work.'

'Ragnar, what did the television reporters say?'

'Your sheriff and Mrs Kevin, they had…' He seemed to struggle for a polite phrase in English.

'Sex?' I was trying to put *Ragnar* at ease?

'No.' The mime-cum-construction stud looked shocked.

'No, no. An event, maybe?' An 'affair,' maybe? But there was no need to correct him. Let Ragnar think that Pavlik and his boss's wife had thrown one great party.

'I'd best be going,' I said, starting to move away.

Ragnar touched me on the arm. I turned. I could see he was blushing. 'I do not like to ask, a time like this.'

Oh, dear. Apparently I had turned him down so obliquely, he hadn't registered it. 'That's all right, Ragnar. I'm very flattered, but I'm also not interested.' Another lie. I was damn interested, but I wasn't going to do anything about it.

'This I understand now. But before you go—' he

dug a white rectangle out of his jeans' pocket—'you take this, yah?' A business card with his phone number and e-mail.

I started to object, but he waved me down. 'Please. You must take.' He pressed the card into my hand, closing my fingers over it. 'Some day you see. You will want Ragnar.' Oh, yeah, some days were like that. But…

'It is then you must call me,' he continued, giving my hand a squeeze before releasing it. 'At any hour.' I was afraid to open my mouth, not sure what might come out of it.

Ragnar held my gaze for a beat of three, four, five. Then, 'I will be good to you, Maggy Thorsen. Better than any other.' I cleared my throat. Or tried to. Something seemed stuck.

'I'm sure you—'

'No, no. We do not speak of it.' He put his finger to my lips.

'But—'

'Ahh, but you must know more, yah? You are a wise woman. I can promise you,' a quick glance around, 'the ten.' The ten? He couldn't possibly mean what I thought he meant.

This time I did manage to clear my throat. 'Umm, did you say ten?'

'That is not enough?' Ragnar looked surprised. 'You demand the fifteen?' Only men truly believe bigger is better, at least in these increments. Ten? Fifteen?

Wait a second. 'Are you talking percentages? As in discounts?'

'Yah, but of course. What is it you believe that I am saying?' Nothing. Absolutely nothing.

'That's very generous of you, Ragnar, and I will cer-

tainly keep it in mind.' Bidding the mime *adieu*, I beat
a hasty retreat around the corner.

Well, if I had to make a fool of myself, at least I'd
done it in the privacy of my own head, I thought as I
unlocked the Escape.

But a lousy fifteen per cent discount? Was that all I
meant to the clown?

Settling in to the driver's seat, I fished out my phone
and flipped it open to 'Contacts'. I scrolled down, but
found no Hampton, Anita *or* Brewster. That made the
decision whether to call ahead or arrive unannounced
a simple one. Of course, it also meant I couldn't ask
for directions.

After their lavish wedding, Anita and Brewster
had built a house about twenty miles beyond Poplar
Creek, which forms the western boundary of the town
of Brookhills. I'd been out there only once, but I should
be able find it again. I hoped.

As I drove west, I switched on the radio to keep me
company and caught a measured, male voice in mid-
pronouncement '...theory is that the events woman—'

'*Affairs* woman,' I said to the dashboard.

'...was still alive when she was placed in the cup.
JoLynne Penn-Williams' tooth-marks were found on the
inflatable, apparently made as the woman struggled to
breathe. Someone—and law enforcement officials fear
it may be one of their own—wanted just the opposite.' I
pushed 'CD' and was rewarded with smooth jazz. Great
music for relaxing, though I wasn't sure anything was
going to help this morning. After talking with Brewster, I'd drive straight to the jail. I needed badly to talk
to Pavlik, to get his take on all this. The county must
have Saturday visiting hours, right?

Twenty minutes later, I turned into a long, brick driveway. Not 'real' brick, but the kind etched into red-stained concrete to simulate the tonier treatment. At least until the concrete cracks, as it always does in Wisconsin, where the earth regularly freezes and thaws.

Still, it beat the rat-a-tat-tat of gravel pocking the undercarriage of the Escape as it rolled into the driveway of my place.

I left the car, hearing immediately the thwock of a tennis ball being struck by racquet strings. Curious, I circled the white mini-manse instead of going directly to its front door.

Wow. A backyard tennis court.

As a kid, I'd begged my dad endlessly to make one for me. Who needed grass and trees anyway? In my ten-year-old imagination, I'd teach myself to play tennis and beat Chris Evert on the way to a grand slam. Then, in the winter, I'd flood the court, learn to figure-skate and win a gold medal at the Olympics, like Dorothy Hamill. All three of us—Chrissy, Dor and me—we'd be best friends.

Oh, lay off the sarcasm, will you? I was ten.

Brewster and Anita Hampton were facing each other across the net on a bright green court. They both wore white, matching the gleaming lines. The whole set-up looked brand new.

As I watched from under a sugar-maple tree, Anita tossed the ball up for a serve, but, instead of swinging at it, she caught the ball. 'Damn wind,' she said.

The leaves on my tree indicated no discernible breeze. She went to toss again, but this time let the ball fall. 'Bugs,' she complained, stomping and swiping at her legs.

Excuses, excuses. I wasn't being bothered in the least. Anita set up to serve once more, this time taking a wild, awkward swing that sent the ball skittering my way.

I emerged from under the tree and retrieved her wild shot from the grass.

'Who wants it?' I called, holding the tennis ball up.

Anita jumped at the sound of my voice and pointed at Brewster. Apparently her last effort had double-faulted the game away.

I threw baseball-style to her husband and kept walking toward them.

'Thanks, Maggy,' Brewster said, his tone of voice pleasant, even welcoming. 'What a nice surprise.' Anita didn't look pleasant, much less welcoming. Probably ticked at being caught by a former subordinate without makeup on her blotchy face. Her tennis dress hung unfashionably from her shoulders like a hand-me-down, and I could make out a stain near the hem.

But who gets dressed up to play in their own backyard? Polite guests, after all, call first.

'I'm sorry to just pop by,' I said, still relishing the fact that Anita wasn't quite as impressive without tailored work clothes or war paint. And she downright sucked at tennis.

'Not at all, Maggy.' She pulled herself up straight to regain some of the ground lost by her appearance. 'Is something wrong? You heard me instruct Kevin to dismantle your staging today.'

After she'd yanked his guys away to do Milwaukee's yesterday. How kind of her. Well, with luck, whatever mixup she and Kevin spoke about yesterday was still giving her fits. 'No, nothing's wrong in Brookhills. They're breaking things down right now.'

'Is he there?' Anita seemed a bit anxious.

'Kevin? No,' I said.

'Why? Do you need to see him?' Brewster's brow furrowed a bit.

'No, no,' Anita said hurriedly. 'Just wondering.'

'So what *is* wrong, Maggy?' her husband asked. 'You look worried.'

'I am. It's Pavlik.' Could the county exec *not* know his own chief law enforcer had been arrested for murder?

'Our sheriff?' Well, that was a start. At least he knew Pavlik's name and title.

'Oh, that's right, Brew.' Anita flapped a hand at her husband.

'Maggy and your sheriff are…seeing each other.' She said it like it was of no consequence to her, despite the fact she'd been acting mighty friendly toward Pavlik during the aborted dedication of the commuter-train.

I looked back and forth between them. 'You do know that he's been arrested.'

'We've been informed,' Anita said, fingernail worrying a spot on her cheek. 'In fact, he's being held in our jail.'

'I'd like to see him. Do you think that's possible?' My question was directed to Brewster, but it was Anita who answered. 'Certainly, dear. Though only during regular visiting hours, of course.' She seemed to feel that no special arrangements were warranted, despite the fact I knew where she lived.

This time I turned my back on Anita, so there could be no question of whom I was addressing. 'You don't honestly think Pavlik killed JoLynne Penn-Williams, do you?' Brewster flushed, but once again it was his wife who did the talking.

'Maggy, he can't possibly answer that. You were in public relations, remember?'

Drained of patience, I wheeled on her. 'I'm not a reporter, Anita, and I sure don't work for you anymore, either. What I want to know, as a friend, is what steps Brewster and "our" county are taking to support and defend Pavlik.' I didn't add, 'Because I'm getting the feeling that the only one who gives a rat's ass about the man is me.' But I sure thought it.

'Brookhills County will do everything appropriate...' Brewster started, as if he were reading a news release. One prepared by his loving wife.

'Oh, shut up, Brewster,' Anita said. OK, make that his not-so-loving wife.

'Honey,' Brewster said, 'Maggy's right. She is a friend and deserves—'

'Fine,' Anita snapped. 'You two "friends" talk.' She was still messing with her zit, but just making it redder. The woman would need spackling a half-inch deep to cover the thing. 'I'm going inside.' With that, she wheeled and stalked off.

Brewster and I watched Anita go. 'Sorry,' I said, when the back door slammed closed.

'Not your fault.' Brewster didn't quite have his usual 'boyish good looks' expression. 'She's been a little touchy the last few days.'

'Work stress?' I guessed, then remembered the tennis dress just hanging on her. 'I couldn't help but notice Anita's losing weight.'

'She is that,' he said, still looking toward the house. 'Even though she tries to hide it.'

'Could she have an eating disorder?' Maybe our barista Amy nailed it when she mentioned that Mrs County Exec looked almost anorexic.

'I don't think so. Anita's just not the same woman, though.'

'As before you were married?' I laughed lightly to put Brewster at ease. 'That's not uncommon, you know. We're all on our best behavior when we're dating.' I, for example, had yet to fart in Pavlik's presence. I figured Frank's chronic flatulence was already enough of a deal-breaker from my side of the relationship.

But Mr County Exec was shaking his head. 'That's not what I meant. It's my—' He broke off.

'Your what?' I asked. After all, Brewster had brought it up. He turned and eyed me, as though approaching a decision.

'Your question to me a few minutes ago?'

'Yes?'

A pause before: 'No.'

'No…what?'

'No, I don't think Pavlik killed Jo.' Abrupt change of subjects.

'The authorities believe he was having an affair with her.'

'Maggy, he wasn't.' There was something about the way the man said it. Flat tone, dead certainty.

The light dawned. 'But you were,' I said to Brewster Hampton.

SEVENTEEN

OF COURSE.

I was remembering Brewster's 'Don't touch her,' when JoLynne's body was found. And his face flushing just minutes ago, when I asked him if he thought Pavlik had killed her.

Kate McNamara, our intrepid reporter, had said that JoLynne was rumored to be bonking someone in our county's government. Rebecca had gone further: a person JoLynne 'worked with'.

Well, Brewster Hampton certainly fit those criteria as well as Pavlik did. Maybe better.

'Does Anita know?' I asked him.

This time, just a glance toward the house. 'I'm not sure.'

'She hasn't said anything?'

He gave an involuntary shiver. 'Anita wouldn't, Maggy. She'd just lower the boom on me without warning.' My God, the man was afraid of his wife. Maybe he had reason. If Anita found out that, having sponsored JoLynne into WoPro, the woman had turned around and started an affair with Anita's own husband… Well, the dragon lady I recalled from the bank would confront JoLynne. And it wouldn't have been pretty.

'Do you think your wife "lowered the boom" on JoLynne instead?' Even as thin as Anita was now, she probably outweighed JoLynne and she certainly stood a good five or six inches taller. If my former boss had managed to get the other woman on the ground, Anita could have suffocated JoLynne the way Kevin had described. Did she have the strength, though, to get her husband's lover up and over the side of our inflated cup?

Brewster was looking confused. 'Do you mean literally? Like Anita...*hurt* JoLynne?'

Like kill her in this case, but: 'Yes.'

He was shaking his head. 'More likely that Anita would suddenly have me served with reams of divorce papers. And at the courthouse, after alerting the media to be there. Maggy, she'd take everything I have.'

'No prenup?' Men are such idiots when love, aka lust and sex, enter the picture.

'Just one with provisions to protect her.' Brewster saw my look. 'Anita's the spouse who brought a dowry into our marriage.'

I hadn't known Anita came from money. But another thought had occurred to me. 'What time did you arrive at the Brookhills depot Wednesday to catch your train to the Milwaukee celebration?'

A frown. 'About ten to six. I wanted to hitch a ride when the train was moved to Milwaukee at six a.m. for the first leg of the dedication ceremony.' Made sense. That way Brewster's car wouldn't be stranded in Milwaukee and have to be recovered after he and Wynona rode the train back to our celebration.

'But Anita was late?'

'It didn't start out that way,' Brewster said. 'Anita drove us to the station, but needed to take care of a few things on the Brookhills end before we left. In fact, I ended up holding the train for her. Not a big deal, I guess, because it wasn't running a regular schedule that day anyway.' Could JoLynne have been one of those 'things' Anita had taken care of?

Brewster's timeline seemed to match the one Jerome had given me. 'When you arrived at our depot, do you remember what was going on?'

'Not much, really. From down below at the platform level, it looked like the saucer to your cup was already inflated on the framework Williams built.'

'Gallows,' I automatically corrected.

'What?'

Better I hadn't said anything, given Pavlik's earlier reaction to the term. Only now I was stuck. 'That's what they called the staging built above the boarding platform. Made it easier to keep the two straight, I think.'

'But…"gallows"?' A shudder. 'Bizarre.'

What wasn't? 'About the cup?'

'Oh, right. Well, I assumed they were getting ready to inflate that, too, because the air-pump started up as I boarded the eastbound train. I remembered thinking we'd likely get complaints about the noise from our depot's neighbors.'

If Brewster was at train-level, it wouldn't help to ask if he had seen anything in the cup. It was dark and he'd have been far too low. 'Is Pavlik aware of your affair with JoLynne?'

'I think he suspects.'

'Is that why you had him taken off the case?'

Afraid, then back to confused. Brewster settled on downright startled. 'I didn't. I swear.'

'Then—'

'Iced tea, anyone?' Anita called out from their house's open back door. She was dressed in lemon-yellow capris and a white shirt. While I, given the distance, couldn't tell how well she'd covered her zit, the woman had definitely applied some make-up.

Anita Hampton's world had seemingly been righted, with her back on top.

'Sounds great, honey,' Brewster replied and made for the house.

I skipped their iced tea in favor of bread and water: the Brookhills County Jail.

I'd never visited anyone behind bars before, so on the drive there I tried Christy Wrigley's cell phone. I figured she'd seen Ronny enough times to have the protocol for our jail down pat. The phone rang five times and then went to voice mail. Hanging up, I turned into the county's parking lot.

On my own.

I stepped through the street door of the apparent visitors' lobby. Lining one wall was a row of lockers, most of them with keys attached to curly orange cords that could be slipped over your wrist.

Looked a little like the changing room in a mammogram clinic. *Remove your top and put this paper gown on, opening to the front. Place all your personal items in the locker and turn the key, taking it with…*

Difference was, this room was coed and both the co's and the ed's were a tad seamy. Also, the chairs were molded black plastic instead of floral-upholstered. And the coffee wasn't free, either.

I waited for a particularly grizzled 'visitor' to cross to the vending machine, his shoes making suck-suck noises on the tacky linoleum floor. Then I approached the uniformed deputy sitting behind a glass window at the far end of the room. His name tag read 'Ernst'.

'Excuse me,' I said.

He didn't look up. 'Photo ID.' I sifted through my handbag to find wallet and driver's license. 'What should I—' Even as I said it, a drawer, like they have at drive-in banking windows, shot out toward me at waist level from what had looked like a flat metal panel.

I dropped my license into the metal maw, and the drawer slid back in silently.

Ernst, a grey-haired man who looked irritated at being relegated to desk duty, picked up my photo ID, studying first it, then me.

Seeming satisfied, he said, 'Hats, bandannas or scarves are not permitted. Put those and your coat, bag and anything in your pockets that could set off a metal detector into one of those lockers. Secure its door and take that key with you.' If I couldn't tell from Ernst's no-pause monotone that it was a jaded spiel, the fact I didn't have coat or hat, bandanna or scarf probably would have clued me. However, I did as requested and returned to the window, orange stretchy cord around my wrist with the locker key dangling from it.

'I'm here to see—' The deputy glanced over his shoulder at the big clock on the wall behind him, then leafed through a stapled bundle of papers until stopping at one.

'It's eleven fifteen. That's Two and Three A East, plus Juvie and East Female. Which?' It was like I'd stumbled into a foreign country without first learning the language. How in the world did our little Christy find her way?

'I'm afraid…' I cleared my throat. 'I'm afraid I don't know which.'

'Ma'am—' the word came from Ernst's throat more like an irritated groan than a solicitation—'there are people behind you. If you don't know where—' My turn to glance over my shoulder. Sure enough. The line was halfway across the lobby. Directly behind me was Grizzled Guy, vending machine coffee in hand. He didn't look happy. Or that he'd ever *been* happy.

Time to roll out the big guns. 'I'm here to see Sheriff Pavlik.'

'Jesus Christ, lady.' This from Grizzled Coffee-Holder.

'Have you tried looking in the man's office?'

I started to answer, but if the guy didn't keep up on the news, I didn't feel compelled to tell him the sheriff was in the slammer. Instead, I turned back to the deputy and lowered my voice. 'Listen, I'm a friend and I really need to talk to him.'

'Sure you do.' Ernst pushed back in his chair. 'But the sheriff's not here.' How stupid of me. Pavlik wouldn't be in the general population of the jail. As a law enforcement officer, he wouldn't be safe.

'Is he being held somewhere else? Can you tell me how to get there?' The deputy shook his head, like he actually pitied anybody so dense. 'Drive fifteen miles due east and stop five blocks before plowing into Lake Michigan.'

It took me a second, but I got it. 'Of course. Pavlik's in the Milwaukee County Jail.'

Ernst clapped twice in slow-motion. 'Correct. What parting gifts do we have for our contestant, Johnny?'

'How about a kick in the butt if she don't get out of line,' Grizzled Coffee-Holder grumbled.

I could take a hint. I stepped away from the window with a 'thank you' to the deputy which I hoped rang as hollow as his 'ma'am.' At least Ernst had told me what

I needed to know, even if the game show shtick was a little unnecessary. I should have realized that if the case had been turned over to Sheriff Walensky in Milwaukee County, Pavlik would be held in Walensky's jail, not his own.

I should have tipped to it when Anita said he was being held at 'our' jail and insisted on answering the questions I was directing to Brewster. She didn't consider Brookhills, the county for which her husband was responsible, her own. 'Ours' meant where *she* worked. Milwaukee County.

I crossed the room to my locker and slipped the key chain off my wrist. Now I could drive fifteen miles and start the whole process over again. At least this time I had some idea of…

'Thank you, Bobby,' a familiar voice called.

I turned to see Christy coming out of the door next to the deputy's cubicle. No wonder she hadn't answered her cell, she was already *visiting* a cell.

'Not a problem,' Deputy Ernst said, giving her a wave.

'Have a good day, Christy.' She's 'Christy', I'm 'ma'am'. Apparently the yellow-gloved one was more personable than I'd realized.

'Maggy?' Christy said when she saw me. 'What are you doing here?'

'I was looking for Sheriff Pavlik.' I gestured toward 'Bobby' behind the glass. 'You must come here a lot.'

'Not a lot.' Christy slipped her key into the lock.

'No?' As she turned the key, I realized she wasn't wearing gloves, yellow or otherwise.

'No,' Christy repeated, opening the locker and retrieving her cell phone. She slid it into her pocket and then delved back and pulled out a pair of the transparent vinyl gloves she reserved for dressy occasions, where yellow rubber just wouldn't do. 'Two A-East inmates can only have visitors on Wednesday, Thursday and Saturday.' Again, I wondered how the woman contained her fear of germs when she was in the pokey. I guess love does conquer all.

'But they won't let you wear your gloves?'

'Sadly, no.' Christy draped the vinyl ones over the edge of the locker door and opened the cap of a small bottle of antibacterial hand gel. 'Like some?'

'Thanks.' I rubbed the gel into my hands and then removed my own stuff from its locker, leaving the key.

Christy, on the other hand, used the gel and then carefully slipped her gloves over clean hands. Then she swung the locker door closed with a forearm. She was wearing long sleeves, naturally.

'You take a shower the moment you get home?'

'Oh, yes.' A sheepish smile. 'Once I was in such a hurry I forgot and left the car's engine running.'

I laughed, doing a 'tack' dance on the sticky floor. 'I can't say I blame you. Heading out?'

'I am.' She held up her gloved hands. 'Would you mind opening the door for me?' I was doing just that when I caught a glimpse of Kevin Williams, coming out the same barred gate that Christy had.

'Kevin,' I called, holding the door with my butt, so I could wave at him.

'The police were just updating me,' he said as he joined me at the exit. His expression was sympathetic. 'I understand Sheriff Pavlik was arrested yesterday.'

'That's what I hear.' I could see Christy standing about twenty feet down the sidewalk, apparently waiting for me. I felt honored she'd selected me over the prospect of a more immediate shower.

I put my hand on Kevin's arm. 'Listen, I have to run, but are you all right?'

His eyes grew shiny and he looked away. 'I know people believe, since JoLynne was fooling around, that I wouldn't be broken up about her death. But I am.' He swiveled his head toward me. 'Why is that?'

'Because you loved her and love…' I interrupted myself.

'Aww, geez, I think we're deteriorating into *Love Story* territory here.'

'Ryan O'Neal and Ali McGraw.'

Kevin grinned, though his eyes were still teary. 'Could be worse. *The Bridges of Madison County*, even.'

'With all due respect to the fact that both our spouses cheated on us,' I said, gesturing for him to walk with me, 'Meryl should have left her husband and run off with Clint. He was hot.'

That got an actual laugh out of Kevin. 'Afraid I'll have to trust you on that one. He's just not my type.'

I sighed. 'Clint Eastwood's *every*body's type. Like Sean Connery or George Clooney.' Kevin stopped at a fork in the sidewalk and pointed toward the lot to the east of us. 'My truck's there. I have to go help the guys break down.'

'And I'm over here.' I indicated the center lot where Christy was still waiting, amazingly patiently. 'You'd better hurry. Ragnar was making good progress when I left. They might be finished already.'

'Even better.' Kevin gave me a two-fingered salute and headed toward his car.

I joined Christy. 'I'm sorry that took so long.' I

wasn't quite sure why she'd waited. Maybe to solicit donations for Ronny's defense fund.

'Who's that?' Christy asked, pointing to Kevin's back.

'Kevin Williams.' I'd forgotten that, though Christy had identified his truck as heading downtown the morning of JoLynne's murder, she had never actually met him. 'Kevin is, or was, JoLynne's husband.'

Christy fell into step with me. 'I saw him in the visiting room.'

'Yup.' We had reached my Escape. 'Well, here I am. Can I give you a lift to your car?'

'Actually, a lift home instead would be wonderful,' Christy said. 'My Kia is in the shop, so I asked Art Jenada if he could drop me off here. Catching a ride with you would save him the trip back.'

'No problem.' I waved her around to my passenger side. We pulled out of the lot behind Kevin and, also like Kevin, turned right toward the depot.

'I wish I'd have known who he was when I saw him inside,' Christy said. 'I need to return something. Not that I have it with me, of course.'

'Return something?' The traffic light turned yellow and I stopped short to the displeasure—conveyed by squealing brakes and blaring horns—of the car tailgating me.

Christy nodded. 'Thursday morning when it looked like rain, I took in the balloon clusters and a microphone that somebody had left on the stage.' She looked sideways at me. 'People are so careless.' Meaning her current chauffeur?

If so, Christy was pretty much right. The light changed and the horn from the car behind me sounded again. I inched out as slowly as I could and the guy zoomed around me through the intersection.

'That's illegal,' Christy said.

'What is?' Now I was both careless *and* a scofflaw?

'What that guy just did. You shouldn't pass in an intersection.'

'Never a cop around when you need one,' I said. 'And speaking of our criminal justice system, how was your visit with Ronny?'

'All right.' Turning left, I tried to gauge her via a single glance.

'Just "all right"?' Christy shrugged. 'I got there a little late. Not that I'm blaming Art. Bless him for taking me in the first place. But by the time I'm across from Ronny, his roommate is in the next chair. Ronny doesn't like Shef very much.' I thought the correct label was 'cell-mate'.

'So your conversation was a little stilted?'

'A *lot* stilted. And that Kevin guy is pretty big, so he was crowding me the whole time. Meanwhile, Shef was giving Ronny dirty looks. I could tell my Ronny was scared.'

'Shef being Ronny's…wait a minute. Did you say Kevin was this Shef's visitor? The Kevin you just—'

'That's why I asked you. And if he's a friend of yours, you should tell him to be more considerate during visits. Happily, it won't be a problem for me very much longer.'

'Why?' My mind was spinning and Christy's hopscotching from subject to subject wasn't helping any.

'Ronny told me Shef is going to Chicago to face some charges.'

'What kind of charges?' Maybe Kevin knew the guy

from the Windy City. Both Kevin and JoLynne had lived in Chicago and, if I remembered right, met in rehab there.

'I don't know, but Ronny said it had something to do with chicken.' Christy craned her neck. 'You can let me off here, if you don't mind.' I pulled the car to the curb in front of her home/piano studio.

'Chicken? You told me Ronny's cell-mate's name. Is that Shef with an "s" or "c"?'

'"C"—C-h-e-f. I told Ronny he should suggest pork chops to Chef.' Christy got out of my Escape and leaned down to talk through the open window. 'Ronny said he didn't think that was a good idea.' Something told me Ronny was right. Wouldn't catch me talking pork in that place.

'I don't know whyever not, though,' Christy was saying.

'Chef might have appreciated the tip and been nicer. Everybody likes a nice breaded pork cutlet or chicken breast.' I was lost. Maggy Thorsen, as Alice in Christyland.

'Pork? Chicken? Whatever are you talking about?' I asked as she went to bump the car door closed with her hip.

For the first time, Christy Wrigley seemed impatient with me. 'Why, Shake 'n Bake, of course.'

EIGHTEEN

Shake 'n Bake?

I could see Hamburger Helper qualifying as a criminal offense, but why arrest someone for dusting innocent chicken or pork?

Christy was obviously, and understandably, enchanted with the seasoned breadcrumb product. Shake 'n Bake kept her hands clean. She just poured the mix into a plastic bag, added meat, shook, dumped it in a pan and popped the pan into the oven.

Like I said, Christy I understood. But Ronny's cellmate Chef? The piano teacher had entered her house before I could catch her to ask. She'd probably already quick-stripped and stepped into the shower. And God knows how long she'd be in there. I hoped she didn't have a knife and a toothbrush with her.

I looked around for Kevin's truck, but there was no sign of it. In fact, there was no sign of Ragnar, the other guys or even the gallows. Life had returned to normal. Just the railroad tracks and depot.

Depot. Uncommon Grounds. I should check in with Sarah, see if business had picked up.

Even as I had the thought, the front door of UG opened and Jerome emerged. I waved and he crossed the street to my Escape.

'Wow,' I said, 'you're looking very handsome.'

'Thank you.' The videographer was wearing a charcoal gray jacket over a blue shirt. His longish blonde hair was artfully wind blown. 'I stopped in to see Amy. I hope that's OK.'

'Of course. If things are as quiet as they were earlier, I'm sure she was happy to have your company.'

'I hope so.' Jerome colored up. 'I sure was happy to have hers.'

I practically broke into a chorus of 'Young love, first love'. Guess I still did believe in the possibility of romance.

At least for other people.

'What about you, Maggy? Having a good day off?'

'Yes, thanks.' In truth, someone his age might well envy me a trip to the jail—as only a visitor, of course—and the county executive's McMansion.

Jerome's face changed instantly, like he'd just remembered he should be sad for me. 'I'm sorry about Sheriff Pavlik. Any news?' I waved off his concerns, feeling badly that I'd been responsible for this emergence from the young man's love stupor.

'Not to worry. Things will turn out fine. I did want to ask you one thing, though.'

'Anything.'

'When you were shooting tape of Kevin Williams inflating the cup, where were you?'

'On the boarding platform.'

'So you were shooting up?' Jerome nodded.

'And therefore you wouldn't have been able to see whether or not JoLynne's body was in the cup.'

Jerome thought about it. 'No, I guess not.'

'But certainly Kevin could have.'

'Uh-unh.' Now Jerome shook his head. 'They were on the same level I was, adjusting their compressor.'

Of course. 'So who was up on the gallows with the cup as it filled with air?'

'Nobody I could see.' Jerome stepped closer to the Escape to avoid getting nailed by a Brookhills Barbie driving her Lincoln Navigator. The four-wheel-drive land yacht barely fit in a traffic lane.

'County Exec Hampton said the saucer was inflated before the cup itself.'

The camera operator tilted his head. 'You know, he's right. The saucer seemed to be a separate piece. Which makes sense, I guess.'

'Why?'

'Because they'd want the base filled and stable. You know, like the foundation for a house? Only the cup had a variable airflow, so it could billow and wiggle. Sweet effect, by the way.' Not so sweet for JoLynne, but I thanked Jerome for his compliment anyway and wished him a good weekend.

As I swung away from the curb, I began mentally revising my timeline. If nobody was on the cup's elevated gallows when the thing was inflating, there was no way of knowing whether the cup was empty—especially since the saucer was already inflated and would have blocked sight lines from even farther back.

Revise my timeline? I'd have to scrap the whole damn thing and start all over again.

By the time I pulled the Escape into my driveway, I'd formulated a plan. First, resolving to learn (for a change) from my earlier mistake, I'd telephone somebody, to make sure that Pavlik was actually *in* the Milwaukee County Jail. Then, assuming the answer came back 'yes', a trip down there.

Before I left, though, I'd take a page out of Christy's

book, and Google 'Shake 'n Bake' for anything beyond seasoned breadcrumbs in a plastic bag. That way, I could talk to Pavlik about it.

Finally, I'd get hold of Kevin Williams to find out who *was* the last person to see the inside of the still-deflated cup. And when.

I was a little surprised I hadn't heard from Pavlik, though that proverbial 'one phone call' should have been to a lawyer. And presumably, he'd know a bunch of criminal defense attorneys. I figured it was like divorce lawyers. Second time around, hire the attorney who took you to the cleaners the first time. In Pavlik's case, that meant retaining one who had helped even clearly guilty bad guys walk. Not that Pavlik was guilty, of course.

If he didn't have a lawyer yet, I'd try Caron's husband, Bernie. Granted, he was a trademark attorney, but he might have a recommendation.

As I unlocked my front door and turned the knob, I heard the rolling, oncoming thunder of Frank's paws pounding our living room's hardwood floor. His unique method of greeting was to chop-block my knees with his shoulders, toppling me on to my rump as he rushed to water a tree.

I opened the door a crack, and Frank's black nose appeared.

'If you step back, I'll let you all the way out.' Mommy having leapt safely aside.

The nose didn't obey.

'Frank…' I drew out the syllable, using the 'Mom' warning tone.

A sniffle.

'I'm serious. Step back or I just close the door and

leave.' Obviously, an empty threat. I had better things to do than cool my heels outside, only to eventually mop up after Frank piddled inside. And besides, I was getting hungry.

Happily, my sheepdog didn't know a bluff when he heard one. His nose retreated. I stepped to the side of the door by the big front window. I could barely see Frank's stub of a tail, wagging like a furry metronome on speed.

'Farther,' I instructed.

When his hips came into sight, I leaned over and gave the door a shove. Frank finished the job with his forehead and darted out into our yard.

'I haven't been gone that long,' I called after him.

Frank ignored me and continued on his rounds: shrub to sniff, lift leg, pee; tree to sniff, lift leg, pee; tire to sniff— 'Away from my car, hairball!' He stopped with his leg nearly halfway up. Frank glanced back at me, weighing his options. Then, decision made, he let fly.

I surrendered and stepped into the house. Passing through my blue-stucco walled living room, I booted up the computer on its small desktop and dropped my purse on the kitchen table. My refrigerator provided the makings of a lettuce, light mayonnaise, low-fat peanut butter and thinly sliced raw onion sandwich. To be toasted.

Don't knock something you've never tried.

After cutting my sandwich in symmetrically diagonal quarters, I carried it and a Diet Coke to the table.

Sitting down, I took a first bite. Nirvana. Finding my cell phone in my purse, I scrolled through the address book to Pavlik's office number. Then I pushed 'SEND'.

'County Sheriff's Office,' a familiar voice answered.

'Cheryl,' I said to Pavlik's office manager. 'I'm so glad you're there. This is Maggy.'

A hesitation. 'Hello, Maggy.'

'Don't worry,' I was quick to assure her, 'I know the sheriff has been arrested.'

'Go on.' Very flat tone. Apparently Pavlik's staff had been ordered to keep their collective mouths shut about the incident.

'You don't need to say anything but "yes" or "no". I understand he's being held at the Milwaukee County Jail. Is that correct?'

'One moment, please.' Click.

I took another bite of my sandwich and waited, figuring Cheryl was merely moving to somewhere she'd have sufficient privacy to talk to me.

Slightly louder click. 'Public Information, McDonald speaking.' Though Cheryl probably had a written directive in front of her requiring that she transfer any call like mine, I still didn't like it. I'd been in public relations and knew all about runarounds. As with most things in life, it is far better to give than to receive.

'Mr McDonald, my name is Maggy Thorsen and I'm a personal friend of Sheriff Pavlik's. Cheryl, his office manager, just transferred me to you for information on how I can get in touch with him.' There. How much more succinct, reasonable and benign could I be?

'Sorry, but I'm not in possession of that information.'

'Fine,' I said through clenched teeth. 'Can you tell me who is? "In possession of" such, I mean?'

'Only the person currently in charge of the department, ma'am.' I decided to brain the next person who called me 'ma'am'.

'In that case, would you connect me with his or her office?'

'I could, ma'am, but it wouldn't do any good. The

interim sheriff is unavailable.' I shoved my plate away. It's not often that my appetite for a peanut butter and onion sandwich can be ruined, but this exchange was leaving me teetering on the edge.

'Well then, if neither Sheriff Pavlik nor his temporary replacement—' using an edge in my voice to chisel the 'temporary' into my approach and McDonald's attitude—'then who is the *next* in command?'

'Sorry, but I'm not in possession—' Snap.

The sound of both my patience and my flip-phone. Hanging up a wireless connection is infinitely less satisfying than slamming down a phone receiver. Maybe somewhere there was a menu of appropriate, downloadable sounds (shrill whistle, primal scream, shotgun blast) to recapture the essence of good old-fashioned hang-ups.

It was even less satisfying and more galling to know that the aforementioned McDonald had maneuvered me into doing exactly what he wanted me to do all along. Go away.

'I feel like I'm trapped in a Kafka novel,' I said out loud. Then I looked around. No Frank. Small loss, though, as I was pretty sure my sheepdog had never read any Kafka.

I picked up the remains of lunch and went to my door. The big goof was waiting on the porch. 'PB & O, Frank?' His back end started to dance a jig his front end couldn't keep up with. I tossed him the sandwich.

Leaving the door open so the dog could return at his leisure, I went back into my kitchen and picked up the phone again. Bernie the Attorney was my last resort.

Caron's voice answered. 'Egan residence.'

'Caron, this is Maggy. I really need to—'

'…We're not home right now, but if you leave your name and number at the beep…' Fighting the urge to throw my cellular across the room, I waited for the outgoing message to end. 'Caron, this is Maggy. I need to get hold of Bernie right away and I don't know his cell phone number. Can you have him call me? It's really important.' I closed my phone, wondering what I should do next. I could go to the Milwaukee County Jail, but even if Pavlik was there, I didn't know which cell block or section he might be in and when visiting would be allowed. A big city slammer seemed likely to be stricter than our suburban Brookhills one, meaning a lot of time invested with perhaps no results.

I looked around in frustration. My eye was caught by a boxed message on my computer screen. In large white-on-black letters, it asked if I wanted to install an update 'NOW'.

Seeing no 'NOT NOW, NOT EVER' option for this chance of a lifetime, I just tapped 'LATER' and sat down.

Opening Google, I typed in 'Shake 'n Bake' and came up with 1,370,000 references to the seasoned coating mix. Chicken recipes, pork recipes, chicken *and* pork recipes, even something called 'Armadillo eggs'. Perhaps not as delectable as my late, lamented peanut butter and onion sandwich, but nothing seemed an extraditable offense that could move Chef from suburban Wisconsin to urban Illinois.

Maybe I shouldn't use the brand name spelling. I tried typing just 'shake and bake' instead.

Two seconds later, there it was, between a misspelled chicken recipe and a scientific procedure:

Shake-and-bake: slang term for a short cut method of making methamphetamine…

Meth? One of the subjects of Pavlik's DEA conference in Chicago.

I followed the link to a news article:

A scourge that is spreading across the Midwest. This amounts to a short cut around typically more elaborate meth production. Shake-and-bake (also called the 'one-pot' method) requires only small amounts of ingredients that are 'shaken' in a plastic, two-liter soda bottle. Like the dangers inherent in traditional meth labs, the process can be highly volatile. However, should there be an explosion, the shake-and-baker cannot dive for cover, much less run away. He's left, figuratively, holding the bomb, since, literally, both his hands have been blown off at the wrists.

Lovely. But the writer had me hooked.

'Them shake-shits can blow theyselves to kingdom come and back,' an inmate serving time for running a traditional meth lab and dealing its product told me. 'They ain't even making no real ice. My clientele, now, they wouldn't touch that crap.'

Pride in product, even amongst drug dealers. Good to know.

I guess.

Next, I clicked on a link to what the interviewee had called 'real'. A photo, center-page, showed what looked like a pile of rock candy or small, irregular ice cubes, flecked with black.

Another showed pink, so-called 'strawberry', meth. Fittingly, 'pink' was one of a hundred additional slang labels listed, along with 'rocks' and 'sugar', 'cookies' and 'glass'. And, lo and behold, 'cristy'. I didn't think

I'd be mentioning that one to our piano-teaching neighbor anytime soon.

I was sitting back to think when Frank traipsed in.

'Did you close it behind you?' I asked.

No answer. My sheepdog was too busy trying to get the peanut butter off the roof of his mouth.

I filled his water bowl and went to secure the door.

When I returned to my desk, I opened a drawer and pulled out a yellow legal pad. Some pieces of the puzzle that was JoLynne Penn-William's murder were starting to fall into place, but it's a lot easier to solve the jigsaw when you've already seen the picture on the box.

Which is an elaborate way of saying I didn't know what the hell to do next. From my bouquet of gel pens in a tall mug, I selected a red one, let it hover for thirty seconds over the pad and then wrote: 1.

Writer's block is nothing. I was suffering from thinker's block, and a bad case of same.

I put my red pen back in the mug and took out a black one. Time to get serious.

Next to the numeral, I put Kevin Williams' name. Christy said he had been visiting Ronny's 'room-mate' this morning. And that Ronny's roomie, Chef, was a convicted drug dealer who was being shipped to Chicago on charges dealing with 'shake-and-bake'.

Since shake-and-bake was a short cut method of making meth, and Chef was a druggie, it made some sense. We knew Kevin Williams had been in rehab because, according to Rebecca, that's where he first met JoLynne. More sense.

And, when Rebecca accused Michael of sleeping with her sister, the accusation that JoLynne was addicted to drugs and alcohol, as well as sex, reared its ugly head. No indication, though, of any addiction on Kevin's side. Or, for that matter, whether one or both spouses were still using.

I swiveled back to the computer and typed in 'meth symptoms'.

A ton of hits came back and I chose one that looked reputable. Symptoms seemed to differ based on a.) severity, b.) length, and c.) depth of addiction. The early-use signs were characteristics like 'energetic', 'excessively happy', and 'needing less sleep'. Symptoms that would be tough to pinpoint, much less prove they were caused by meth and not bipolar disorder, other drugs or even an unbearably cheery disposition.

In contrast, the final stage included teeth and hair falling out, plus a bunch more awful things, any of which I certainly would have noticed in the people around me. 'Excuse me, but is that your bicuspid on the floor?' I ran my finger down the list for a mid-stage addiction. Meaning, I surmised, when you were no longer 'energetic', but before you were reduced to scalp and gums. The middle-ground symptoms: weight loss; dry, itchy skin; mood swings; acne…

Geez, change weight 'loss' to weight 'gain' and you had menopause.

The list continued: '…or sores caused by picking at imagined acne or bugs or lice.' Bugs or lice? What a horrible, horrible drug. Why would anyone ever *do* this to themselves? But neither JoLynne or Kevin appeared to match even the mid-stage picture painted.

However, someone else I knew sure did.

Anita Hampton, skinny as a rail, picking at the supposed 'pimple' on her face. The skin, dry and blotchy, probably from scratching. Mood swings, such as storming into the house like a rabid wraith and then coming back out with lemonade on a tray like Mrs Cleaver in *Leave it to Beaver*. Even the early-use symptoms fit Anita. All that energy she'd had when I worked for her at the bank. The tirelessness. The nothing-is-ever-good-enough perfectionist attitude.

Anita hadn't been just a pain in the butt as a boss. She was then—and continued to be now—a certifiable meth-head.

I abandoned my numbering system and wrote down thoughts as they came to me.

OK, so if Anita was hooked on meth, shake-and-bake or traditional, did her husband Brewster know?

Was Kevin Williams involved? That would explain his jail visit with Chef, as well as the twenty minutes between the Hamptons arriving together to take the train to the Milwaukee dedication and Anita's tardy boarding. Maybe Kevin was her drug connection and they were…connecting.

But how did all this tie into JoLynne's murder? Pure coincidence seemed unlikely.

What if JoLynne, unlike Kevin, *had* given up the drugs? When she found out her husband was dealing again, she might have threatened to blow the whistle on him. JoLynne worked for Brookhills County, so it would have been easy enough for her to make an appointment with someone in the sheriff's department, even Pavlik himself. Maybe that's why she was killed: JoLynne told someone she was…

I stopped, my black gel pen trembling over the pad.

'…JoLynne Penn-Williams was,' I wrote unsteadily, '*seeing* Pavlik.'

NINETEEN

'SEEING' PAVLIK.

Rebecca had said JoLynne was banging Pavlik 'like a drum'. I knew I wasn't wrong about that. The phrase was immediately and permanently burned into my brain. But had JoLynne also used those exact words in talking to her younger sister?

Or had Rebecca, blinded by jealousy, misinterpreted JoLynne's admittedly ambiguous—and far more innocent—expression: 'seeing Pavlik.' Perhaps JoLynne was killed, not because she was having an affair with Pavlik, but because she had threatened to report husband Kevin for dealing.

Assuming he had, indeed, been dealing. Right now, all this was based on his visit to a jailed drug dealer and the fact that Chef was from Chicago, like JoLynne, Kevin...

And, of course, a couple million other people.

I didn't know why Kevin had visited Chef. Not to *buy* drugs, certainly. Even though I hadn't gotten very far into the jail's labyrinth, I was fairly certain drug exchanges would be vigorously discouraged.

It was possible, I supposed, that Kevin was getting instructions from Chef. I had no way of finding out, though, without asking the recent widower. And I sure wasn't going to do that.

While I tried to think of something I *could* do, Frank

padded across the kitchen, put one hairy paw on his water bowl and flipped it.

'That trick's getting mighty old,' I told him. 'Besides, have you noticed we do nothing but eat and drink around here? Go catch a movie or take up a sport. It'll make you a more well-rounded companion for me. Give us something new to talk about.' Frank padded back out of the kitchen.

I slipped my cell phone into my handbag. I hoped that I'd hear from Pavlik or Bernie soon, but, in the meantime, I could be productive.

Levering myself out of the desk chair, I picked up my car keys. I couldn't interrogate Kevin, but it should be harmless enough to ask Rebecca if she remembered her sister's exact words about Pavlik. I also wanted to find out in what context she and JoLynne had spoken and, importantly—maybe even most importantly—who else had been there.

As I rumbled across the railroad tracks to Uncommon Grounds, I saw Christy, wearing a gardening apron and centering mums and their roots in ceramic pots on the front deck of her piano studio. She waved a yellow-gloved hand and I gave her a thumbs-up for the large clay planter she'd already apparently finished.

Continuing down Junction Drive, I passed Art Jenada's catering operation and parked in front of Penn and Ink. Unlike Christy, Rebecca and Michael didn't live behind their storefront—or above it, as in Art's case—so I wasn't sure I'd catch either of them there.

Since I had no idea where they *did* live or even if they cohabited, I was relieved when Michael answered my knock.

'Hi,' I said. 'Is Rebecca here?'

A shadow crossed his face. 'Why?'

'I just wanted to talk to her.'

'Why?' Ahh. Stonewalling, because Michael was worried I'd tell Rebecca that he'd admitted to a fling with her sister.

'Nothing to do with you,' I said, thinking the reply would merely sound like I was being abrupt if Rebecca was nearby.

Michael, though, read between the lines. 'Sure, Maggy. OK.' He stood aside, the relief in his voice evident on his face as well. The walls of the front foyer of their converted house were lined with framed ads the duo had produced, as well as watercolors I knew to be Rebecca's own. If I was any judge, the woman displayed genuine talent.

And, speak of the devil, Rebecca careened around a corner.

'Michael, have you seen our—' She stopped. 'What are you doing here?' Talented, maybe, but rude. Genuinely rude.

'I need to talk with you.' I looked at Michael apologetically.

'Alone, though.' I didn't, necessarily, but I wanted to convey the appropriate gravitas.

But gravitas, shmavitas, Rebecca was having none of it.

'Anything you want to say to me, you can say in front of Michael.' She linked her arm with his, flashing a large, pear-shaped diamond on her left ring-finger in the process.

Explained the change from 'you bastard, Michael, you're shtupping my sister.' I decided not to comment on either the ring or the Hyde-to-Jekyll personality switch.

'Rebecca, you told me that JoLynne and Pavlik had a relationship, correct?'

'Yes.' But wary.

'And that your sister told you…how did she put it?'

That earned a roll of the eyes. 'Are you asking if she said he was "banging her like a drum"? No. Even my sister had more class than that.' More than her surviving sibling, certainly.

'So, not quite the slut you thought?'

'JoLynne did the best she could.' Rebecca's eyes filled with tears. Maybe I'd misjudged the artist. Or maybe she was willing to let bygones-be-bygones now that JoLynne was no longer a threat to her own romantic relationship.

'My sister conquered a lot of demons,' Rebecca continued.

'The drugs, the alcohol.'

'So, she was clean?' I asked. 'I mean, as far as you know?'

'Absolutely.' Such a positive assertion was a little much for me, considering the way Rebecca had bad-mouthed JoLynne both before and after her death.

Rebecca must have seen my eyebrows rise, because she flushed. 'I know. I was awful about my sister that morning we found her. I had this idea that JoLynne had seduced my Michael.' She threw a smile at 'her' Michael.

He had the smarts to say, 'Sorry, ladies, I have to make a phone call,' and then to leave us before the bullshit got too deep for him to wade through.

When Michael was out of earshot, I said, 'Enough beating around the bush, Rebecca. There are a couple of things I need to know. Now.' Rebecca seemed surprised, but just nodded.

'Number one.' I held up my index finger. 'Do you know without a doubt that JoLynne was not using or dealing?'

'Drugs?'

No, playing cards, you twit. 'Yes, drugs.'

'Absolutely,' she repeated. 'And the police told me there were no drugs—or alcohol—in her system when she died.' Nothing like sisterly 'faith' confirmed by lab tests.

'What about Anita Hampton?'

More wary now. 'What about Anita?'

'Does she do drugs? Maybe uppers of some sort?'

'How should I know?' Rebecca asked. 'The only time I see her is at the monthly WoPro meetings.'

'You're a member of WoPro?'

Rebecca's face flushed again at my reaction. 'Why wouldn't I be? I'm a female entrepreneur, too. A mover-and-shaker.' Shaker-and-baker came to mind.

'Did JoLynne sponsor you?' The flush that had started to slowly recede came roaring back a third time.

'Yes, but I would have qualified for membership regardless.' Right. Like I would have long ago, if Anita hadn't required that I apply and then sponsored me to boot.

'In fact,' Rebecca continued, 'I'm surprised being JoLynne's sister didn't work against me.'

'Are you saying she wasn't well liked? Why? Too pretty?'

Rebecca ignored the bait. 'Too straight. I thought it was an act. She didn't drink, didn't smoke, or...' Rebecca stopped herself. 'Listen, I don't have time for—'

My turn to interrupt. 'Spill it. Or I'll call out the drug-sniffing dogs.'

'It wasn't that.' She looked around to make sure Michael hadn't returned. 'Just things like super-energy drinks. Caffeine.' I looked at her.

'OK, OK. Cold tablets, too,' Rebecca admitted. 'And—but only occasionally—Ritalin.' Good God almighty.

'What do you do? Get your kid diagnosed with a sinus infection or attention deficit disorder, then pilfer from the prescriptions?'

'I don't have kids,' Rebecca protested, 'so I tried not to judge. Remember, I was new to the group.'

'But JoLynne did…judge?'

'Not really even that.' Rebecca squirmed. 'JoLynne would leave when talk turned to those kinds of things. In fact, she seemed more upset that Kevin was getting so many jobs from WoPro.'

'Did JoLynne feel it was a conflict of interest?' I asked, hoping for something more.

'Maybe.' The artist looked uncertain. 'But I also thought she might be jealous because a lot of the women liked Kevin. Sort of cozied up to him.'

I bet they did. 'Especially Anita Hampton?'

'Yes.' Now Rebecca's eyes narrowed. 'But how could you know that?'

I shrugged. 'Just a guess. Did your sister talk with you about it?'

'No. We…uh, didn't have that kind of relationship.' Meaning, to me, that their sibling conversations had run more along the 'I hate your guts, you slut' line.

'But,' Rebecca continued, 'JoLynne had it out with Kevin in the parking lot after the WoPro meeting Tuesday night. I heard her say she was getting him back. That she was seeing Pavlik.' Thank you, Lord!

'This is really important, Rebecca. Is that what your sister said, *exactly*?'

A blink, followed by another. 'I think so. Why?' Why? JoLynne discovers Kevin is not only using again, but apparently dealing. And, to make matters worse, his best customers are her professional contacts at WoPro. She'd be 'seeing' Pavlik to blow the criminal whistle on her husband.

Rebecca might have misinterpreted her sister's comment, but Kevin would know just what his wife had in mind.

It was no coincidence that JoLynne died the next morning.

'Do you remember what your sister was wearing at the WoPro meeting?'

'What she…? Of course.'

I waited. But not for long. 'Well? Are you going to tell me?'

Rebecca shrugged. 'A pencil skirt and silk blouse, but then you already knew that.'

I did? And then I realized she was right. I did. 'You mean the same outfit we found on her corpse?' God forgive me, I was trying to hurt Rebecca.

She swallowed hard, before a weak, 'Yes.'

'Did you tell the police?'

'No. I didn't think—'

'I guess you didn't,' I said, sounding exactly like my mother.

'Listen,' Rebecca said. 'I was trying to be sensitive. I thought you, of all people, would appreciate that. My sister's clothes could have dragged your sheriff into a scandal.'

'Oh, I see.' Slowly, now, Maggy. 'You figured JoLynne spent Tuesday night with Pavlik and hadn't gone home to change. But didn't you say she was railing at Kevin in the parking lot following WoPro's Tuesday meeting?'

'Of course. He picked her up. But believe me, JoLynne wouldn't have had any problem with dumping him for the evening.' I had a feeling it was Kevin who dumped JoLynne that night.

And right into my coffee cup.

The problem with formulating theories, I thought as I thanked Rebecca and walked outside, is knowing where to take them.

My theory, that JoLynne threatened to turn Kevin and his jailhouse connection in to the authorities and had been killed for it, seemed pretty darned good. Problem was, I had no actual, physical proof. And even if I did, who would listen to me?

My only law enforcement connection was in the slammer and I'd gotten little cooperation from anyone else at Pavlik's office. I checked my phone. No return call from Bernie.

Nor any word from Pavlik himself.

I slipped the cell back into my handbag and took out the car keys. As I walked toward my Escape, I saw Christy awkwardly hefting a potted mum on to the wide railing of her deck.

As she struggled under the weight of the dirt-filled planter, I pocketed my keys and climbed her steps to help.

'Thanks,' she said as we finally positioned the first

plant on a corner over its post, where the ceramic would
be more stable.

'They're awfully heavy,' I said, as we picked up a
second pot for the opposite corner. 'Maybe you should
lift the planters up here empty, *then* fill them with soil.'

'But the dirt would fly all over,' Christy objected as
we set the second one down. The index finger of her
glove got stuck under the pot and she was struggling
to ease it out. 'However, if I pour the top soil over my
newspaper-strewn planking, I can control the mess.'
Mess? I looked at Christy's 'newspaper-strewn planking' and didn't see a speck of dirt. What had she done,
drib-drabbed the soil into the pots through a funnel?
The fact that on one front page rested both a soup spoon
and a toothbrush, supported the spirit, if not the letter
of my...

I picked up the toothbrush. While the bristles were
pristine, the handle end was black with top soil and...
sharpened?

'What's this?' I held the brush out to Christy.

'Oh, that?' She took the thing from me. 'It's a shiv,
Maggy.'

'But do you know what a "shiv" is?' I asked, aghast.

'Prisoners take an everyday object like this and file it
into a blade with a point. Then they use it to stab people.
To *death*.' But Christy seemed unconcerned. 'I know.
I found a bunch of articles online, remember? A shiv
can be surprisingly efficient when inserted correctly.'

'Correctly?'

'Like into the right place on the human anatomy.
Only, I use mine just for making sure there are no air
pockets in the soil.' She knocked dirt off the sharpened
handle and slipped the shiv into her apron pocket.

I was still reeling from the 'human anatomy' comment.

'Did you make that thing?'

'Don't be silly, Maggy. Ronny gave it to me.' Back for another adventure in Christyland.

'Wait, wait. You carried that thing out of the jail?'

'A lot easier than smuggling it *in*.' Christy began delving through her other apron pocket. 'Ronny found the shiv one day underneath his roommate's mattress. At first, I figured Chef was probably cleaning those tiny intersections where the bars connect.' A sigh. 'It's really tough to scrape out what gets in there.'

'Let me guess. Ronny didn't embrace your reasoning?'

'Uh-unh.' Christy's apron-exploration came up with a handful of decorative stones. 'He was afraid Chef would "gut him like a pig" in his sleep, though, according to my research, gutting somebody is a pretty *in*efficient technique for—'

'Christy? Stop. Now!'

'OK. But I thought you wanted to know why Ronny gave Chef's shiv to me.' The Chef's shiv. It even alliterated, sort of. And, of course, the whole scenario made perfect sense. At least in Christyland.

She began arranging some stones on the surfaces of soil in her pots.

'Pretty,' I said, relieved to be back on the planet Earth. Suddenly, though, I was struck by a déjà vu moment. Then, too, it had to do with rocks.

I picked up one Christy had just placed. 'What is this?' She didn't look at me. 'Quartz.' I worked the stone around in my palm and picked up a smaller, pink one. 'Where'd you get these?'

'Nowhere.' Christy had moved away, her back now to me.

'Christy?' The same 'mom' tone I'd used on Frank. Happily our piano teacher was more easily snowed than the sheepdog.

'All right.' She turned, face bright red. 'I admit it. I stole them.'

'From the bowls that anchored the balloons.' It wasn't a question. 'The ones you said you brought in from the rain for Kevin so they wouldn't be ruined.' But why would bowls and the rocks in them be 'ruined' by rain? And, as we've already established, Mylar balloons will likely outlive cockroaches.

There was only one thing that made sense. Christy had coveted her neighbor's rocks.

'Maggy, I just kept ten or twelve.' I thought she was going to cry.

'Ten or twelve?' I turned over the two in my palm. 'What did you do with the rest of them? The ones you didn't keep?'

'I returned them in the bowls, of course. But these were so different—I didn't think anyone would miss a stone or two.' I was developing a bad feeling about this. 'Christy, who did you give the bowls and...um, their contents to?'

'Me,' a voice behind us said. I turned.

TWENTY

KEVIN WILLIAMS STOOD at the bottom of the deck stairs, right hand in his jacket pocket.

'Hi, Kevin.' I decided to play stupid since, as Sarah Kingston has often told me, I'm really good at it. 'Poor Christy is feeling so awful about some rocks she took from your pots.' I smiled in what I hoped was a disarming way and held out the two I had. 'I told her that was silly, but you'd better take them so she can sleep at night.' And, preferably not with the fishes.

Kevin returned my smile, but his hand stayed in its pocket. He did have the nicest, backlit brown eyes.

'Let's go inside.' The hand in his pocket gesturing accordingly.

'Inside?' Christy chirped. 'But everything's such a mess.'

'I'm sure not,' Kevin said, gallantly. 'Now you two gather up the…rocks from those pots.' We did and preceded Kevin into Christy's house. The front room was—where do I register my surprise—immaculate. An ebony piano gleamed in one corner, in contrast to the spare, matte-flat mission furniture.

'Put them there.' Kevin gestured to a square table in front of the couch.

Christy quailed. 'But they're dirty, from the—'

'Do it,' Kevin ordered, less gallantly now.

'No.' Great. Our neighborhood neat-freak was going

to get herself—and, far worse, *me*—killed. I dumped my load on the table, but Christy still hesitated.

'Maggy—' Kevin's free hand pointing at me—'already got your table dirty. Now, you do it, too.' With a final anguished look, Christy complied. A quick scan of the stones.

'Where's the rest of our ice?'

'I think that's all there is.' I turned to the piano teacher, who was sniffling. 'Right, Christy?'

'I don't understand,' she said. 'It's not ice. They're just…rocks.' Kevin laughed, but this time there was no light behind the brown eyes. They might as well have been two olive pits.

Then he turned toward me, and I realized I wasn't fooling him. Kevin knew that I knew.

'"Ice" is actually right, Christy,' I said. 'A nickname for crystal meth. Tell us, Kevin, did you kill JoLynne over it?' A gasp from my fellow hostage.

Kevin ignored her. 'I didn't kill Jo. Just ask your sheriff friend in his jail cell. Or that kid with the camera. Hell, ask anybody who was there that morning. They all saw I wasn't alone for a minute. I did not kill my wife.'

'Nice collective alibi.' As moving as Kevin's speech was, it was secondary to Christy and me getting out of her 'living' room still doing so. Living, I mean. First, I needed to find out whether Kevin really had a gun.

'I was thinking, though,' I continued. 'When JoLynne's body was found, her clothes were identical to the ones she'd worn the night before. Not very fashion-conscious of her. So, maybe you killed your wife that night, and brought her to the depot early Wednesday morning, wrapped up in the un-inflated cup.'

A flicker and then: 'That's crazy. Why would anyone in their right mind kill somebody in private and
then dump the body in the middle of a public train
dedication?'

'It does seem a little far-fetched, Maggy,' Christy
offered in a hushed tone.

Couldn't expect much help from her corner, though
maybe she was trying to keep Kevin calm. Cross-
purposes: I wanted to fire him up, but without our getting fired *upon*.

'Maybe, maybe…' Roadblocks became real problems
when you were making things up on the fly. 'Maybe
you wanted JoLynne's body discovered with plenty of
witnesses around. Because you knew there was evidence on the balloon that would point to you.' I had a
brainstorm. Or at least a drizzle. 'Evidence like…tooth
marks.' A flicker, then Kevin forced a grin. 'Please.
How could I set up the balloon and inflate it without
*some*body seeing the body? Like you just said, Maggy,
there were a lot of people around.' He lifted his pocketed hand, and I saw the tell-tale impression of a muzzle
pushing forward against the fabric of his jacket. OK—or
not—first major question answered: Kevin had a gun.

I had a purse and car keys.

A sound outside drew my attention to Christy's big
front window. I saw Sarah step through the doorway of
Uncommon Grounds across the way and look down the
street. Hope surged. She would see my Escape parked
and wonder where I was. Maybe come looking.

Instead, though, she took out a cigarette.

'That liar,' I said, involuntarily. Kevin looked startled.

I didn't want him startled. Hair-trigger and all that
jazz.

'Sarah, I mean.' I pointed toward the glass. 'She said she quit the cancer sticks.' My friend had her mouth open, blowing a smoke ring, though I had to admit I couldn't see it.

'Filthy habit.' Christy chiming in.

I started toward the door. 'I'm going to give that woman a piece of my mind—'

The gun came out of Kevin's pocket. 'Maggy, I don't think so.' As he said it, Sarah took one final puff, pulled the cigarette out of her mouth and stuck it back into her apron pocket.

'Was she pretending?' Christy asked. 'Or is she going to catch on fire?'

'Just going through the motions,' I said, as the door jangled closed behind Sarah. 'She used to smoke whenever she was stressed. I guess I shouldn't have left her alone to run the coffeehouse.' The way things were heading, however, I *was* going to leave her, period. Not to mention Frank. And Pavlik. And...Eric.

Unacceptable. Not without a fight. 'Do you really want me to tell her?'

Kevin and Christy exchanged confused looks. He said, 'I think she's talking to you.'

'Me?' From Christy. 'About what?' Admittedly, I am a queen of the non sequitur.

'Umm, actually, that question was for Kevin. I was asking if he wanted me to explain to you how he finessed JoLynne's body.'

'Not really,' the props man said.

'I do, I do.' Christy waved a gloved hand. Kevin's gun waved back.

'The saucer was inflated when Kevin started the compressor for the cup,' I said, stepping forward to keep his attention. If he was going to shoot me, at least Christy might have a chance to duck and run. 'JoLynne's body was already lying on the bottom of the cup. Jerome and his camera were on the train platform, shooting from below, so he couldn't have seen her by looking up. Neither could anyone else on the platform, much less on ground level.'

'And why would I do that?' Kevin sounded confident, but I had a feeling he'd been shaken by how much I'd put together.

'How could I possibly know the cup would fall off and Jo's body would be discovered?' Uh-oh. Kevin was right. For the cover-up/alibi to work, his wife's corpse had to be revealed during… 'Ragnar. He was in on it with you.'

'Shhh.' I turned toward the sound to see Ragnar Norstaadt in full mime regalia. Short pants, suspenders, striped shirt, beret. He had one white-gloved index finger to his lips. 'Mum is the word, Maggy Thorsen.'

TWENTY-ONE

'THE MIME TALKED.' Christy shook an accusatory finger at Ragnar. 'It's just not right.'

That was what she found unsettling in our situation? Ragnar turned to Kevin. Or on him. 'Stupid, stupid man. Better I leave you in Chicago.'

'You think I'm going to cover for you?' Kevin's words were defiant, but despite his burly body, he seemed genuinely scared of the tall man in the short pants. 'I go down, you go down.'

'I do not go down, and you do not go down. If you keep your stupid mouth shut. I have performance and delivery tonight, but first now I have to clean up the mess you make?' As part of said 'mess', I was just fine with both of them leaving it be. I glanced at Christy, still wearing her gardening apron and yellow gloves. The piano teacher might not be great in a fight, but at least she wouldn't leave fingerprints.

'So, then, Kevin, who *did* kill JoLynne?' I asked. 'Did her loving husband bark her, like you described to me?'

'Burk,' Ragnar corrected. 'And the coward cannot do even such right. I must finish that job, too.'

Kevin glared in anger. 'It was your pushing me off Jo that gave her the chance to leave tooth marks on the balloon's material.' Now he withdrew a little. 'No marks and we wouldn't have had to use the cup at all. We could have just dumped her body in the lake. But if my wife disappeared and they found traces—'

'Why?' Both men turned to me, but I was addressing Kevin. 'Why did you do it?'

'He made me. I didn't want to. I loved her.' What a weenie.

Ragnar: 'Then you never should tell your woman of our business.'

'For the last time,' Kevin protested, 'I didn't *tell* her. But Jo was smart. When I started sucking up to her female druggie friends and spending more time at your place than ours, she tipped to it.'

Wait a second. 'Ragnar's place, in the country? Is that where you made the meth?' It was so hard to keep up. 'What about the "shake-and-bake"?'

'Garbage,' Ragnar said. 'Our clientele pay for only the best and we do not disappoint.'

'OK. Then what about Chef, the guy Kevin visited in jail? Is he part of your operation?' A sharp intake of breath from Kevin, and Ragnar wheeled on him.

'You go to see the Chef? Why would you do this?'

I came up with some fuel to be added to the fire. 'Or, Kevin, did you work for Chef? Maybe inherit his business after he was busted?'

'Inherit?' said Ragnar. 'Like from a father?' A guttural rumbling from the mime's throat. 'No, no. The Chef and his product are both garbage. They need…taking out.' I was going to miss Ragnar's sense of humor.

'So why,' I said, shaking my head, 'why, oh, why would Kevin visit him in jail?'

'Good question.' Those two words coming from a man wearing comical clothes shouldn't have had such emotional impact. Especially since Kevin was the one holding a gun.

'I, I...' the props man stuttered, eyes wide.

'Choose your words with much care, my friend.' Ragnar sounded like a character in an old spy movie. I'd succeeded in putting the two bad guys at odds. Problem was, if they started shooting, both us hostages would be in the crossfire.

Then, instead of waving as she had before, Christy timidly raised a yellow-gloved hand.

'Yes?' I said, since I didn't think either man would call on her.

Christy lowered the latex. 'I think Kevin was just being nice, since Chef is leaving for Chicago soon.'

'Christy should know,' I told Ragnar. 'She was visiting the jail at the same time.'

'That's right,' our yellow-gloved one said. 'It was a little awkward, of course, Chef being my Ronny's roommate, but they were perfectly civil. He—' she angled her head toward Kevin—'was saying how much everyone missed Chef.' Christy gave Kevin a small smile. 'I thought it was sweet of you.' And I thought Kevin was going to be sick.

Before Ragnar could say anything—or just break all our necks—I weighed in on Kevin's side. 'Very smart. Assuming the two of you dropped the dime on Chef in the first place. You must have gotten one hell of a client list. And keeping in his good graces could only help future business. Even allow you to...diversify your product lines?' Ragnar looked at me with black-button, dead-mime eyes. This guy was no dunce. Oh, for two of the moron criminals we all see on TV.

'Uh, you know,' I continued, '"keep your friends close and your enemies closer".'

Kevin puffed out his chest. 'Just doing my job.' Ahh, there was one. Moron, I mean.

'Behind my back.' From Ragnar. 'You cry to me over your cut of our money. Maybe Kevin is not so loyal as he pretend.' Christy made a little whimpering sound and pulled a tissue from her apron pocket to wipe her nose.

Ragnar and Kevin both ignored her.

'I don't know what your problem is.' Kevin was blustering now. 'I'm the one who called you in Chicago and told you southeastern Wisconsin was ripe for the picking. Chef had gone to a hundred per cent shake-and-bake and the upscale users were complaining.' People like Anita Hampton, I wagered.

'Sure. Why settle for fast-food burgers when you're willing and able to pay for steak?'

Kevin threw me a startled glance. 'I like that, Maggy. Mind if we use it?' Moron material, for sure.

'Go ahead.' Nothing would probably be gained by trying to negotiate any cut for me, should the publicity campaign be successful.

'So, *you* take all the credit for our success here?' Ragnar's tone was flat.

'It was my idea,' Kevin protested. 'My connections.'

'Don't you mean JoLynne's?' I piped up.

He looked stricken at the mention of her name, like it was a total stranger who had smothered his wife and deposited her body in a giant coffee cup. 'I told you, I loved Jo. I was proud of what she'd accomplished.'

'So was JoLynne, Kevin,' I told him. 'That's why she couldn't let you destroy it.'

'Enough.' Ragnar crossed to the table and picked up a hunk of what I guessed was crystal meth. 'The rest of this—where?'

'That's all there is,' said Christy.

Ragnar's eyes lasered and he took a step toward her. Again, it should have been hard to take him seriously in his mime outfit, but the clothes and make-up—even his blonde braid—just made him that much creepier.

'Christy's not lying.' I stepped between them. 'Can't you see how scared she is? If either one of us knew where your product was, don't you think we'd tell you?' Ragnar seemed to consider that.

'Maybe somebody else took a few,' I said. 'I mean, there were two whole bowls of them just sitting there.'

'Don't be a schmuck,' Ragnar said. 'Most of the stones were only quartz. Genius here made a mess of just one pickup, thank God.' Kevin started to protest, but I rode over him.

'Did you say "schmuck"? What happened to the language barrier, Ragnar?' A smile.

'And the accent.'

'What accent?'

'I don't know, Swedish? Norwegian?'

'Actually, generic Nordic, of my own creation.' Ragnar said. 'Did you like it?'

'Very much.' I couldn't believe I'd let this man play me.

'And that's not all you liked. *Wanted,* even.' Ragnar slid effortlessly back into character, or lack thereof. 'Is that not right, Maggy Thorsen?' When I didn't answer, Ragnar lifted his eyebrows. 'Lost your sense of humor, I see. Just as well, we have business to conduct. Now. Our ice?'

'I told you we don't have it. Have you tried Anita Hampton?'

'Who?' This from Kevin. He still held the gun, but it was shaking as it hung by his side.

'Nice try, Kevin, but I know she's one of your major clients. The "crossed signals" you both talked about on Thursday? The failed hand-off from Wednesday.'

'If our Kevvie *had* bloody well handed it to her instead of getting "creative", the pick-up wouldn't have been buggered beyond recognition.' Ragnar seemed to have morphed again, now into the English *Im*patient. The guy really *was* an actor.

'How many times do I have to tell you?' Kevin protested.

'I *did* pass the product to Anita when she stepped off the train from Milwaukee.' The prolonged handshake I'd seen between the two at the edge of the stage.

'Then the balloon with Jo's body crashed down, practically cutting her toes off, and Anita stashed the rocks in one of the bowls, so she wouldn't be caught holding. She told me she came back when the police were gone the next day, but…nothing.' No wonder Anita looked so crappy yesterday. She was probably going through a cold-turkey withdrawal.

'Stupid,' Ragnar said. It appeared to still be his favorite word. 'And then you just walk away and leave the ice for anybody who likes pretty sparkles, like glove-girl here?' Given that the mime, himself, was wearing gloves, I thought it was a low blow. I sensed Christy tensing.

Kevin, however, was too deep in debate mode to mind anybody but Ragnar. 'And just what was I supposed to do? The cops had sealed off the stage, the boarding platform, even the gallows. They were questioning me. Then, at some point—' he raised his finger toward Christy—'she must have taken both pots.'

Christy's face—showing no tension now—bopped up and down in agreement like a bobble-head doll. 'It began to rain, you see.' That was her story, and she was sticking to it.

But Ragnar had begun fingering the rock in his hand. 'You girls ever try ice?' Another complete change of voice and tone. Coaxing, now, like encouraging a couple of kindergarten kids to swing on to 'real' bicycles without training wheels.

Christy's eyes—and probably mine, as well—went big and round.

'Maybe this'd be a good time.' Ragnar, still persuading.

'That way, Kevin and I can be here to help. It would be a shame if you sampled our ice on your own and made a mistake. Tragically overdosed, perhaps.' A chill went up my spine. We were going to die.

How long would it take the authorities to find our bodies? And even then, would they realize we'd been murdered?

Apparently having found something the two men could agree upon, Kevin herded us from the living room into Christy's tiny kitchen. Ragnar followed.

A round table was centered in the room. Two chairs, but a single place mat, signaling a perennially hopeful, but usually solitary, diner. Ragnar put the meth on the mat, the rock already leaving powdery white traces on the dark blue cloth.

A whimper from Christy. 'I have newspapers you can spread. If you like.'

'Not necessary, bird. Better to leave traces of your... experiment.' Eric would be told I'd overdosed. My son was only nineteen. Oh, God—what would that do to him?

'Silverware?' Index finger shaking, Christy pointed to a drawer next to her sink.

Ragnar pulled out a serrated steak knife. 'Straws?'

Christy shook her head, 'I don't have—' Kevin was uneasy.

'Then how can they snort? Maybe they should smoke it.'

'Inspired. Do you have a pipe?'

'No. You?' Ragnar looked skyward, then reached into the obviously empty pockets of his mime-pants and pulled them inside out.

'I don't smoke, either,' Christy said. 'But Maggy's friend Sarah does. Maybe I should go across the street—'

'Good of you to offer,' Ragnar said. 'But snorting should do fine. Would you have playing cards, by any chance?' Christy shook her head. If her eyes got any bigger, I wouldn't be able to see her nose.

'Not to worry, luv. A dollar bill—rolled right—will do the job.'

'But how can we make them inhale?' Kevin gestured carelessly with the gun, like he'd forgotten it was still in his hand.

'Hold their mouths closed.' Ragnar's tone changed again.

'You'd know all about that, Kevvie. Am I right?' Kevvie, wisely, I thought, kept his own mouth closed.

'Don't worry.' Ragnar back to the silky, coaxing tone.

'Practice does make perfect.' The mime sat down at the table with Christy's steak knife and pulled the place mat toward him. 'You might want to stop waving that gun, though, Kevvie, and keep it trained on them. I have to concentrate on what I'm doing here.' Ragnar swiveled toward me, his back to Christy near the sink. 'Spare a dollar?'

'You really think I'm going to lend you a dollar to kill us with?'

'Not a loan, really, luv, since that implies—' Ragnar's head jerked back convulsively, and the steak knife hit the place mat as though its handle had gone red-hot in the mime's palm.

'Don't move.' The words came from Christy, but the low, raspy voice didn't sound like hers. The piano teacher was standing directly behind Ragnar now, her left hand grasping his braid, pulling back on it to expose his throat. Her right hand, though, was against the back of the mime's neck, whatever she was holding lost in those yellow gloves.

'What, the—' Kevin started to raise his gun.

'Either of you moves, he dies.' Christy yanked the braid again, canting Ragnar's chair on to just its back legs.

I felt like we were in a roadshow of *The Exorcist*. Unearthly voice, supernatural strength. Pretty soon Christy'd be spouting Latin and pea soup from a spinning head.

Ragnar started to speak, but I heard him cry out in pain.

'Mimes…don't…talk,' Christy said, underlining each word. 'What part of that didn't you understand?'

'Best lay your gun on the table, Kevin,' I suggested.

The props man still had his weapon half-raised in the direction of Ragnar and Christy. Now he began to turn toward me.

'Freeze!' The word hit the kitchen like a thunderclap, and we all did as told. Then I recognized the…'Pavlik?'

'Police,' he roared, nearly deafening me again. 'Drop the gun. Now!' Kevin, resident moron, just stayed… well, 'frozen'.

The butt end of a wickedly impressive assault rifle came down on Kevin's mighty forearm.

I cringed reflexively and suddenly the room was alive with sheriff's deputies stomping all around us. Gravity, if not shattered bones, had sent Kevin's handgun clattering harmlessly to the floor, the man following, screaming in pain.

Pavlik's own weapon was trained on Ragnar. The muzzle looked about six inches wide to me. 'Hands on your head!' Fortunately for Ragnar, the mime seemed to know the drill. Even after he complied, though, Pavlik's aim never wavered off Ragnar's chest. 'Now, Christy. One small step at a time. Move back and away from him.' Christy released Ragnar's braid as part of her first movement, so his chair rocked back on to all four of its legs. Every firearm in the room seemed at the ready until Pavlik moved himself between the piano teacher and Ragnar.

Releasing one hand from his pistol grip, the sheriff swept the steak knife from the table and back toward a deputy, who stepped on the tip of its blade. 'Cuff this silly sonofabitch.' Christy had circled around to me by the time two deputies snapped clasps on Ragnar's wrists, both behind his back and twisted toward the spine, palms out.

As they jerked Ragnar to his feet, blood ran down the side of the mime's neck from a spot below and slightly behind his right ear.

'What did you…' I waved vaguely toward Ragnar, now nearly out of the room. I heard a deputy calling the EMTs for Kevin Williams, who had been reduced to blubbering and rocking like a lovelorn walrus on Christy's floor.

The piano teacher didn't seem concerned about the 'mess' in her kitchen. She held out her yellow-gloved right hand to me. In it was the shiv-toothbrush, long handle tapered down, the blood on its sharp point a bright crimson.

'Ohhh, Maggy.' Christy Wrigley practically levitating with joy. 'Ronny's going to be *so* proud of me.'

TWENTY-TWO

'A SHIV?' PAVLIK finally asked, incredulously. 'Where on God's green earth did Christy Wrigley get a shiv?' He and I were standing on the sidewalk in front of her piano studio. She herself was being ministered to by paramedics. I wasn't sure if she was really going into delayed shock or was just mesmerized by the sight of so many men wearing gloves.

'Your jail,' I said. 'Ronny was afraid he'd be gutted by his roommate's shiv, so he gave it to Christy.' I hesitated. 'It is *your* jail again, right?'

Pavlik did a quick scan to make sure no one was looking directly at us, then he pressed his lips to mine. 'I'm so sorry.'

'What? For letting me believe you'd been arrested for murder?'

Pavlik waggled his head. 'Not that, so much. We'd been watching Williams and Norstaadt even before the DEA conference. We suspected they'd taken over the drug trade in southeastern Wisconsin, but JoLynne Penn-Williams calling for an appointment with me while I was physically at the Chicago event, persuaded us.'

'Did she actually come…see you?' The misunderstood word more 'tripped' than 'came trippingly' off my tongue.

Pavlik met my eyes, pure regret and not just a little

guilt in his. 'Never had a chance. She called my office Tuesday, but didn't leave her name or number. The next morning, my assistant Cheryl checked the telephone logs and reached me on my cell as I drove back from Chicago. I tried Ms Penn-Williams' number over and over, but no answer. When I arrived at the dedication, I realized why.' No more JoLynne. I linked my arm with Pavlik's and laid my head on his shoulder.

'I'm sorry, too.'

He brushed the hair away from my face. 'Maggy, neither of us killed her.'

'No.' I raised my head. 'But we could have killed us.'

'*You*, literally,' Pavlik said, as we watched the bad guys leave us—Ragnar by cruiser and Kevin by ambulance.

'Yes, but I meant me and you.' I stared into his eyes again, not getting anything back. 'As a couple.'

'I knew that's what you meant.' And that was all Pavlik said.

In the following days, I learned many things.

I'd guessed that Pavlik's 'arrest' had been a hoax: an effort to make Ragnar and Kevin, especially the latter, feel safe enough to do something stupid. Not that Kevin needed much encouragement.

Ragnar's real name was Harold Hart, neither Nordic nor, at least any longer, a mime. In fact, Harold was talking such a blue streak these days that I feared a lot of folks were going to pay more for his memoirs than they had for his crystal meth.

Kevin Williams, on the other hand, was both dupe and dope. His business faring poorly, and unhappy with his share of the profits from Ragnar/Harold, the props man tried to strike a side deal with Chef for the shake-

and-bake trade. Kevin figured the profit margin would be larger on the lesser-quality meth, since the stuff wouldn't cost him very much in overheads to produce.

Instead, his plan had cost him everything.

But the fact that Kevin was a moron didn't mean he wasn't a villain. JoLynne had fallen in love with a man she believed wanted to turn his life around. She wasn't perfect, but she'd done her part while he had first betrayed and then conspired to murder her. I hoped Kevin Williams and his brown eyes would burn in an especially torrid circle of Hades, with Ragnar tied to the next stake.

The news media had broken the story and poor Brewster had done his best to weather the storm. To his credit, in my opinion, the county exec was standing beside his woman *and* his county. At least so far.

WoPro was on temporary hiatus, since so many of their members had opted for 'vacation time'. In rehab. Anita included.

Rebecca Penn and Michael Inkel remained engaged, though with no date set. I suspected Michael'd gotten a cautionary case of cold feet when Rebecca acted so nutsy. I hoped one of the things listed on their gift registry, eventually, was a pair of nice, warm slippers for him, because I had a feeling the marriage wouldn't keep the groom's toes warm for long.

All was still fair in love for our unexpected warrior, Christy Wrigley. She visited Ronny regularly, but also had added Kevin to her shortlist of special convict friends. My theory was that someone like Christy needed an antiseptic relationship. A man she *couldn't* have physical contact with—say an inmate awaiting trial for a capital crime—felt 'safe' to her. I'd love to be a fly on her wall when she Googled 'conjugal visit'. Not that a fly stood a chance in Christy's house.

Uncommon Grounds continued to prosper, except on Saturdays. Since the lack of business had driven Sarah to pretend-smoke, we'd temporarily gone to being open just weekdays. Down the road, we'd likely expand our hours, but right now all of us—Sarah and Tien, Amy and I—needed the time more than the money.

As for me, the following Saturday I awoke to the morning sun with a heaviness in my chest.

'Frank, damn you. Get off me!' The sheepdog opened one eye.

'Off, Frank.' The other eye opened, but still no movement.

'Wanna go out?' I tried. 'Huh? Huh?' Frank took his ole-boy time to lever all limbs up. Then he stood for a moment, body shading my face, two hairy legs on each side of me.

I shielded my eyes with a forearm, preferring that his private parts remain as private as possible. When the bed finally rocked, I shifted my arm to look up. No more sheepdog.

'Thank God,' said a voice in my ear. 'I thought he'd never leave.'

* * * * *

REQUEST YOUR FREE BOOKS!
2 FREE NOVELS PLUS 2 FREE GIFTS!

HARLEQUIN

INTRIGUE

BREATHTAKING ROMANTIC SUSPENSE

YES! Please send me 2 FREE Harlequin Intrigue® novels and my 2 FREE gifts (gifts are worth about $10). After receiving them, if I don't wish to receive any more books, I can return the shipping statement marked "cancel." If I don't cancel, I will receive 6 brand-new novels every month and be billed just $4.74 per book in the U.S. or $5.24 per book in Canada. That's a savings of at least 14% off the cover price! It's quite a bargain! Shipping and handling is just 50¢ per book in the U.S. and 75¢ per book in Canada.* I understand that accepting the 2 free books and gifts places me under no obligation to buy anything. I can always return a shipment and cancel at any time. Even if I never buy another book, the two free books and gifts are mine to keep forever.

182/382 HDN F43C

Name _____ (PLEASE PRINT)

Address _____ Apt. #

City _____ State/Prov. _____ Zip/Postal Code

Signature (if under 18, a parent or guardian must sign)

Mail to the **Harlequin® Reader Service:**
IN U.S.A.: P.O. Box 1867, Buffalo, NY 14240-1867
IN CANADA: P.O. Box 609, Fort Erie, Ontario L2A 5X3

**Are you a subscriber to Harlequin Intrigue books
and want to receive the larger-print edition?
Call 1-800-873-8635 or visit www.ReaderService.com.**

* Terms and prices subject to change without notice. Prices do not include applicable taxes. Sales tax applicable in N.Y. Canadian residents will be charged applicable taxes. Offer not valid in Quebec. This offer is limited to one order per household. Not valid for current subscribers to Harlequin Intrigue books. All orders subject to credit approval. Credit or debit balances in a customer's account(s) may be offset by any other outstanding balance owed by or to the customer. Please allow 4 to 6 weeks for delivery. Offer available while quantities last.

Your Privacy—The Harlequin® Reader Service is committed to protecting your privacy. Our Privacy Policy is available online at www.ReaderService.com or upon request from the Harlequin Reader Service.

We make a portion of our mailing list available to reputable third parties that offer products we believe may interest you. If you prefer that we not exchange your name with third parties, or if you wish to clarify or modify your communication preferences, please visit us at www.ReaderService.com/consumerschoice or write to us at Harlequin Reader Service Preference Service, P.O. Box 9062, Buffalo, NY 14269. Include your complete name and address.

HIDIR13R

REQUEST YOUR FREE BOOKS!

2 FREE NOVELS
PLUS 2 FREE GIFTS!

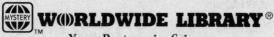

W❂RLDWIDE LIBRARY®
Your Partner in Crime

ReaderService.com

Manage your account online!

- Review your order history
- Manage your payments
- Update your address

> **We've designed
> the Harlequin® Reader Service
> website just for you.**

Enjoy all the features!

- Reader excerpts from any series
- Respond to mailings and
  special monthly offers
- Discover new series available to you
- Browse the Bonus Bucks catalog
- Share your feedback

Visit us at:

ReaderService.com